Menace and Memory

Whitney Hill

BENU
MEDIA

Benu Media
6409 Fayetteville Rd
Ste 120 #155
Durham, NC 27713
(984) 244-0250
benumedia.com

To receive special offers, release updates, and bonus content, sign up for our newsletter: go.benumedia.com/newsletter

ISBN (ebook): 978-1-7376311-5-6
ISBN (pbook): 978-1-7376311-6-3

Library of Congress Control Number: 2022902434

Cover Designer: Pintado (99Designs)
Editor: Jeni Chappelle (Jeni Chappelle Editorial)

Content Warnings

This book contains strong physical violence and gore, blood-drinking, on-page death, swearing, slurs (not toward any real racial or ethnic group/identity), alcohol use, knife violence, threat of sexual violence, mention of the off-page death of a parent, and consensual on-page sex scenes involving bondage, knife play, and consensual non-consent.

It's also a steamy vampire romance with a happy ending, so make sure you have something to cool down with afterward!

For those who have struggled to break free from toxic environments or people, but who are determined to make their own way, rewrite their stories, and not look back.

Chapter 1: Lya

I was trapped, and there was no escaping my bonds. I'd tried.

I could barely hear circling footsteps in the dark, the faint inhale of anticipation. A hand ghosted over my throat, and I gasped, arching and straining against the loops of rope pulling me spread-eagle on the bed.

I'd been tied up a few times in my life but never erotically…until now.

Cade was infuriatingly patient, as one apparently was after almost five hundred years. As a vampire he also had much better senses—night vision that pierced the dark of the new moon, a nose that would pick up every scent my body threw off and tell him whether I was panting in arousal or fear.

At the moment, it was definitely arousal, spurred by anticipation.

"Don't you dare keep me waiting," I snarled.

A satisfied chuckle from the dark pulled my head in the opposite direction from where I'd thought he was. I was a good bounty hunter. He was an excellent predator. The scales tipped in his favor.

Unless I used magic.

I jerked against the ropes again, a distraction while I drew on Aether. Before I could speak a spell or a command, he was on me. His weight pinned my hips, and his hand closed firmly around my throat in warning.

"Don't," he whispered. "Trust me, the punishment will be far worse. Shall I show you?"

I shivered, groaning as his fangs scraped along my neck and down to my breasts. With a quick lick to my nipple, he was gone.

"Cade!" I jumped as two fingers rested on my lips and opened my mouth to them, suckling.

"This is going to be even more fun than I'd imagined. All that impatience and demand and drive, restrained and stretching tighter by the second." He took his fingers back. "You have no idea how delicious you smell right now."

Before I could answer, the fingers that'd been in my mouth slipped between the folds of my lower lips, cool against my heat.

I bucked, gasping again as he pushed deeper and curled them, slowly at first, then faster, pumping them and touching me nowhere else. His thumb pressed, making me cry out with pleasure and need, almost to climax—and then he was gone.

"Goddess damn you!"

His cool breath whispered against my ear. "I told you the punishment would be worse."

He kept going, taking me to the edge and pulling back at the critical moment, until I finally gave in and begged him to bite me, first with reluctance, trying to keep hold of my pride, then with increasing desperation. He couldn't fuck me until he'd bitten me, and all he was doing was *teasing* me as everything I was slowly unraveled and was replaced by need.

When I was down to breathless, whispered pleas, he slipped away again. Sulfur and light flared as he lit a match then the candle on the nightstand. Cade gazed at me, his naked body covered in the scars he'd taken as a pirate before he died his first death, his dark hair in complete disarray.

He looked too hungry to be pleased with his work, his eyes fully black and his expression tight. "Do you still trust me to bite you bound like this?"

"Yes." I wouldn't have agreed to it to begin with if I didn't, but he was big on consent.

"May I bite your thigh?"

"Yes, for the love of the Goddess, bite me anywhere, please, Cade—"

His tongue flicked over his lips as his gaze roved over me. Not all solidaires were also sex partners, as I was to him. But we both enjoyed a bite and bang, so here I was, girlfriend and buffet.

"Please," I whispered once more, fighting the ropes again, even as I met his eyes for the glamour that'd put me under and take the pain of a bite to a whole new level of pleasure.

A pleased, dangerous smile curled his lips. He cupped my jaw, and everything spiraled into euphoria as his glamour fell over me. Now he moved with more urgency, slipping between my spread legs and kissing the femoral artery of the left one before sinking fang.

A low, guttural moan slid from me as I finally came. I was vaguely aware when Cade withdrew his fangs and pressed his tongue to the bite to stop the bleeding but definitely aware when he turned his attention to my pussy, lavishing attention on it until enough blood was moving through him to get hard.

Then he was in me, moving fast and rough as he took me over every edge he'd pulled away from earlier.

Another lance of pleasure shot through me as he bit again, my neck this time, taking a few more swallows before pulling away and spreading his hand where any movement of mine would press my throat against it.

"You're mine," he whispered.

I was too busy drowning in glamour and orgasmic pleasure to voice my agreement, but I did agree. Especially if it meant more of this.

Then his wrist was against my mouth and liquid fire poured into me as he fed me in return. As I pulled on him, he thrust harder into me, grunting as he finished. Heat spread in me above and below, filling me in a way it could only now that I was his solidaire and thus permitted to have his blood.

I whimpered as he both pulled his arm away and pulled out. The glamour was fading, but his blood still carved through my veins as he untied me. It lit a fiery path through me, searing in a new layer of pleasure. When it ran its course I lay as I was, boneless in the aftermath of it all, as he checked me over, massaged my wrists and ankles, and then gathered me close to him.

"Are you okay?" he asked in low, soothing tones.

I jerked my head in a nod as the paralytic effect started wearing off then managed a "Yes," because I knew if I didn't manage a verbal he'd worry.

"Did you enjoy yourself?"

"Yes," I groaned, as much from the aftershocks of pleasure rippling over me with his ongoing caresses as from pure sexual exhaustion.

"Good. You're the most incredible person I've ever met. Thank you for trusting me." He brushed light kisses over my shoulder then leaned to reach for the glass on the nightstand.

I drank greedily when he held it for me. It was oral rehydration solution, which tasted like dog's bollocks but would do more for me than plain water after the exertion and blood loss. Drinking from him helped as well, but we knew from experience I'd crash from that high soon and I needed to hydrate before then.

When I finished the glass, he asked, "More?"

"No. Hold me."

Cade shifted us so that he could fully envelop me and tightened his arms. "With pleasure."

I drifted. We had a good life here in St. Augustine. Quiet. Private. Settling into slightly new routines, now that I was his acknowledged solidaire—executor, trusted associate, girlfriend, blood source, and daylight bodyguard all in one. With the role came more protection and status than I'd ever had as a half-elf in Otherside, and for once, I was breathing easy. I had a few new responsibilities, but a weight had been lifted. I knew where I belonged and that someone would have my back. Trusted someone completely for the first time in my life.

I was weirdly happy…and deep down, I didn't trust it would last. But for now, things were going well, so I pushed the thought aside.

With a contented sigh, I snuggled closer to Cade. He made a pleased sound and rolled us to our sides, still curled around me as he stroked my hair.

"I wasn't sure how you'd feel about being tied up," he murmured. "Thank you for humoring me."

"Humor's for comedians. I'm your solidaire." After eight months together and five in my expanded role, it was still slightly bonkers to me that was the case—typically the role of solidaire was restricted to humans—but he'd asked, and I'd eventually accepted with pleasure that only grew by the night.

"That doesn't come with this kind of obligation," he replied sternly. "You know that, right?"

"Mm-hmm." I was too sleepy with satiation and blood loss to argue him. "Don't worry. I liked it, and I'd happily do it again."

That got him to relax. His arms tightened around me, and we dozed a little, as we did every new moon, until the full effects of the glamour wore off and my hunger rose. It'd gotten harder to ignore since I'd started drinking from Cade. All of my hungers had. Food, drink, sex—I seemed to need even more of what life had to offer and experienced it with more intensity.

It was ironic to me, given vampires were undead, but Cade seemed to have expected it. I had to trust he knew what he was doing, since it was rare for a vampire to take a half-elf as a solidaire given the unpredictability introduced by crossing Aether with glamour.

My stomach rumbled at the same time I said, "I need to eat."

Cade laughed into my hair. "So I hear. In or out?"

"Out," I said after a moment's thought. "The eclipse is making me restless." As one of the elf-blooded, my magic spiked at new moons. Eclipses took it up another notch. "Besides, we haven't been seen in a while."

"Hmm. True."

The air that swept in behind him when he shifted away was cold, but that wasn't all that made me shiver. "What's wrong?"

"Just wondering what the hell Alejandro did with that treasure. I'd expected to see him skulking around by now." The look on Cade's face explained the rest: he was still worried the blood witch's interest in me hadn't run its course.

I started to offer the usual placations then paused and tried a different tack. "We weren't in any shape to hunt him down before, even if you were going to break the deal I'd made with him. And if he comes back, you've done everything possible to strengthen me."

"I think that's what I'm most afraid of," Cade admitted in a whisper barely louder than that made by his clothes as he dressed. "I might have made you into a more tempting target for some."

I started to huff a sigh then turned it into getting up and out of bed. He wasn't wrong, but I'd done well enough on my own for more than thirty years before meeting him.

Okay, so "well enough" included getting exiled and shot, but that was beside the point.

"That's why we're building a community," I said instead. "Right?"

"Of course." But he didn't sound completely convinced.

I let him be in his mood. There really was nothing more to do about it; he was just being overprotective again. Part him and part vampire instinct when a prime blood source was threatened. I was learning to live with it, since it wasn't worth leaving him over, but it did irk me sometimes.

Once we were both dressed, I let him drive us over to one of the beachside bar and grill restaurants on A1A. A steak would have done me better, but this place had an amazing coconut shrimp appetizer. A couple of burgers would do just as well for the protein I needed, even if it confused the servers when they caught me eating the food on both my plate and Cade's.

Suddenly I wasn't in the mood to deal with that confusion tonight though, and not just because the eclipse was setting me on edge. "You wanna eat at the beach?"

He glanced at me to see if I was serious. It wasn't just that I was contradicting what I'd said earlier about being seen by any of our fellow Othersiders who might be passing through or the annoyance of the eclipse or that it was February and therefore cold. It was more that I'd avoided the beach, especially at night, since being attacked by sirens a few months ago. But I missed it, and it wasn't like we were going to summon them to shore like we had then.

"Will you be able to see to eat?" he asked.

It was a wiser question than he might have asked, and I reached over to squeeze his arm. "I don't have a high-blood's night vision, or a vampire's, but I can manage to find my mouth in the dark."

He snorted a laugh. "As you wish, my love."

The beach was technically closed at this time of night, but who was going to tell a vampire and a half-elf we couldn't be there? With the bag of food in hand, Cade let his glamour loose in an undirected calming wave, and I muttered a "don't see me" spell—carefully, given the eclipse—that would amplify the effects. If anyone was watching from one of the bungalows lining the road down to the public beach access, they'd feel compelled to look the other way and forget what they'd noticed. I hoped.

Eclipses made things wonky sometimes. Unexpectedly stronger or weaker, sometimes with disastrous results. It was probably for the best that Cade had stopped me earlier.

I spread the blanket I'd brought from the car, and Cade anchored it against the wind as I stood there, looking out over the dark, crashing waves.

"Everything okay?" he asked.

I hugged myself, struck for a moment by memories.

"Lya?"

I shuddered and sat down, reaching for one of the black Styrofoam containers of food. "I'm fine. Or I will be. I just need to get used to it again. No time like the present, right?"

He didn't answer, and I knew he was probably beating himself up over what'd happened.

"Cade. Enough."

That got me a sharper look. He didn't like being ordered about. He'd deal with it, but deep down—or maybe not so deep—he liked being in charge. It made him feel safe, and it was why I'd agreed to his hesitant request to explore bondage as a sex thing.

I leaned against his arm to soften my rebuke.

He kissed the top of my head and wrapped the second blanket we'd brought around us both. "I'm proud of you. Of all you're building here to turn your experiences into something good. There's not enough of that in Otherside."

"Tell me about it." My words were muffled by a mouthful of burger, and my embarrassment made me sound extra surly. I swallowed and cleared my throat. "Thank you though. Really. I…nobody's ever told me that."

Cade leaned away. I couldn't quite read his expression in the dark, but his better vision could probably let him see mine. "Never told you what?"

"That they were proud of me." I shrugged and munched on a yucca fry. "I was practically a bastard in my mother's House. My father was barely tolerated, especially after they broke tradition to raise me as a pair rather than sending him away. I was housed, clothed, fed, and when I was old enough, trained alongside the Darkwatch, until they got into the magical part of the training and washed me out of the program." I sipped my water to get the food past the lump in my throat at the memory of the benign neglect my existence had merited. "Nobody's ever wanted me, Cade. Not like you. They certainly were never *proud* of me."

He was silent long enough for me to finish my food. As I packed up the trash, he said, "What would you have been if you'd made a different choice? One that let you stay there?"

I snorted. "Nothing. Nobody. I'd be absolutely nothing other than an embarrassment. Because there's nothing for people like me. Low-bloods don't get titles or honors." My lips twisted at the term. I preferred "half-elf," but I was speaking as they would. "Or choices, unless we leave and make our own way."

"Every time you tell me more about your life, I pray they stay out of it going forward."

Something twisted in my chest at the heaviness of his tone. "Why's that?"

His gaze weighed on me in the dark. "Because I'm not sure I could resist draining them if they did anything other than beg your forgiveness, and I don't know if you could find it in your heart to forgive me after that."

I leaned over to kiss his cheek and rose. "Then it's a good thing we'll never have to find out, hey?"

Cade didn't respond, and I turned the conversation back to business as we shook the sand out of the blankets and made our way back to the car. Some things were more important than a meeting that was never going to happen.

Chapter 2: Cade

Cade woke early the next sunset, as he often did now that he was getting monthly meals of Otherside blood. The stronger he made Lya with infusions of his own, the stronger what came back to him got. The sun bothered him less, and although he still didn't risk it, he was less irritated by its presence.

Beside him, Lya slept on, as she often did after a new moon. He didn't give back as much as he took, and she was usually exhausted the next day.

He'd been counting on that.

Brushing a light kiss on her temple, he wrestled down the surge of hunger and slid from the sheets. It wasn't just Lya's hungers that grew the longer they were together and exchanging blood. With the vitality of her blood, his own hungers had undergone a resurgence after a century of settling. He didn't *need* to feed; on the contrary, he could survive longer than ever without doing so and could go a few nights rather than just one without losing the warmth and smoothness of motion a good feed offered.

But now, instead of going three or four nights without a bite, he found himself hunting every two to three nights. More if Lya was occupied—or horny, which she was often these days, much to his delight. If he could feed from her every night, he would, but he'd experienced that firsthand and wouldn't subject her to it. If he was quick, he could duck out for a quick sip and take care of the other business he attended to after a new moon.

Business Lya would be pissed about if she knew but which he couldn't dissuade himself from.

Cade idly kept an eye on the bars as he wandered through the Old Town. Downtown St. Augustine wasn't really big enough to sustain a vampire his age feeding as frequently as he was, but so far, the tourists had made up for that. The university students were a reasonable bet as well, given he could pass for a slightly older one himself if he had to. Lya was happy here, with the safehouses she'd set up and work that involved helping people more often than bringing in bounties these days, so he was reluctant to pull her away from that. But his feeding habits weren't the only reason he was trying to figure out how to talk her into taking up a more mobile lifestyle.

Alejandro was still out there, and he knew exactly where to find them.

It was a risk Cade couldn't abide. The blood witch had nearly taken Lya from him twice in a week's time, and only her quick wits and courage had saved her. Then he'd had to let the bastard go to save Lya's life.

He snorted, chastising himself as he pulled out his phone and dialed Maria.

It wasn't just the risk. It was vengeance Cade wanted. Alejandro had broken their agreement. Threatened her. Cut her up to lift the blood curse on the treasure that should have bought out the cost of Lya's exile, then stolen what should have gone to her. That was half the point of making her his solidaire— bestowing the wealth he'd inherited on her in turn, freeing her from the weight of an unjust sentence and giving her options the rest of Otherside refused to.

Alejandro had spoiled that plan. He'd pay sooner or later. Cade had an eternity to be sure of it.

The phone rang almost long enough to go to voicemail.

"Muffin!" Maria said a little too cheerfully when she finally picked up. "The usual?"

"If you please."

"Hmm. A moment." The sound of footsteps and a door closing followed by a clattering keyboard reached him. "A few suspicious animal deaths but unless Callista's Watchers are cleaning something up, there's no sign of him. You're sure the witch is still in the Triangle?"

Cade blew out an annoyed sigh. "No. That's the trouble. He could be anywhere on the Southeast coast, unless he's branched out in the last century and a half."

"And yet you're certain he's either here or biding his time there."

"He wants Lya, I'm sure of it. He's never gotten a taste of a target and not taken the whole. There are only two places she's been on this side of the Atlantic, and he swore not to go back to Europe after what he had to do to escape Interpol the last time."

"Cade." Maria's tone switched to chiding. "This is backward. Your solidaire is supposed to guard *you*, and you know it."

"Fuck that."

"Of course you'd say that. Rogue."

She sounded equal parts exasperated and affectionate, and Cade wondered when their sometimes-tense business relationship had become more friendly. She didn't seem to begrudge him the loss of access to Lya, with whom she'd had an arrangement before Cade had come into the picture.

"Why are you helping me?" he blurted out.

A long silence hung between them. "I suppose because I see what you two are trying to do. I'm trying to do the same in my own way. Modernize. Update Otherside. Make things fairer. Drag us into the future. We're running out of time, and you're the only one my age who can see it." Her tone sharpened. "I'm pissed that you grabbed sweet Lydia out from under me, but she's her own woman."

Cade frowned. "What do you mean 'running out of time'? What have you heard?"

"Nothing. Call it a feeling. Or an observation. Or common fucking sense. Come on, muffin. Don't tell me you don't see it too."

"There's no more room." The words jerked from him as he slipped through the crowd of holidaymakers, a shark making his way through schools of fish, knowing there weren't enough to sustain him if he gorged himself the way he wanted to. The way he once had. "We're losing ground."

"There you have it. Otherside will have to come out sooner or later. My bet is sooner. But where? How? Which of us gets exposed first?" Her voice lowered, almost too quiet to hear and laced with silky danger. "I don't have the answers. But if the Raleigh coterie is going to survive, I need to…rearrange a few things."

Cade halted in his tracks, raising a hand in apology when someone bumped into him before ducking into the doorway of a knick-knack shop, closed for the day but with lights making a display of cut-crystal animal figurines glitter. "Are you saying what I think you're saying?"

"I'm saying if helping you look for a blood witch gains me a potential friend that might repay a favor in a decade, well, it's a small thing in the big picture. Wouldn't you say?"

"I see your point." He looked out into the night, slightly dizzied by what Maria was suggesting. Reading between the lines, she wanted to take Aron's place as second in the coterie and then become Mistress of Raleigh herself. It'd damn near be a coup for a vampire her age—*their* age; she was only a few years younger than him in death—to head up a city the size of Raleigh with the resources to sustain a nest the size of the one Torsten led.

"Do I have your affection?" Maria asked, too lightly.

In other words, would he support her coup?

He didn't waste time thinking it over, since there was only one question that mattered. "Will it keep Lya safe?"

"Yes. Should something happen to you, I'll adopt her in. Blood and free will intact, no obligations."

"Then yes. Just keep me posted, should you hear anything that might be Alejandro."

"Good doing business, muffin. Speak at the next new moon, if I don't hear anything first. Better still, make an appearance before then. We should talk in person. Oaths and all that."

She hung up, leaving Cade with a spinning head and a racing mind. Maria wouldn't be the first *moroi* with ambitions, but hers would require a lot of powerful blood very quickly. Probably the other reason she was helping with his search for Alejandro; if they could capture him, his blood would provide an incredible boost to whoever drained him.

If. A blood witch wasn't a necromancer or a sorcerer but had the potential to become either or both. And either or both could, with enough time and power, become a lich lord that could control undead up to and including vampires—especially if a vampire failed to recognize the danger and was taken as a bounty. It was a dangerous game, and with the treasure Alejandro had stolen, he could afford to dabble, even if the soul gems that'd been in the cache had gone to the djinn.

Shit. The djinn.

There had to be a reason they wanted the soul gems, beyond denying Callista. Who knew why the djinn did anything though? Their reasons were as myriad as they were and just as capricious.

Cade kept turning the problem over in his mind as he slipped into a house party near the university, glamouring and sipping lightly from multiple people amidst the blare of dancehall music before disentangling himself and leaving. His thoughts went nowhere, but he knew, deep down, that Maria was right. Something was coming to a head, and he had to protect Lya from it.

Talk to her. You thought you knew better last time, and it almost got her killed.

He turned that over in his head as well, trying to find the right angle. They'd been together long enough—and failed to communicate often enough—that he'd learned how important honesty and clarity was for them, especially given the power imbalance his greater age and power afforded. She'd been treated as less-than her entire life, and he had to be careful that he didn't perpetuate the problem in his zeal to protect her.

He'd just about worked out what to say when he got home. A familiar scent and laughter from inside the house made him pause in disbelief because not only were the scent and sound not Lya's, but he knew them.

Donatien.

Cade burst into the house, glamour rolling from him in a heavy wave, ready to kill.

Lya's surprised jump pulled him up short. "There you are. We have a new applicant for one of the guesthouses."

The vampire seated across from her smiled, almost but not quite showing fangs, exactly as he used to when he and Cade had gotten up to some terrible mischief that had ended with as much blood on the floor as in their bellies. He still looked the same too: olive skin, dark hair falling past his shoulders in waves, shorter than Cade but thicker in build. His hazel eyes were just as sharp, just as mocking, as he turned to an angle Lya wouldn't be able to see from where she was sitting and smirked at Cade.

I've discovered your secret, the look said. *And I'm going to make you wish I hadn't.*

It was all Cade could do not to react. All thoughts of talking to Lya about Alejandro and Raleigh fled. If it had been bad for Lya to meet Alejandro, Donatien's reappearance was a disaster.

Cade's acquaintance with Alejandro had been two bad jobs, all business.

Donatien had been over half a century of carving a bloody swath through the then-new city of New Orleans while Cade tried to escape the memories of what Morris had done to him and Donatien had delightedly encouraged every single depravity.

"An applicant? No, I don't think we do." Cade moved to stand behind Lya with all the quickness of his age and strength, a warning to Donatien.

The other *moroi* pursed his lips, clearly noting both the situation between Cade and his solidaire and the benefits he'd gained from it. "That's a shame." His English was still accented with a touch of French even after all these years. "I've missed the area."

Lya tensed as she picked up something unsaid between the two men but said nothing.

"I'm sure you can understand the situation with the hunting grounds here. Tourist town and all that." As much as Cade tried to moderate his tone, an edge still cut through it. "Perhaps you should try Jacksonville."

Donatien studied them, his gaze flicking from Lya to Cade and back. They all knew why nobody had claimed Jacksonville or even spent enough time there to look like they were thinking about it: Santiago would see it as a direct threat to his hold on Miami. "As you say. Perhaps I could beg one day then, before moving on?"

Lya's lean against Cade signaled that she was willing to let him lead here. He couldn't help but slide a hand over her shoulder, wrapping it lightly around her throat in a clear signal of ownership. He would apologize for it later, when Donatien was out of his nest or, better yet, out of his city.

"One day." Cade's instincts told him it was a mistake to make the concession, but Lya would be suspicious enough as it was. "No deaths. No property damage. No turnings or pets. No excess."

Rage flickered in Donatien's gaze and was gone so quickly Cade almost thought he'd imagined it, but the other *moroi* simply inclined his head before letting his pleasant mask slip into place once more as he took in Cade's hand still bracketing Lya's throat. "Merci bien." He rose. "Shall we?"

Cade went for the drawer where the keys were before Lya could shift, digging out the set for the property farthest from them. "After you."

With a last mocking smile, blocked from Lya's view by Cade between them, Donatien bowed. "A pleasure to make your acquaintance, Mademoiselle Lya. My thanks for your warm welcome."

A rebuke of Cade's. He didn't care. He wanted Donatien out of his nest before everything went to hell. Lya would have questions, questions he'd answer if he had to but would desperately rather not. The less she had to go on, the better.

She'll understand.

The thought was more of a prayer than anything else, but she'd been accepting of his long history before.

But for how long? How many times could the dregs of the past come back to threaten what he'd managed to carve out of all the blood and death? How could he forge a closer connection with her, one that would make her stay for good, if his past kept intruding?

Cade turned down the street toward the small apartment Lya had secured as one of their guesthouses. It'd made sense at the time; there was a long way between Miami and the next

Otherside city, and sometimes help was needed on a journey. St. Augustine offered a reasonable pit stop for those heading north and who preferred a quieter location than the much more populous Jacksonville forty miles to the north. Cade just hadn't expected Donatien to be one of those travelers.

The other *moroi* wasn't silent for long. "She's—"

"Completely off limits."

Donatien pouted. "I was merely curious about—"

"Don't be."

"You're smitten." He laughed. "And she doesn't know, does she? About anything from La Nouvelle-Orléans?"

Cade glared at his one-time partner in chaos and death. "Don't do this, Donatien. Let the past lie."

"But we had so much fun!" With a skipping spin, Donatien put himself in front of Cade, walking backward. "Didn't we? Don't you remember when we—"

"I remember all of it. Painfully clearly. And if you know what's good for you, you won't speak of it again."

His full lips pursed in a disappointed pout. "As you wish. For now."

"Not for now. Ever."

"Completely smitten then. Would she be so easily lost, this dusk walker? Perhaps I should—"

Cade loosed his glamour, and a small group of mundanes turned and headed down a side street without knowing why. He kept his fangs behind his lips. Barely.

"Last warning, Donatien." The soft tone that slithered out of Cade came from the depths, that dark place he'd mostly, but not quite, buried. The place he found himself tapping when Lya was threatened because he'd do anything—even become the devil he'd once been—to keep her safe.

His companion inclined his head in acquiescence, but the small smirk said everything. Donatien had always gotten under

Cade's skin. And every time, it was in service to something bloody.

"Why are you here, anyway?" Cade asked.

Donatien shrugged. "Word about your little project is getting around. I was guesting in Miami for a time." A sideways glance and another sly smile. "Luz finds all of this hilarious, by the way. Collecting misfits and strays."

"Which you appear to be."

"And always have been, so long as it means I can do whatever my evil little heart desires." His voice dropped. "Come on, Cade. What's the point of immortality if you don't have *fun* with it? We can do anything we want, anything at all. And you want to— what? Play house with a woman who's only half in the world? Save stray animals?" He scoffed. "What a waste. We were *gods*, my friend."

That grated. It shouldn't have, but it did. The superior attitude, the words digging at Cade's existing worry about staying so long in one place. He drew power from Lya, but there was safety in wandering…and he wanted both.

"Silent treatment?" Laughter danced in Donatien's tone, even if it didn't spring from his lips. "I must have hit a nerve to make you go all broody."

"We're here." Cade stopped and pointed at the building. "Ground floor. Unit A. Leave the keys in the mailbox at the house by sunset tomorrow and get the hell out of town."

"Yes, sir." Donatien saluted then took the keys. "Much obliged, sir."

With a last glare for the sarcastic tone, Cade spun on his heel and left, dreading what he'd walk into when he got home.

Chapter 3: Lya

I waited for Cade at the kitchen table with a glass of iced tea—normal, unsweetened black tea, not the syrupy-sweet shit US Southerners drank—mulling over the bizarre encounter with this Donatien. It wasn't the first time we'd had a vampire vagabond or some other traveler stop by. We'd painted the stylized eclipse symbol for Otherside on the front gate for a reason. He'd approached properly, stepping into the gate and hailing the house just as I slunk out the back to check the tripped ward. He'd been perfectly polite, meek even, as he mentioned having met Cade some time ago. Hell, he'd been decent to talk to, when most vampires his age were all haughty superiority.

None of which squared with Cade's immediate, almost frightening, possessively defensive reaction on arriving home or Donatien's own reaction to it, a mask slipping to make my stomach clench as my blood froze. My instincts were usually better than that. They had to be.

There was a story here.

Who had I invited into our home? Had I gotten overconfident in my new vamp-blood strength? Complacent in my happiness? Or was this asshole just that dangerous?

So I sat and waited, drinking fucking tea when I would rather have had whiskey or wine, wondering about Donatien. Wondering if we had another Alejandro situation on our hands and what we were going to do if we did.

Mostly, wondering what the hell had happened between the two vampires for all of *that* to be Cade's reaction.

The ring I'd given him warned me he was on his way back, and the ward passed him through without tripping, recognizing him as an extension of me. He blew in the front door, suppressed fury crackling off him like heat lightning, dark eyes distant.

I stayed where I was, not quite as still as the dead but as still as I could be. Love me or not, he was a vampire, and accidents happened. I'd survived one and didn't see any reason to tempt fate with another if it could be helped.

He stopped short at the kitchen table, looking almost surprised to see me. "You're still here."

I nodded, meeting his eyes so he'd know I was cautious but not scared and not running. Yet. He needed that trust from me to come down from his predatorial headspace sometimes. He must have been in deep this time not to pay attention to his ring telling him I was still where he'd left me.

"I imagine you have questions," he said.

I did. I really did. But this was something I'd had to make peace with months ago. "Cade, our pasts always catch up with us. Yours is just a few hundred years longer than mine and apparently filled with much more dangerous people."

His flat look seemed almost angry. "You don't want to know why I had to claim you like that?"

"I do. I definitely do. But there's clearly more going on here." I tilted my head and frowned, reading his tells. He didn't have many, but the little finger on his left hand was spasming and he was standing far too still, a vampire trying to hide in plain sight. "Are we in danger?"

"Alejandro is still loose, and now Donatien is back. Yes, we're in danger. Staying still is dangerous. It's how we get found. How we get *killed*."

The sharpness of his tone stung. It sounded like a rebuke of me, but it had to be about more than either of the other men. Something deeper had been triggered by this recent arrival. Still, he stayed as unmoving as only the undead could. I'd be pacing if I was this agitated.

That he wasn't moving scared me. Not fear of him but fear *for* him.

I swallowed past a lump in my throat. Fear was fear as far as his predator's senses were concerned, and as on edge as he was, I needed to calm it down. "Cade—"

He rushed me.

It took everything in me not to move. Not to flee like prey or react like a bounty hunter who'd been cornered by a dangerous target but to sit and stare him down, like an equal. My breathing and heart rate picked up though, and his pupils dilated.

Slowly, he extended a single finger and traced it from the corner of my jaw to my chin, tipping it up. "Why do you trust me? You have no idea who I am, really. What I've done."

"Whoever you *were* and whatever it *was*, I wasn't there," I said softly. "If you want to tell me what this is about, I'll listen."

Fear made his eyes fill with black, and I steeled myself against the lapping waves of glamour.

"You'd leave," he whispered.

"You hung me from your ceiling and threatened to drain me once, but I'm still here," I snapped. Whatever this was, I was already tired of it. I could be patient—he was carrying around a boatload of trauma—but I wasn't going to be a doormat. "You complicated the situation with Callista enough that it nearly got me killed, but I still agreed to be your solidaire. Yes, I fucking trust you. Trust me to accept that the past is in the past." I narrowed my eyes at him. "Unless it's not and you have a confession to make."

He jerked his hand away like I'd burned him. Blinked a few times. Inhaled deeply, even though the undead didn't really need to breathe, then closed his eyes. "I'm sorry."

"Okay. Is there something you want to say? Or should I start packing?"

His eyes flew open, the whites of his sclera fully lost to black.

I kicked myself. "For *us* to go, not for me to leave you. Goddess, Cade. You didn't act like you did in front of Donatien with Alejandro or Callista, which tells me something much worse is possible now."

Or that something much worse happened in the past. Maybe Cade hadn't always been the measured, self-contained man he was now. Okay, obviously he hadn't been, and whatever he had been must have been terrible.

My heart thudded a little harder.

He knelt in front of me with vampiric speed, pushing between my knees to bury his face against my belly. "Lya, you have no idea. And I don't want to tell you because I can't bear to see your face."

I hovered my hands over him, not sure if I should touch him. Fury pushed aside fear as I cursed Morris's dead ass for making Cade into this.

"Why are you angry?" he asked, words muffled.

"I can't help but think this is Morris's fault."

"No. It's mine. I was free of him when it all happened. Donatien just gave me an outlet after two hundred years of madness and pain."

My heart broke for him, harder than it ever had. "Taking accountability is good."

I gently laid my hands on him then started running them through his hair when he nuzzled closer. The throb of the big artery in my abdomen felt more obvious than ever, but he wouldn't go for a belly bite…would he? Given all this, I was starting to think he might and that all the carefully affirmative consent he insisted on might have a source beyond wanting to do right by me.

"Cade."

"Mm."

"Own what's yours. Not what others made you. You're trying. You take care of me. That's what matters to me. Fuck everyone else. It's you and me." I prayed he didn't hear the catch in my voice as I said that or take the fear he had to be able to smell to be fear of him.

It was me, all me.

It was realizing how fucking much I loved this man despite the fuck-ups and the misunderstandings and the tears.

He was *trying*. We both were.

Maybe one day that wouldn't be enough, but for tonight? Tonight, it would be.

I'd wondered a few times what I'd do if Henri ever came back into my life. I'd loved him enough to go into exile for daring to try to be with him.

Right now, at this moment, I knew I'd follow Cade to places much worse than exile.

"Look at me," I said. It felt powerful, to be the one telling him that. Usually, it was the other way around. "Hey, look at me."

He did, with the slow reluctance of guilt.

"Am I—" No, that wasn't it. Asking if I was keeping him here would come out wrong, and I suddenly cared very much how this night ended.

Don't make it about me. This needs to be about him. Which was a foreign concept, even after eight months with him. I'd learned self-reliance and even selfishness the hard way.

I started again. "Would you feel better if we got out of town for a little while?"

The black in his eyes receded a little. "You'd do that?"

Biting back a snarky response, I leaned forward to kiss the crown of his head. "Whatever you need. I love you."

"But *you* need—"

"For you to be okay. Othersiders got along just fine without us here before we opened the safehouses. Yes, I want to help people who've been cast aside, like me. But *you* took me in first, Cade. You're my priority."

He gazed up at me long enough that my heart fluttered with anxiety.

What the hell was going through his head?

Then he took my hands in his and kissed them. "I would feel better if we went somewhere else, at least for a little while."

"Okay." I smiled, trying to make it encouraging. "Then we will."

"Tomorrow? I want to be sure Donatien leaves town before he does something that'll mean we can never come back."

"Sure. We can pack tonight and be ready to go whenever." At least this time leaving a place that felt like home was a choice rather than a punishment. I could deal with that, and we could make a new home.

Cade still watched me like he was waiting for a trap to spring shut. "It shouldn't be this easy to be with you."

I laughed. Couldn't help it. "Easy? You think it's easy? The last man who thought that got beat nearly to death. *You* had to piss off Callista to secure the questionable pleasure of my company."

He rose and cupped my jaw, drawing me in for a kiss. "I almost didn't come home tonight because I didn't know what you'd do about earlier. So yes, this was easy."

I nipped his lower lip. "To be honest, it was kind of hot. Being claimed like that."

"It was?" He frowned in consternation.

Fair, given I usually would have had his balls for acting like I was some kind of damsel in distress—or worse, like I was a Happy Meal two kids were fighting over. I was a bounty hunter who'd done just fine on her own, thanks much. But our bedroom play had always been on the rougher side, with more things like last night's bondage coming as we got a better understanding of our likes and desires.

And being wanted was always a turn-on for me. He gave a damn.

"I mean, it is now that I know I'm not imminently going to be caught in the middle of a vampire fight." I tipped my head back to expose the length of my neck, which still bore two fast-healing dimples from last night's bite, knowing it'd be a tease for him.

Cade took the bait. Fingers dragged along my collarbone, pressing almost hard enough for me to be pushed back against the chair before they closed around my throat. "Like this?"

"Yes," I whispered. I couldn't help the flutter of my eyelashes any more than I could that of my heart, and he squeezed lightly when he felt the change in my pulse.

"I want you. I want—" Another light squeeze before his words tumbled out in a rush. "I want to be sure you're *mine*." He pulled lightly, drawing me up and out of the chair by the throat. "Donatien is very charming. I *hate* that he was here with you."

"You have nothing to be jealous of," I said.

"Being a vampire *is* jealousy. We have to share everything or be alone." He leaned over to kiss me. "Everything except solidaires. Even a city master would be censured for it."

"Then take me. I'm all yours." I ran my hands up under his shirt, dragging them back down over his chest with clawed fingers to make him hiss.

His next kiss did exactly that, falling hungrily on my mouth as his tongue invaded. His other hand gripped my hip, hard, and pulled me tight against him. From the developing situation in his trousers, he'd gotten a bite in sometime this evening.

Lucky, lucky me.

I wrapped my arms around his waist, willing him to find comfort in me. This was new for me—wanting to give rather than take, to be what someone else needed me to be instead of clutching my own needs so damn close. To let him in and be…vulnerable, I guess, rather than keeping walls up and keeping my heart safe. Keeping him out, blocking a deeper connection.

Cade wasn't Henri. Cade needed me.

"Take me," I whispered again when I pulled away for a breath. "Please, Cade. Right now."

He did just that, throwing me over his shoulder with a speed I could just barely follow with the improvements his blood had slowly made to my senses and reflexes. We were in the bedroom before I could do more than gasp, and I was on the bed in the next heartbeat. He followed me down, pinning me against the mattress with his body, wrists trapped in one of his hands. The other came back to bracket my throat as he stared down at me.

For a moment, the planes of his face looked almost cruel in the harsh light making it in from the kitchen. A flashback, maybe, to something Donatien had reminded him of. Then they softened just a little, and he kissed me again.

I intentionally knicked my tongue on a fang, and he groaned as he got a taste of me.

Pulling away, he said, "You'll know if someone approaches the house?"

"Yes," I panted. "Wards are up."

Cade released me long enough to yank my clothes off, hurling them somewhere in the dark as I did the same with his. He turned me over, checking that I was ready before guiding himself into me and then gripping my hip to push hard and deep, wrapping his other arm around my neck. Not so hard that he'd hurt me but enough that the pressure would take my pleasure up a notch.

His hips slammed against my ass. He'd taken me at my word, and I didn't say or do anything to stop him. Fangs grazed my shoulder, but he kept them in check even if I wished he'd bite me. He wouldn't, not after doing so last night, but the temptation was clearly there.

I wiggled and fought, a token resistance to make him go harder.

"You're not going anywhere," he growled next to my ear.

And as though that idea was the hottest thing ever, he came, thrusting hard and deep as his arm tightened around my neck until I saw stars.

"Shit." He pulled out. "Sorry."

"I said 'take me,' not 'make me come.'" I rolled over and grinned at him. "Would you like to watch me finish myself off?"

His eyes flashed. "Yes."

I leaned back against the pillows and spread my knees wide, enjoying his avid attention as I did just that.

We still had to pack tonight, but that could wait. Right now was for healing damaged pasts and cementing uncertain futures. Wherever we ended up going tomorrow, we'd need the connection between us to be strong.

Something told me that whatever the reason Donatien had come looking for Cade, he wouldn't be put off lightly.

Chapter 4: Lya

I woke before dawn with Cade sprawled across me, rather than our usual—the other way around. He was too heavy for it to be comfortable, which was probably why I was up so early, but I didn't move.

Normally, this would have irritated me.

Being needed. Seeing my partner as needy, rather than us both as independently powerful beings. But there was a kind of strength in this. A power and reassurance in being needed, rather than a burdensome obligation. We'd been together long enough that I knew how powerful he was…and where he needed me to shore him up.

Needed me.

Bizarre, outrageous even, to think of a vampire needing a half-elf. Yeah, we had more powerful blood than humans yet more accessible blood than the rest of Otherside, but he was more than sixteen times my senior. And yet, just like humans seemed to stop maturing in their teens, Cade might still be closest to the age he appeared—mid-twenties or early thirties at the latest. He looked to be my age when he didn't let the beard he'd died with grow out.

I ran my fingers through his hair as I thought all this through. He made an agreeable noise and nuzzled closer to the juncture of my shoulder and my neck.

Fangs scraped, sending a shiver over me. Then he was out again.

How had I not realized before how much he needed me? How much it felt good to *be* needed? Independence was important, but with Cade, I was discovering the beginnings of interdependence. What it meant to be in community, rather than standing at the margins, peering in through the window as everyone else who belonged enjoyed their ice cream together.

He might be nearly five hundred years old and seemingly invincible with it, but he was still mine. Mine to nurture. Mine to protect during the day. Or when he got lost in his long, difficult past.

I could be a light in the dark, not just a meal and a fuck.

My arms tightened around him with the thought, and I flushed at the realization that deep down I was still thinking of myself as a thing—blood and sex—rather than as a full partner. That was a me problem but one I'd been unconsciously projecting on Cade for months.

Like, yeah, I was creating Otherside safehouses so those like me had a refuge.

But I was also doing it so I had proof I was more than flesh and the sustenance that could be gained from it. That I was more than a glorified cow.

"Ly?" Cade mumbled as I squeezed him again.

"Shh. We're fine. Sleep."

He subsided immediately, clutching me tighter for the bare moment it took for him to fall back into the sleep of the undead. With nothing even close to the wards at the edge of the property, I followed him.

***

The wards jangled my nerves, and my eyes snapped open.

"Babe," I hissed.

With the sun already at the horizon, Cade was awake in an instant, alerted by my tone and the tension in my body. "What's wrong?"

"Wards."

We were in the golden period where both of us were equally effective. Him, by virtue of night coming on and being a well-fed vampire. Me, by virtue of it being sunset and close enough to the new moon that I was still at peak magical strength. I snatched the Sawback I'd recently purchased to replace my old one—no silver edging on this one but it'd have to do—and headed out the back as Cade confronted whatever it was from the front.

I was in the side yard when I heard Cade's voice. "Toss the keys, Donatien."

"I'd rather bring them straight to you, mon cher."

"No."

A taut silence stretched as I eased around the edges of the property to get behind Donatien, off to the side. *Give me a reason, asshole.*

The jangle of keys reached me in the semi-dark, followed by the muffled thump as they hit Cade's palm.

"Now get the fuck out of my city," he said.

"So possessive," Donatien replied. "I like it."

I eased behind a live oak and peered around it, hidden by the girth of the tree as much by the Spanish moss dripping from its branches. The two vampires stared at each other, a frighteningly deep longing in Donatien's gaze.

"You truly don't want the old days back?"

Cade snarled. "No. I've moved on."

"Don't you remember the joy of sharing prey between us?" Donatien glanced around, his eyes skipping over my tree without seeing me. "Where is your woman, come to think of it?"

"None of your fucking business. She's my solidaire."

"And you wouldn't share her with an old friend?"

I went cold at that.

I'd thought it was completely against vampire law or custom or both to share a solidaire. That being one would keep me completely safe from at least one faction of Otherside.

Apparently, I'd been wrong.

Cade ghosted down the front steps. "No. She's *mine*. Mine alone."

"We'll see, I suppose." Donatien's small, knowing smile made my blood run cold.

After everything I'd done, was I still prey? Even among the vampires?

"No, we won't. Don't push me, Donatien." Cade was in striking distance of the other vampire, but he had the rigid look he got when he was really hanging onto his instincts.

"But it's so *fun* to push you. Don't you remember?"

"I do, and I wish I didn't." Cade's voice was full of remembered hunger, and his knuckles were white where they fisted around the keys Donatien had returned. "Those days are past."

Donatien studied Cade, as though he was looking for a chink in his armor.

I'd had enough of all of this. Mindful of the wind direction and my steps in the fallen leaves and gravelly soil, I slunk close to Donatien and was rewarded with a flinch when I hovered my machete alongside his neck.

"Time to go," I said.

For just an instant, I caught a glimpse of everything Donatien had hidden from me last night. Malice. Evil. Sadistic intent—not like Cade's, which had a limit, but something more on par with those Othersiders who believed they were close to godlike power and didn't care who had to learn it the hard way.

Then his gaze darted to Cade. Back to me. He inclined his head, although his expression was pinched with disgust and annoyance. "As you wish, mademoiselle."

I couldn't help myself. "Dégage. Va te faire enculer."

"Lya!"

I didn't take my eyes off Donatien despite the sharp rebuke in Cade's tone. I didn't get to use my native French much in this part of the world, and it was clear as day Donatien was a prime outlet and well deserving of it. He could shove the idea to share me straight up his ass.

All I did was wave at Cade and sneer at Donatien as I pressed a little harder on the edge now at Donatien's throat.

"Dégage," I repeated with a shooing motion of my free hand, using the familiar tense rather than the respectful one I really should have with a generally unknown vampire who was definitely older and stronger than me.

"Tu vas le regretter." Donatien's gaze promised every ounce of the vengeance in his words. Maybe more, given his clenched fists and bared fangs. Naked sharps were like unholstered guns. You didn't take them out unless you were happy to use them and deal with the consequences or too crazy to give a damn either way.

I didn't give a shit.

Whatever past he was trying to drag Cade back into, I wasn't about to allow it. I might be Cade's, but he was equally *mine*. And this bastard wasn't going to slink back into Cade's life. Not like Alejandro had. Not at all.

I was Cade's solidaire, and I counted this under protecting him from shit he couldn't defend against himself. Because if he could, this asshole would've dropped the keys and left. Whatever had passed between them, there was a weakness Donatien thought he could exploit in Cade. One that Cade himself might well slip into, now that I thought about it, given my vagabond had restricted himself to a single city for months now.

Shit. This was definitely in my job description, and it explained Cade's struggles last night.

Fortunately for all of us, Donatien caught the resolve in my uptilted chin, hard eyes, and colorful language. Raised his hands. Backed up, then another step, and another, until he was at the gate.

I lowered the machete to avoid drawing mundane attention but kept pace with him the whole way, proving I wasn't afraid of him and that Cade was more important either way. Whatever ideas these two had about solidaires, I was going to shove them down both their throats and carve out my own definition, in blood if I had to.

The rings I'd gotten for us told me Cade was approaching, so I didn't shame myself by jumping when he touched my shoulder.

"My thanks, love," he murmured. "I'll see him gone."

His glance at the car told me to make sure we were ready to go too.

I nodded. "Yes, sir."

That got me a blank stare. I never used any kind of acknowledgment of Cade's superior—in vampire society—role. I refused to call him "master" as a real solidaire or fledgling would, but for the sake of playing my role, I'd cede a little more ground to him, even after last night's submission.

Life in Otherside was a dangerous game, and I was a player, whether I wanted to be or not. I could swallow my pride if it meant security.

Cade jerked his chin in the direction of the gate, and Donatien left with one last dark look at me. I got the feeling I really didn't want to find out who would be worse between him and Alejandro and pulled on Aether, a threat of my own, to cover my shiver.

In the time it took them to reach the gate, I debated putting a tracking tag on Donatien, like I had on Alejandro. I fully embraced paranoia as a survival skill, and although magical trespass was a killing offense in Otherside, tracking tags were light enough not to be noticed and would break within a few weeks. No harm, no death.

Besides, he'd pulled fangs first.

But no. We were leaving town. The whole point was to have less baggage and put this aside for a while.

I watched until the vampires rounded the corner at the end of the block and then headed back inside to take care of closing the house up. We'd managed to pack after last night's romp, and the witch who helped me take care of the other properties had agreed to look after this one in exchange for a pay raise. Fair enough. Cade could afford it.

After triple-checking everything was unplugged, the rubbish was out, and all the doors and windows were locked with the blinds and curtains closed, I got our suitcases out to my Ford Escape. We'd packed light, enough for a couple weeks only. Whatever we needed, Cade's money could buy when we got wherever we were going.

Not having a destination beyond "Let's go north and get away from the sun for a while" bugged me, but Cade seemed at ease. He assured me he had safehouses or boltholes all over the East Coast.

It'll be fine. You always wanted to go on a road trip, right?

I was just getting the last things loaded when Cade reappeared. He hugged me from behind and kissed my neck before peering into the car.

"You already took care of everything?" he asked.

"Yeah. Just needed you. Is he gone?"

"He should be. Not much we can do at this point. All of Florida is technically Santiago's demesne, and if I'm not here, then it can't be said I should have controlled Donatien if he misbehaves." Cade squeezed me and inhaled before letting me go. "Thanks for getting everything ready."

"Sure, babe. You need anything from inside?"

"I'll give it a last sweep and then lock up."

"Works for me." I got into the driver's seat and waited, finding music I liked and mentally preparing for a long night of driving. I might have adapted to nocturnal living, but driving at night meant only seeing as far as your headlights could shine.

In Otherside, what you couldn't see coming was especially deadly.

The lanai screen door slammed as Cade leapt straight to the ground and got into the passenger seat. "All set."

I couldn't help grinning at his obviously better mood.

"What?" he said.

"You seem like a weight is being lifted. It's nice."

"Oh." He settled back in his chair and let the hint of a smile curl into a fuller one. "I do like being on the move. Ships first, cars now. There's always a new horizon."

I got the car started and us out the gate, letting him out to lock that up as well. Then we were on our way.

"I guess I didn't realize how much you needed to be going places," I said softly as we made our way through town.

His gaze cut to me. "Is that—"

"It's fine. I... Well, I guess I realized I'm naturally pretty selfish. I wanted a home somewhere, so I made you anchor yourself with me."

"Ly." His hand settled on my thigh with a quick squeeze. "You didn't make me do anything I didn't want to do. This is nice. What you started here is sorely needed. It's just..." He trailed off and shifted in his chair, and the little finger twitched against my leg. "Put it this way. I only stayed in Raleigh as long as I did because I was getting desperate. In a bad way. I needed to take some time to figure out what I was looking for, and then you walked into Nightshade and showed me."

I'd showed him a whole lot that first night. I smirked before sobering. "So you're telling me not to get used to staying still."

He winced. "If it means a lot to you, we'll figure something out."

"There's a compromise in it somewhere. And hey, maybe I'll like the whole vagabond lifestyle. It's worked out so far." We sat in a companionable silence until I got to the freeway. "Where we going? Other than north."

"I was thinking to stop in Raleigh, actually. There's a large coterie in Charlotte as well, but I don't have ties there I can lean on in such short notice."

I glanced at him, surprised, even as a shameful little quiver started in my belly. I liked the Triangle in principle, but I'd been shot there, then held captive, beaten and sliced to hell, and escaped only with the temporary good graces of a blood witch who'd openly threatened me and a forced promise to the local Arbiter.

I suddenly wasn't sure how keen I was on returning. "Really? Why? Is Torsten even going to let you back into the territory?"

"I'm sure he's moved on from Callista's little smear campaign." He went very still. "Which is good because I need to make an appearance for Maria's sake. We've been invited."

Which meant there was something going on and he'd decided not to tell me. The quiver turned into a twist in my guts, and I pressed my lips together to stop myself from going off. That was the problem with telling him he didn't need to tell me all his secrets. I actually had to abide by what I'd said, and I couldn't even be mad about it. My light mood soured, and we'd barely left town.

This might be a longer drive than I'd anticipated.

Chapter 5: Cade

The sharp tinge of anger cutting through Lya's scent told Cade what she thought of his plan as much as the thin line of her lips did. He waited for the question, any question, but she just kept driving.

If I tell her now, will it make it better or worse?

"Raleigh it is," she said finally. The tightness in her voice told him she wasn't just angry. He stayed as still and blank as he could, trying not to set off a further reaction as he scrambled to figure out where her mind had gone.

Talk to her. You can't keep doing this and keep her, let alone draw her closer.

"There's something you're not saying," he said in a low voice he hoped would project calm rather than accusation.

She eyed him for a bare second before putting her attention back on the road. Opened her mouth and shut it again. The car accelerated another ten miles per hour, and half a mile passed in silence.

"I'm scared to go back." Her whisper had the sound of a confession, one being dragged from her. "I *hate* being scared. And I hate saying it out loud. Bad shit happens to me there, and the power sharing agreement makes it impossible to guess who's going to take a shot at me."

Shit. Of course.

Before Cade could formulate a reply though, her phone rang. The center console display showed an unknown number, and Lya stiffened.

"That's the country code for France," she said. "There is no fucking reason for anyone to be calling me from there."

When she let it ring, Cade said, "Are you going to answer it?"

She hesitated then tapped to reject the call. "No. I don't give a shit what anyone there has to say. And we're having a discussion. That's more important to me." This time, her glance held a tinge of wry amusement. "I can't exactly run off just now, can I?"

He snorted, unable to help a relieved laugh. "I suppose not."

Still, Lya said nothing for another mile. He held his silence, settling in to wait. Elves were predators. Humans were not, though they fancied themselves to be. She was half human, and he hadn't been anything close in nearly half a millennium.

Five more miles slipped away before she growled.

"You're annoyingly good at waiting me out," she grumbled.

"I've had time to learn." Cade studied her without looking at her directly.

"I know when you're watching me, creeper."

He smiled with the side of his face she couldn't see. If she was calling him names, she'd at least halfway forgiven him.

"I'm mad at you, but I think I'm madder at myself." The words fell out of her in a tumble like a rockslide. "Which makes me more mad."

"Because of Donatien?"

"No. Yes. No—fuck, I don't know." She chewed her lip. "I realized I've been projecting on you. That half the reason I'm trying to help people is to prove I'm not a walking buffet. And then just as I tell myself I'm being stupid, some random comes slithering out of your past, fools me into thinking he's harmless—"

Cade grunted.

"Okay, not harmless but at least no more dangerous than any other vampire. And then he asks you to *share me*, like that's a thing that's done, when I thought I was finally safe." Her sideways glance at him was as sharp as one of her knives. "Am I safe, Cade?"

He couldn't help his snarl. "That you even have to ask makes me sick with myself. That should never be in question."

She started to reply then pressed her lips together firmly as two more mile markers passed.

Okay, so maybe she was good at the waiting game too. Cade's earlier thought came back to him, that whenever he thought he knew better or that keeping things from her would be the best course of action, it backfired spectacularly and usually at Lya's expense.

"Donatien found me in a half-flooded warehouse on the banks of the Gulf." His words came from him as slow as the Mississippi, quiet as an owl's wing.

Lya could hear him though. She stiffened.

"It was as far as I'd had the money and fortitude to get after fleeing what should have been Morris's pyre. I hadn't fed properly in weeks and was more than half dead and more than ready to go the rest of the way. Donatien…he saved me."

The memory flashed through his mind. The choking fear that'd washed over him at the ash-and-iron scent of another *moroi*—not his master but, at that time, all of Cade's experiences with Otherside had been brutal ones. He hadn't been prepared for the gentleness of Donatien's touch after he'd slapped him awake or the teasing words that'd followed instead of a beating or other abuse.

Cade cleared his throat. "He took me to a flophouse, a hole in the wall owned by one of the fae. I was too out of it to know it then, but he nursed me back to health on a diet of urchins and whores. And when I was better, he gave me an outlet for all the rage and pain I'd held inside for two hundred years while Morris—"

His voice cracked. He hadn't meant to talk about this. He didn't have the strength for it even now.

Closing his eyes, he let just a little of the darkness slip out and curl through him. Just a little of the old rage and savagery that'd insulated him from everything that'd come before and everything he'd done after.

Lya shifted, smelling of shame and misery. "I'm sorry. I didn't mean to—"

"It's not you. Nothing you have to be sorry for." He swallowed hard and shifted in his seat.

Lya always smelled better than usual with his blood freshly in her, and the memories he was dredging up now reminded him how long he'd used blood to drown anything he'd rather have forgotten. He'd broken away—eventually—but seventy years of bloody carnage along the Mississippi was hard to forget.

Especially when sometimes he dearly missed the days when it was easier to sate his hungers without getting caught by mundanes and without having to worry about what his partner would think of him.

"Still," she whispered. When he didn't take the out she offered, the car sped up again before she winced and eased off the gas pedal. "You know I trust you not to hurt me, right? Whatever you did is in the past."

"What I did still lives in me. You should have run last night. Leashes fray and break, and I don't trust the one I have on my hungers with Donatien around."

"Then it's a good thing we left." The stubborn snap to her tone made him look at her. Anger pinched her brow and suffused the car, confusing him. What had he done now?

She cleared it up for him. "If I see Donatien again, I'll kill him."

He blinked, startled out of the darkness by her own. "What? You have no grounds."

"I do." She glanced at him, quickly so she could put her eyes back on the road but long enough for him to see grim determination. "I'm your solidaire, and he's a threat to you. I won't have it."

"I'm stronger than he is now. I—"

"Stop. I saw you last night, and I'm listening to you now. You're on a knife's edge. Every single one of the guests we've housed has had a similar story: the humans are getting closer to discovering Otherside. If you slip, if he pushes you…" She shook her head. "You smell like hunger personified, Cade. I would rather pre-emptively kill him and take the punishment for it than be forced to kill you."

The words hit him like a box to the ears. "I smell like hunger?"

"I didn't notice it before now. Maybe it's being in the car and both of us agitated. But don't think I haven't noticed you hunting more often."

Cade grimaced. "As your hungers have increased, so have my own. A predictable side effect but one I hadn't expected to hit quite so hard. It'll fade again eventually."

Another sideways glance from her. "Okay. Thank you for being honest."

"Ly—"

"I'm not sniping at you for not saying anything sooner. I'm glad you've said something now, rather than letting me confirm it by having to clean up whatever it is Donatien would have dragged you into doing."

Cade couldn't bring himself to tell her that she wouldn't have been able to clean up whatever Donatien dragged him into because, if he was that far gone, Lya herself would have been their first target. Donatien would have made sure of it. He hadn't been a lover, but the bond of… Friendship was probably too generous a word. Something darker was needed.

But the ties that bound them ran deep.

Instead, he addressed something she'd said earlier. "Sharing solidaires is not done, whatever Donatien would like to think."

He could read her flash of expression almost as well as if she'd spoken, despite the darkness. She'd figured out what he hadn't said.

All she said in reply was, "Okay." Then she sent a chill racing through his guts. "Does Donatien know Alejandro?"

The disaster it would be if the two of them did know each other sent Cade into fight mode. The car swerved as his glamour hit Lya hard, and he pulled it back in as he caught the wheel until she shook it off.

"Is that a yes or a no?" Her voice quavered ever so slightly.

"I don't think so." He looked at her, seeing her for a moment with the predator's calculation rather than the lover's adoration.

Yes, he'd strengthened her considerably already. Almost to the level of a weak high-blood. But she was still human-blooded, and there were plenty of Othersiders who wouldn't give a damn about a solidaire bond even if they cared to ask first.

"Either way," he said, "we need to keep our stay in Raleigh short. If Alejandro didn't slink back to St. Augustine, he might well still be there."

Lya tensed, flooding the car with enough fear that Cade had to roll his window down and stick his head out like a damn dog.

When he'd brought himself down again, she asked, "Is your business with Maria going to take long?"

"Not if I can help it," he growled. "We'll make an appearance in Raleigh, stay a day, and keep going. Annapolis, I think. The nearest Otherside presences are the Richmond Conclave of Queens, a couple of werewolf packs in the mountains of Virginia and North Carolina, and a small coterie in Philadelphia."

Lya frowned. "Nobody in D.C.?"

He shook his head. "Part of the local terms of the Détente. No established groups within a hundred miles, although the Richmond Conclave is pushing it." He couldn't help his grin. "The mundanes teach that the British burned the White House in 1814, but it was really werewolves and vampires burning the elves out."

She snorted. "Of course you did. Wait, were you there?"

"No." Melancholy slipped over him again. "I was still in the Louisiana Territory then."

Lya must have heard the soft pain in his voice because she just nodded and sped up again without asking any more questions.

***

The winter nights stretched long enough for them to arrive before dawn, especially with Lya driving. At mid-month, there were fewer speed traps, and Lya's intuition for where the state troopers would be hiding was good, even in South Carolina where they were busier and sneakier. It would be, Cade thought with pride. Despite his earlier thoughts, she was a predator in her own right. Not as much of one as he was, of course, but she'd made a living as a bounty hunter in Otherside, despite her human heritage.

"Where we staying?" she asked as they took the exit for downtown Raleigh.

"We'll check in at Claret then see what Maria's preference is."

Lya navigated the empty streets. Her scent and the stiffness of her posture gave away her anxiety, but she didn't protest. Cade had called to give Maria a heads-up when they crossed the border into South Carolina then taken care of the courtesies with Callista. Maria had been overjoyed he was doing as she'd asked so soon.

Callista had been…Callista. Unreadable and yet full of vague threats, for all she'd kept both Cade and Lya on her payroll.

Cade directed Lya to the parking garage next to the secondary entrance to the coterie's nest. She ground her teeth at being told to leave her weapons in the car's safe, so he relented and allowed her the silver-edged tanto she'd gotten to replace the one lost to the sirens last autumn. She was solidaire to a vagabond. It could be overlooked as an eccentricity.

Her mood lightened at the sight of the golden-skinned vampire leaning against the door.

"Noah," she said. "Long time no see."

"I'm just surprised to see you again, Desmarais." Maria's fledgling gave Cade a long look that said *I know who you are, and what you've done.* "I suppose this one had better control of his instincts than I thought, given past history."

Lya frowned, and Cade allowed his eyes to blacken in warning. Noah was only around two hundred years old, if Cade recalled correctly—a snack for a *moroi* of Cade's age. That'd never stopped the other vampire from testing the limits before though.

Noah's mood flipped to geniality, even as the skin around his eyes tightened. "In any case, welcome back to Raleigh. Maria bid me wait for you and escort you to the Master."

Tight prickles of…not fear, but healthy apprehension, raced over Cade. "I hadn't thought—"

"Of course you hadn't, vagabond. You're only welcome because Callista smoothed things over, but the Viking didn't live this long by giving master-killers easy access."

Lya snorted. "Technically, *I* killed Morris, thank you very much."

"Just so." Noah raised his brows as though it should have been obvious that Lya was included in the master-killer comment. "And now"—he sniffed—"you're one flesh. So much the better a team for killing city-level masters or at least for making an almighty mess." He cocked his head and smiled grimly. "Which you've both already demonstrated an unholy talent for."

Cade rested a hand on Lya's shoulder to stop the bubbling question about the one flesh part. He'd explain it later. "Lead on then, if you please. It's been an eight-hour drive, and I have a feeling the hours till dawn will stretch longer than I might like now."

With a last cryptic look, Noah unlocked the door and led them down a series of stairs, through two more doors, and then through a heavy leather curtain.

Lya would have halted as she pushed through, had Cade not kept her momentum going with a hand around her wrist, drawing her forward behind him.

The room was full of vampires, including Torsten, the old Viking himself, sprawled in his throne with one booted foot over the other knee and a broadsword propped against the arm of the chair. The Master of Raleigh had a power signature that fit his status, a heavy metaphysical throb like the beat of a dying heart. Cade didn't always sense it—most of the old ones learned to tamp it down enough not to set off the mundanes they hid among or at least enough that they wouldn't consciously perceive it.

That Torsten wasn't doing so now boded ill for them.

A roaring fire blazed in the massive hearth on the far side of the room from the secondary entrance they'd used, welcome in chasing out the chill and damp of both the cooler northern climes and being underground. Standing at Torsten's right hand was Aron and, at his left, Maria.

Though he stood almost completely still, something was off about Aron, a skittering edge of—

Bloody flaming hell.

Madness.

Aron was in the early stages of mental decay, of becoming a rakshasa.

Torsten's line was known for it, and Cade suspected it was what drove Maria's relentless hunt for Otherside blood as much as chafing at her number three position did. The affliction was growing more common as the Détente combined with human technology to make it harder to get powerful blood without the kind of fight that couldn't go undetected.

Cade was on autopilot as he steered Lya toward the dais, mind racing. An audience like this meant one of two things: a reward or a punishment. Cade hadn't done anything to be rewarded, so it was to be a punishment. Not death. Callista had cleared him of that, and she was the ruling power here. But Torsten couldn't let something like attempted murder of one's master go without comment.

He'd miscalculated in bringing Lya here. Either that or Maria had lured him.

She stared back blank faced when he narrowed his eyes at her then at Aron just for good measure, before kneeling and bowing his head to Torsten. At his side, Lya did the same, staying slightly behind and to his left, as he'd instructed her in the event of just this possibility.

"Master of Raleigh," Cade started, "my thanks for the grace you offer my solidaire and me in a day's respite."

"Grace?" Torsten put his foot on the floor and leaned forward to rest his elbows on his knees. "Interesting choice of words. I suppose it is. Or is it?" Cade glanced up in time to see him gesture at Aron. "I suppose you will tell me when we're finished here."

Aron ghosted down the few steps to the floor, eyes fixed on Lya—and Cade got a very bad feeling about what was about to happen.

Chapter 6: Lya

I'd seen Aron once in my visits to Maria. He'd stared at me with hot, jealous eyes. He might be Torsten's number two, but Maria had claimed me first and our arrangement didn't require her to share. I understood better now why Maria had been so keen on snapping me up, but that didn't prepare me for the intensity he approached with now.

"Cade?" I whispered so quietly that it was less than a breath.

He flicked his hand in the signal to hold then rose as Aron stopped in front of him. "What's the meaning of this?"

The other vampire's anticipation weighted the air more oppressively than the heat from the oversized fire. "Cade the vagabond, you're accused of attacking your master with intent to kill. How do you plead?"

"I don't," he snapped. "That is done with. The Arbiter—"

"Doesn't rule in Raleigh," Torsten said.

I dared a glance at him, but he was reclining with steepled fingers, like he was about to watch a dogfight and just waiting for the good part to start.

"She advises," Torsten continued. "She *arbitrates*. But I am Master here, and I can't have such behavior go unpunished."

I swept my gaze around the room. That was why it was full of vampires, all of them standing deathly still and expressionless. Except for maybe Maria. I thought I detected a hint of frustration in her gaze. Had she betrayed us?

As though she'd heard my thought, she caught me looking and gave her head a fractional shake. This wasn't her doing.

So she said.

Aron smiled, slow and cruel. "Very well. The plea entered is no contest."

Cade stiffened. "I didn't—"

Turning to me, Aron spoke over him. "Lydia of House Desmarais, solidaire to Cade, you killed Morris of Bayswater, the Wolf of the Sea. How plead you?"

I shot to my feet and started to answer as my fear and anger spiked.

Cade unerringly reached back and gripped my wrist. "She has no need to plead. Morris was in breach of the Détente."

Maria shifted. "As I already said, Master."

Torsten cut a glance at her, completely unconcerned. "Yes, fine. Funny how you always seem to be in the thick of things, Maria."

She dropped her eyes, lips pressing into a firm line. Maybe she was in almost as much trouble as we were.

The Master of Raleigh turned his attention back to us—to me—and I wavered as the full weight of his power hit me. Or not quite full. It grew stronger by the heartbeat, and mine was running pretty damn quick. Dropping my head, I shook it as a buzzing pressure built in my mind, and I locked my knees to keep from falling.

Cade gripped my wrist tighter, enough that the bones ground together, as he stepped in front of me.

Between the pain and his body between us, the power broke.

I gasped, panting as though I'd run a marathon at full speed and wavering on my feet.

Pull it together, Desmarais.

Whatever was happening here wasn't over. I held my breath to force it and my heartbeat to slow then looked up, narrowly avoiding Aron's gaze.

"Let her be, Master of Raleigh." Cade's tone was barely polite, more cold than anything else. I knew him well enough to hear the rage in it.

Aron chuckled, and something in it put every hair on my body on end. "I think not," he said. "In penance for your crimes, you'll surrender your solidaire to me."

Gasps broke the silence of the other vampires, even as I reeled in shock.

Being Cade's solidaire was supposed to make me untouchable. I should have been safe here, protected, even if Cade died. That'd been half the point of formalizing our relationship to begin with.

"Over my twice-dead body," Cade snarled.

Torsten sat forward. "Then by all means. Begin."

It hit me then that this whole audience was a trap, and Cade had just sprung it.

I backpedaled as Cade released me to block Aron's strike. Then I jumped when that put me too close to the vampires on Maria's side of the room.

A hand grabbed me, and I snarled as I whirled to fight its owner.

Grim-faced, Noah shook his head so tightly I almost missed it and tugged me closer to his side. "I am sorry you got pulled into this," he breathed into my ear. "My mistress said she will ensure you're protected if he loses. It was her promise to Cade."

I didn't dare open my mouth to ask what the hell was going on between Cade and Maria for her to offer that kind of promise or what Cade had demanded in return.

A sharp crack yanked my head back around to the fight.

Aron snarled savagely at Cade, clutching his right arm to his body and massaging his hand. As I watched, he snapped two fingers straight.

Cade snarled right back, a hint of triumph in the curl of his lip. "You know I'm no easy meat."

They circled each other, silent and menacing. The fluidity in Aron's movements said he'd fed this evening. Cade hadn't, but he'd been drinking from me often enough that he didn't *need* to feed nightly.

Both of them still had more speed than I'd know what to do with if they were coming at me.

I could take a vampire in their first or second century, although I wouldn't want to try Noah, who felt to me like he was at the top end of that range. Morris had been weakened by his condition, even if he was still faster than the motherfucker had a right to be.

Cade and Aron? Made me glad Cade hadn't wanted to hurt me when I hunted him last summer.

Their fight was a bizarre mix of boxing, animalistic strikes, and on Cade's side, some martial arts. Aron seemed to rely on the greater speed and strength his age gave him, and Cade was just holding his own with better training and the power conveyed by my Otherside blood.

Their movements blurred.

The only sounds in the room were the crackling fire, the sounds of hits connecting with flesh, and my own heartbeat and breathing.

My thought from the other night came back to me. I was a good bounty hunter. But Cade was an excellent predator, and even as I watched, he sank into a new level of savagery I'd only seen hinted at once before.

I loved the man, yet I had no fucking clue who he was or what he was capable of. Something about that scared me almost as much as this situation did. But if I ran now, we would both die.

So I anchored my feet to the floor and willed my support to him.

It wasn't enough. Aron broke through a block and hooked Cade's ankle. Then they were on the floor. Cade had reach, but Aron had mass. And up close, mass won.

Aron knocked Cade dizzy with a battering blow to the face, followed swiftly by a second. Blood sprayed across the floor, and Cade choked as Aron gripped his throat and glanced at me.

"You broke the bitch in better than Maria would have, given your showing here," Aron snarled. "I'll enjoy her."

He reared back, fangs bared like a snake while a dazed Cade struggled.

Something snapped in me.

I was nobody's prize, and I'd be damned if anybody but me killed Cade.

Drawing my blade from its back sheath, I launched myself toward them, easily breaking Noah's grasp with my unexpected movement. "Like hell!"

I collided with Aron, knocking him off Cade, only to be thrown against the far wall as the vampire used my momentum to kick me off. A sharp crack and a sudden pain in my lungs told me I'd broken a rib. But the important thing was I'd kept my grip on my knife and my attack had given Cade time to recover and drag himself to his feet.

Aron's full attention was on me though. "Not completely broken in then. Good. I like a bit of fight."

"Fight this," Cade growled.

Aron whirled.

I drew on Aether. Whether from desperation or the boost I'd gotten from drinking Cade's blood or both, more came to me than usual, almost high-blood strength. I didn't stop to wonder at it, just lashed out at Aron with a spear of magic. "Drop dead!"

He went down.

And in a burst of dizziness that told me I'd pushed my ability to handle Aether to the limit, so did I. Not even the jabbing pain of my broken ribs hitting the floor could keep me conscious—and it might have sent me on my way into darkness a little faster.

***

Arguing voices woke me, although I was careful to keep my eyes shut and my breathing even.

"—completely fucking unacceptable, Maria. You have my affection, but that is *not* this."

Cade.

He was still alive. Good. Because if there was a thing between him and Maria, I wanted to be the one to kill them both. I did not nearly burn out my aura for a tryst.

Maria's scoff held more than a little sour frustration. "Why would I ask your support if it wasn't this bad?" she hissed. "Think, *muffin*. When have you ever heard of a solidaire being collateral for their master's sins?"

That must have caught Cade because silence stretched taut in the room.

"What brought you north this quickly anyway? I was expecting to have to work months to get you here."

"Donatien. He tracked us down in St. Augustine. Had Lya alone." A brief hesitation before he continued, shame lacing his tone. "I panicked."

"Mm." Maria's small sound was equally pensive and disapproving. "So you were spoiling for blood before you even got here. No wonder."

"Aron had it coming." Cade's snarl was full of a deep, abiding hatred. Aron had made a lifelong enemy tonight.

On one hand, I didn't like it. On the other, it felt good.

"Oh, I don't disagree, darling boy. But you cannot go back to being the Butcher of the Bayou. Not in this day and age. You're lucky Torsten found the fight so fucking entertaining."

My breath almost caught then, as much for the title—because I could hear the capitals in it—as for the sound of flesh on flesh.

"I will be whatever I have to be to keep Lya safe, and you will *never* say that name again." Cade's voice was darker and colder than I'd ever heard it, like it was coming from a completely different person.

"Then don't act like him." A pause before Maria's light tone dipped into the dangerous range. "Let go of me, Cade. I'm your only ally here and the only one who will defend Lydia if you're gone rather than blood raping her until she dies of it." Another pause. "I mean it. You saw how they looked at her. The rest will pity her, but they will not dare to lift a finger to help her unless it's to smother her in her sleep."

A rustle of fabric said he'd obeyed her. Then the bed sank. Cade's familiar touch smoothed a curl off my face.

"She doesn't know," he said. "I've been trying to figure out how to tell her."

She bloody well knows now.

"Then how did you explain Donatien?"

"The truth. Some of it anyway." His voice cracked. "I mean it, Maria. I'm not—not *him* anymore. I'm just me. And I'm hers."

That eased me a little. Whatever they'd meant by "affection" had to be some kind of vampire thing. An oath, maybe.

Before I could figure out how to pretend to wake up, the door banged open, and the weight left the bed. It was all I could do to keep pretending to be out of it. Some flicker of intuition said not to draw attention to myself right now.

Or maybe not intuition. Rather, the weight of a power signature.

Torsten.

"Impressive showing," the master vampire said in a low, cold voice. "From both of you. I thought your solidaire was only a low-blood?"

"Her father is human," Cade replied. The icily polite rage was back. "The human-blooded are fair game as solidaires."

Next thing I knew, a hand closed around my throat as my efforts to be unnoticed failed.

My eyes flew open as it strangled me.

Torsten leaned over me, his attention on Cade and Maria as he casually held me down. I fought his grip with my whole body and clawed his arms by reflex, even as my broken ribs screamed with the excruciating pain of my struggles and nearly made me black out again.

I was not dying. Not here. Not like this.

But despite the vampire's small, wiry frame, nothing I did dislodged him.

He didn't even bother to look at me. "If she is half human, then how is it that she had enough Aether to command my second, a *moroi* of nearly eight centuries? How is it that you faced him with a strength beyond your five?"

"Torsten—Master, please." Cade sounded frantic, but he didn't move as I kept fighting.

I didn't blame him, even as black spots started hazing my vision.

Aron was one thing. A millennia-old city master was quite another.

"Please!" Cade dropped to his knees.

The pressure around my throat eased enough that I managed to snatch a breath, coughing and hacking, nearly blacking out from the pain of it.

My gaze met Cade's.

His was the full black of a vampire who'd lost it, and he was quivering with the effort not to come to my rescue.

I gripped Torsten's wrist with one hand as I tried to get fingers between his hand and my throat, to no avail.

His grip tightened again. "I should kill her for what you've made her, before she turns maenad or worse. How much blood have you given her?"

From the look of despair on Cade's face and the grimness on Maria's, there was no good answer to that question.

And yet Torsten chuckled as he tilted his head and studied Cade. "The Butcher on his knees. I always thought you had more pride than that."

Cade flinched then bowed his head. "Once, I did. But I am not that man anymore, and there is a powerful blood witch with an interest in my solidaire. I had cause to strengthen her faster than is normally proper. Master."

The grip on my throat eased, only to flex painfully against the bruise already forming before relaxing and flexing again. The uneven blood flow to my head combined with my overuse of Aether and my hammering heart to give me the mother of all headaches, but I didn't know where my knife was and drawing on Aether again was beyond me just now.

And what was I, a thirty-one-year-old half-elf, going to do against a vampire city master with a power signature that could probably set off mundanes for a full city block?

With a shudder, I surrendered, belatedly remembering that my struggling only heightened the predatory instincts in a vampire. With Cade, it was bedroom fun. With Torsten? Working myself up was making me even more edible, and I was risking a lung puncture.

The master vampire's gaze finally flicked to me, and I averted my eyes before he could catch me.

"Not entirely brainless then," he said.

"She was only protecting me. As is her duty." Cade's voice rasped with strain. "I told her we'd be safe here. Finding ourselves threatened… She would not have gone after Aron otherwise. She takes her position deadly seriously."

Pressure weighed on me again as Torsten turned his attention back to me. "Is that so, halfling?"

Biting back renewed fury at the slur, I jerked my head in a nod. "Yes, Master."

The word "master" burned on my tongue, but life was worth more than pride or dignity at this juncture. And both mine and Cade's hung in the balance.

Besides, I wouldn't find out who the hell the Butcher of the Bayou had been if I died now.

Another caress to my throat. "Will you seek vengeance against Aron for this night? Against me?"

I glanced at Cade then back at Torsten's chin and forced some more words out, something I thought a vampire of Torsten's age and position would want to hear. "I obey my masters."

Plural. Because I knew Torsten wanted to hear me acknowledge him as well as Cade.

With a last squeeze, he released me. "Fortunately for you, Cade, your solidaire seems to know her place." He sighed, looking annoyed for a moment before deadly disinterest blanked his face again. "I didn't want any of this. Solidaires are to be treasured, especially those loyal enough to attack a vampire centuries older than their own master in his defense. Now my people will think me unduly harsh. But little Maria put me in a bad position with this Morris business, even if I hated the old fucker."

I held as still as I could, keeping my eyes averted as Torsten pondered and his power signature swirled.

"Maria," he finally said.

She jumped at the harshness of Torsten's tone. "Master?"

"You'll be punished for this. Don't think I'm unaware of your machinations and their role in this mess. Your cleverness makes me glad I saved you from burning at the stake most days, but lately you cause as much trouble as you avert."

"Yes, Master," she said faintly.

"Fine. Cade is properly humbled. Half the coterie saw his solidaire broken, and they'll scent truth when I say I punished her further."

My blood boiled at the amusement in his tone, but I kept my mouth shut.

"The point has been made," Torsten concluded. "Get them out."

"Do you have a preference where, Master?" Maria asked.

Torsten snorted. "Now she seeks my approval." He was silent long enough that I darted a glance at him to find him looking at Cade, who was in turn watching me through his lashes while trying to look like he had his eyes on the floor. "Get them one of the coterie-held rooms at The Umstead. Punishment has been served, so we'll put it behind us and treat our vagabond with the required guest privilege—as long as he doesn't dare step foot in my nest again. Ever."

"Yes, Master," both Cade and Maria said.

With a last weighing look at me, Torsten left the room, the broadsword swinging lightly in his grip.

Cade rose with the jerky slowness I'd expect if he hadn't fed in a week, taking a step to the bed and starting to sink down on it before stiffening. "I'm sorry for this. I imagine you have questions."

That was an understatement. I just looked at him, a nasty blend of emotions curling through my gut to sicken me.

Chapter 7: Cade

Lya didn't say a word the entire drive over to The Umstead, the city's five-star hotel. That it was owned by the Raleigh coterie via a series of shell companies and fronts was, of course, a carefully maintained secret.

Certainly one that was holding up better than Cade's own.

His eyes told him she wished she could run right now, be anywhere that wasn't here. His nose told him she was feeling equal parts furious, betrayed, scared, and in physical pain.

When they arrived, she found a neutral expression and let him handle the arrangements at the front desk. It was going on five in the morning, and they looked bedraggled and beaten, though Lya hid under a hood and a scarf. Fortunately, Cade's black titanium credit card, Maria's calling ahead, a push of glamour, and the hotel's own high class got them a pair of room key cards with no questions asked.

Unusually for her, Lya stayed icily silent as the lift descended a floor to their rooms. Garden-level. Not the most defensible in an attack but below the line of the sun's rays and therefore more comfortable for him.

As though there was any comfort to be had with his love acting like he was true-dead and rotting.

The door shut behind them with a barely audible click, but Lya made up for it by practically hurling her suitcase to the floor when he handed it to her then flinching and wrapping an arm around herself with a whimper.

"Lya…" he started.

She ignored him, too furious and hurt even to shout at him. After digging some clothes out of her suitcase, she marched into the bathroom and slammed the door behind her. The click of the lock felt like an accusation. After a moment, the shower started running.

Fuck.

Fury of his own flashed through Cade. He indulged it for all of one minute, cursing the Raleigh coterie in general; Torsten, Aron, and Maria in particular; and himself most especially to Hekate. Then he boxed it up and pushed it down, trying to calm himself before Lya came out of the bathroom. They needed to talk, and she smelled exceedingly good when she was this agitated, which had him salivating, even as his stomach twisted so hard he didn't think he'd ever feed again.

The shower switched off, and a few minutes later, the door swung open.

Lya stalked out in a cloud of steam and floral-scented body lotion. The hotel's. She'd always been more of a woods or musk kind of woman. Without her scarf to cover it, a black-and-green bruise wrapped her neck above the collar of her T-shirt.

"Lydia," he started again, unable to completely mask his fury from her. That Torsten had dared harm a solidaire, *his* solidaire—

"I don't want to talk to you right now. I don't even want to look at you."

"You're hurt," he said stubbornly. "I can smell it."

"Yeah, well, it wouldn't be the first time I broke a rib or three."

That explained the breathiness and the flinch.

Cade tried again. "At least let me—"

"Who the fuck are you?" Her words snapped out like a lash.

He'd been waiting for them, but they still hurt. Waiting for them didn't mean he had an answer he was willing or able to give her yet. Not when she was like this.

When he didn't respond, she whirled on him, her face twisted in a snarl and her words breathy. "The *only* reason I didn't drop you off and keep driving is because I can barely breathe and I genuinely trust that you would never knowingly or intentionally put me in a situation like that. But for the rest?" She shook her head, wincing as she clasped her ribs again. "I keep thinking I know you, and tonight, I realized I never will."

The words cut more deeply into him than Morris's knife had in his throat last summer. Blinking fast, he tried to recover his equilibrium, but she just kept throwing verbal punches in a raspy voice that said she was hurting as much physically as emotionally.

"You'd think I'd have learned my lesson with Henri. I must be the stupidest fucking woman on earth to keep falling in love with men who can't—who won't even—" Shuddering, she looked away as tears fell. "I can't be here."

Cade was between her and the sliding glass door to the patio before she could finish turning toward it. Her sudden wariness made his heart hurt, but he couldn't let her leave. Not like this. Not this time.

"Move." She glared at him, her expression angry but her scent aching with too much pain. The anger was a mask.

"No."

When she started for the main room door, he slid into her path again. Aron had beaten the hell out of him, but he was healing fast and could still outpace her.

"Don't do this, Cade."

A silly mental voice noted how odd it was that even with him blocking her exits, she didn't smell of fear. She truly didn't think he'd hurt her, even after hearing his old moniker tossed out by two other *moroi*. He couldn't let her leave thinking that made her gullible or foolish.

Tired of everything, Cade gave in to his instincts, flowed into her space, and caught her around both arms. Not hard enough to add more bruises to what she was already wearing but firmly enough they both knew she wasn't going anywhere.

He'd expected her to fight him, not for her knees to give out and for him to be holding her up. Quickly, he shifted his hands so he could scoop her up and deposit her on the bed, where she sat stiff and trembling. Spent adrenaline burned his nose as the scent of it came off her in waves that matched the pounding of her heart.

She might try to run, but she wouldn't get far.

A new moon with him, a night drive almost halfway up the East Coast, whatever the hell she'd done to drop Aron at Torsten's, then being attacked by Torsten…she had nothing left and was still trying to run the motor that drove her.

Oh, love. This is how you die, if you're not careful.

Aron should accept the draw, but if he didn't, if he'd sent underlings after them, Lya was an unknowing target.

Rather than voicing the thought, he said, "We're bandaging those ribs before you do anything else."

He couldn't quite erase the growl from his tone, but he was suddenly done with her running. Dead tired of it and then some. He'd bent and bent, and now he was going to break if he had to watch her walk away one more time. It was her gods-damned *running* that kept him from telling her the very thing that had set her off this time.

Even so, part of the keeping of a solidaire was recognizing when they had no more to give and needed to rest. "You are *mine*," he said, "and that means mine to take care of, especially when I couldn't protect you before."

The growing lump in his throat choked him off. He hadn't been able to protect her after telling her she'd be safe. He should have let her go if that was what she wanted, Aron and his goons or not, but the old resolution to let her do as she wished was holding by the thinnest of threads now.

He'd live if she did leave. They both would.

But it'd be painful for them both in more ways than one.

Torsten had been right to ask how much blood he'd given Lya, because it was far more, far faster, than was sensible. Better that than leaving her completely vulnerable to someone like Alejandro or Donatien.

Rather than fighting him, she just sat, silent and distant, allowing him to move her like a doll as he stripped off her T-shirt as gently as he could then went for the first aid kit in his suitcase.

If she thinks she has no way out, something worse than this will happen.

Cade mulled that over as he carefully wrapped her ribs. He could feed her his blood and they'd heal more quickly, but if she couldn't bear to look at him—and her gaze was fixed on a tasteful black-and-white photograph of flowers across the room—then she wouldn't bear tasting him either.

She gritted her teeth, flinched once, and subsided. Cade dipped back into the kit for arnica cream, and she flinched again as he started smoothing it over the bruise around her throat. She'd heal all this by morning, even without his attentions. Her own elven blood, and the infusion of his, ensured it.

But that wasn't the point.

She felt threatened, abandoned, unsafe. She'd been hurt. And it was his fault. Worse, it was reinforcing her worldview that she didn't matter and would be hurt no matter where she went or who she was with.

He couldn't fix that for her, and he couldn't protect her from everything. It was a reminder to himself, both about him and her.

What he could do was show her he'd be there afterward, Butcher or not. He wanted to apologize but had a feeling this was one of the times an apology would spark the rage that always lived in her heart rather than soothing it.

"Where else does it hurt?" he asked softly when he was done with her neck.

She closed her eyes in a long blink. "I'm just tired."

"Hungry? Thirsty?"

Another long pause. "No. I just… I need not to be for a little bit."

Cade barely stopped himself from flinching again at that. None of this was in her usual behavior. She should be starving and parched. Demanding an ibuprofen, at the very least. But as he tried to figure out how to get her to eat something, she laid down gingerly and turned onto the side that he assumed wasn't hurting her.

Fuck.

There was a way to fix this. They'd fixed everything else.

He slumped. But everything else had been different. Not this bad. Because even if he'd been partially responsible before, he hadn't given the instruction that'd led to her harm. This time, she'd gone into danger because he'd told her to. Told her she'd be safe.

She's better off without me.

That thought had him up and off the bed with vampiric speed, as though staying near Lya would infect her with it. He fled to the bathroom, taking his turn at a shower, frustrated that he couldn't wash away the memory of the night's bullshit as easily as he did the dirt of the fight.

If you were the Butcher again, you could find a way to be rid of Aron. And Alejandro and Donatien and everyone else who threatened her. Squeezing his eyes shut, Cade shook his head in an effort to clear the thought, letting the shower spray hit him in the face. *She might leave you. But at least everyone who threatened her because of you would be dead or so broken they wouldn't dare go after her again.*

Unbidden memories of old Louisiana swam up, and he pushed them back down before they could fully take shape. He wasn't that monster anymore. He wasn't what Morris had done to him, what Morris had made him.

He was Cade. He didn't murder for the hell of it. Or dismember bodies or torture the innocent to regain the power he himself had lost.

Not anymore.

He thought he'd been clear when he'd drawn that line with Donatien, but he needed to be clearer. He had something to lose now—some*one*—and he valued Lya even more than his own soul, if he even had one anymore.

As he shut the water off, he resolved to confess. His past kept coming closer, as though the ghosts could sense he was finally happy and were taking their vengeance. Lya was worth it though, even if half-elves were common enough that he could find another.

He didn't want another.

He wanted *her.*

Which meant, even if she told him she didn't need to know the depths of his past, he needed to tell her before she got hurt again.

Even if she ran.

Decided, Cade switched off the shower and dried off. The mirror showed his reflection—modern ones weren't made of silver anymore—and he winced at the dark circles under his eyes. Those were guilt, as though the crimes on his soul were determined to mark his body. He left the beard growing in. Lya liked it, and it created a visual differentiation between past and present that he could hold onto.

I'm not the monster I was. I'm a man, and I have a good woman who loves me.

Faith. He had to have faith in that love and in her.

Faith or not, he half expected her to be gone when he came out of the bathroom, but she was still there. His shoulders came down a notch then jerked back up as he considered whether she'd want him to share the bed. The suite's couch was too small for his height, and sleeping on the floor seemed dramatic, as likely to backfire as to soothe her.

Teeth gritted, he circled the bed to the empty side, freezing when he saw her still awake and watching him, not asleep as he'd thought. Her eyelids were heavy enough that she wouldn't stay conscious for much longer, but he settled into the stillness of the undead, not wanting to break the moment or push her one way or another.

Lya blinked, another long, slow drop of her eyelids that seemed like it would end with her asleep, but she wrestled them open again. "I need to know." Her voice slurred with exhaustion. "I know I said I didn't, but I need to know to be safe."

"Okay, love." Cade took a step closer to the bed and, when she didn't react, eased down onto it, keeping distance between them as he stretched out and propped his head on his hand.

She watched him, obviously struggling to stay awake. "I'm still mad at you."

"That's fair."

Her frown said that wasn't what she'd expected him to say. "Why aren't you defending yourself?"

"I have no need to defend myself from you."

Her frown deepened.

He scrambled to explain before she could take offense. "My sins are many, Lya. I know it. I don't deny it. If I couldn't accept them, accept what I am, then I would have found a way to die long before now." He dropped his gaze then flicked it back up. "You're still here. I have to believe that means you'll at least hear me out."

"Still mad." Her eyelids drooped.

"That's okay, love."

"Not mad I'm mad?"

"No." That was absurd, but he didn't want to minimize her by saying so. Too many people had done that to her already. He was frustrated as hell, scared he'd finally gone too far. But not angry.

"You stopped me running. Didn't do that before."

"I need you." The words that slipped from him weren't the ones he meant to say, but they were Hekate's honest truth.

That jerked her eyes open again, although they didn't stay wide for long. "Tomorrow. You tell me. Tomorrow."

"I will," Cade promised. His heart beat with fear, and his mouth was strangely dry. But he'd do as she asked.

It'd be a relief to tell her finally. When Alejandro had turned up, all of his misdeeds had floated to the surface of his consciousness. Accept them or not, they seemed especially ugly now that he had to consider what the person he loved might think.

Slowly, and with a wince, she extended a hand to the middle of the bed.

Equally as slowly, he reached out and brushed her fingers. When she didn't pull away, he wrapped his hand around hers, although he didn't dare to edge closer and gather her to him like he really wanted.

This small peace offering would have to be enough.

Cade watched her slump then tense and relax again as she fought sleep and lost. The sun rose, pushing him to follow her as he prayed to Hekate she'd still be here when he woke.

70

Chapter 8: Lya

I woke a few hours before sunset with a stomach so empty it ached and a thirst so strong I could barely open my mouth. I inhaled deeply before I remembered my ribs were broken and froze then frowned, unwrapped the bandages, and did it again when nothing hurt. Prodding at my neck didn't draw a throb of pain from the aching bruises Torsten had left me with last night.

I was fine.

Groggy, starving, dehydrated, and hearthurt. But otherwise fine. Still alive, which had been seriously in question last night.

Cade had to have known I would be fully healed by morning, but he'd tended me anyway. Stopped me from running when doing so would have caused me to hurt myself more, when he'd always let me go before. We had the rings. He'd know where I was. So that wasn't why, unless he'd been afraid I'd take mine off. I looked at his big hand on top of mine, slack as he slept on, his brow pinched in worry.

I didn't really want to know about his past. I didn't want to hear the man I loved had been a horrible murderer or a worse murderer than most vampires were just by their natures.

At the same time, not knowing kept hurting me. I hadn't wanted to come back to Raleigh. Other than meeting Cade here—and Maria—my time in the Triangle had been pretty bad. Aside from the memories, there was Callista as well, an ever-present menace at the back of my mind. She hadn't summoned us yet, and I dared to hope that she wouldn't.

My thoughts kept spinning in a haze of brain fog until I remembered I needed to eat something, badly. I started to pull my hand from Cade's, only for him to tighten his grip and make a sound I'd never heard from him before, halfway between a whine and a whimper, almost too quiet to catch. His brow puckered as he slept on, still in the same position he'd been in when he'd joined me on the bed last night.

I fought the urge to comfort him, childishly wanting to punish him for my hurts, but a twist in my heart wouldn't let me. Whether I liked it or not, Raleigh was a logical stop for us heading north. Cade had been active on the East Coast for centuries. Most of his connections and safehouses were no farther west than this. Given what I'd learned last night, I had to assume anything farther west was probably not somewhere we should go. Trying to stay anywhere else in the Carolinas would have been a mess, given the short notice for our arrival, and trying to drive farther north before stopping would have pushed me too far into exhaustion. The sun bothered Cade less than it had before he'd started drinking from me regularly, but he still got burned easily enough—and cranky enough about the pain of it—that we didn't travel by daylight unless it was necessary.

Fine. So he might not have considered my PTSD or whatever it was, my exceedingly bad memories of the Triangle, but that didn't mean he hadn't accounted for everything he could have.

A traitorous voice told me I was making excuses for him and being a doormat. How many times would I excuse him? What would it take for me to finally decide I was being stupid over him? Most people got their hearts broken and buried themselves in a pint of ice cream. I'd gotten myself exiled, and it'd all been downhill from there.

Except for Cade.

He's kept things from you. He's not safe, and he can't keep you safe.

But when I'd really gotten into trouble, he'd been there.

He'd made some of the trouble, but he hadn't abandoned me. Ever. He'd always come for me. But was that enough?

Nobody's perfect.

I didn't know if the counterthought was excusing him or myself or us both. But I couldn't stay here arguing with myself until I starved to death, and I needed to take care of my needs before sunset so we could hit the road.

I tried again to extract my hand, and again, he tightened his grip. The noise was the same, a hint of fear to it.

I'd live another few minutes without eating, so I snuggled closer, pulling his arm up and over me and tucking myself under his chin. His arm tightened around me, and one of his legs tangled in mine. Before meeting him, I'd have called the sensation I felt "trapped." Now it felt like being needed. Being wanted. I huffed an annoyed sigh at myself then breathed in the scent of ash, iron, and granite that rose with the heat of my breath.

Cade inhaled sharply, gripping me hard as his brain told him someone had gotten close to him in his sleep and he wrestled his instinct to violently subdue the threat as my scent came to him.

He pulled away, blinking groggily. "Lya."

"Still here." I smiled wryly.

His hands sprang away. "Did I hurt you?"

"No. I'm all healed up from yesterday. Which you knew would happen, despite my not being hurt that badly in a while."

Cade grunted an affirmative and relaxed. The near-black depths of his gaze locked on me—not vampire black, just the unusually dark brown of his irises. "That's why I've been feeding you so often."

I frowned, vaguely remembering Torsten asking him about that while I tried not to be strangled to death. "Should you not be?"

"No. He was right to ask. Especially with you being a half-elf and all the attendant risks of blending glamour with Aether."

"Is that why he…" I swallowed hard against the remembered feeling of my throat being closed off.

"No. That was to make a point to me. I'm sorry you bore the brunt of it."

"What point?"

"That being outside the coterie system might give me certain privileges but he's still powerful enough that he can revoke or deny those as he pleases." He hesitated, searching my face. "Are you still mad?"

The abrupt change in subject threw me for a moment. "I want to be. But honestly, I've been thinking it over, and I can't see how you—we—might have done anything differently."

I thought he'd relax then, but he didn't.

"Thank you." He tilted his head. "Do you trust me?"

"Yes."

He smiled at my lack of hesitation, but it was a brief flicker.

Before I could process anything more, I was on my back, pinned beneath him. His knees on either side of my thighs immobilized my legs, one hand had my crossed wrists trapped over my head, and the other caught my chin and forced me to look at him. His eyes had gone full black, and his fangs were bared.

Glamour lapped at me, just shy of pushing into my mind and subduing me as he caught my gaze.

"You're sure about that?" he asked.

I was trapped. I was prey. And yet my racing heart and panting breath weren't driven by fear.

His nostrils flared and he frowned. "You're aroused? I hunt you, and it turns you on?"

"Stupid, stupid half-elf, huh?"

Cade swallowed hard, and his eyelids flickered as he tilted his head back, the way he did when he was trying to bring himself down.

But he didn't let me go.

I stayed as still as I could, trying to get my own response under control. What the hell was this?

After another few heartbeats, he shuddered and released me, getting up to pace at a speed far above human normal. Hell, above my normal.

"Between being starving and your moving fast enough to dizzy me, I'm gonna pass out," I said lightly.

His attention snapped to me. "You haven't eaten yet?"

I shook my head. "It's early."

He snatched the menu from the desk and thrust it at me. "Order something. Don't go downstairs yet though."

"If I order, will you explain what the hell this is all about?"

"Yes. All of it. Or as much as you care to hear. On my word." He gave me a tight smile. "Since that didn't scare you off, maybe the rest won't either."

Good enough for me. I ordered two steaks, one rare with a baked potato and one medium-rare with a side salad so they'd think two people were eating. I'd finish it all, but I did try to vary it enough to keep that from being obvious.

"Talk," I said as soon as I'd hung up.

"First, as to why I ask you not to go alone while you're here." He threw himself into an armchair, and all I could think was it was unfair that he looked that good. He was dead, for fuck's sake, or undead rather.

He arched an eyebrow at my admiration, and I cleared my throat as I got up and got dressed.

"I don't trust that Aron didn't have us followed," Cade said. "He tipped his hand last night. He wants you, badly, and for all that Maria has promised her protection, I'd rather not test it if I'm still around to prevent it."

I couldn't help an outraged snarl. "He'd kidnap me? I thought solidaires were sacred!"

"You are. But there's something not right with him." Cade pressed his lips together, looking grim as his eyes went distant. "I think he's becoming a rakshasa."

I went cold. "Shit."

Mental decay happened sooner or later to all vampires. The brain needed the most resources, and as good as the vampire virus was at preserving what was, effectively, an animated corpse, it couldn't last forever. Drinking from Othersiders held it off, which was part of why Cade was so keen to keep me. Rakshasas were put down like rabid dogs before their lack of control and excessive hunger could drive them to inadvertently break the Détente.

"Shit, indeed." He came out of his thoughts and refocused on me. "Aside from Aron, I have to assume Donatien might turn up again. Alejandro as well. He fixated on you even before I strengthened you." He tilted his head again. "There's something about you that calls to us monsters, love."

I grimaced. "Here I thought it was just assholes."

He barked a laugh. "Are you calling me an asshole?"

"Maybe."

"Well, I leave that up to you. But I'm certainly a monster, and so are the others, no matter how genteel a façade we put on for everyone else."

I assumed this was the segue into his past, but before he could say more, my phone rang with a ringtone I hadn't heard in months.

Callista.

I stared at the phone like it was a slavering werewolf. "Why is she calling me if you arranged passage through her territory?"

"I don't know. But I don't like it."

Steeling myself, I picked up the phone and answered it. "Desmarais."

"Little Lydia. I hear you had quite the experience in Raleigh last night."

As usual when dealing with Callista, I didn't answer what wasn't a question.

"If you're recovered, girl, I have a job for you. One that suits your talents."

I darted a glance at Cade. He was scowling but shook his head. We couldn't decline without causing an incident, given we'd agreed to be on Callista's payroll the last time we'd been in the state and to come when she called.

"I'm listening." I strove for neutrality.

But she chuckled as though she could hear the strain. "I have reason to believe there's a blood witch active in my territory."

My stomach flopped then clenched as I froze.

Cade shot to his feet to pace closer to me.

"What makes you say that?" I finally said.

"The usual signs. An uptick in missing pets. Mutilated wildlife left as roadkill. A certain edge to the magic coating what remains. It started small, but we're up to deer now."

"The local coven has nothing to say?"

"This is beyond them, and I think you know it because I think you know who it is."

"Alejandro," I whispered.

"He does seem to be the logical suspect. Which means you, my dear, and your vagabond, are currently my best resources to track him down and kill him before he moves on to humans and risks breaking the Détente. Especially given that you're already in the state."

A knock at the door pulled my attention. Cade waved, indicating I should keep talking while he got the food. I moved into the bathroom and shut the door, to avoid being overheard.

"How much?" I asked. We were supposed to be on her payroll. I wasn't working gratis, not even for the head bitch in charge of the Carolinas.

"Two hundred."

"Thousand?" Couldn't hurt to be clear.

"Yes."

I chewed my lower lip. Blood witches were a big job. The price was not even close to fair, and I assumed it was total and not for each of Cade and me, which made it even less than fair. Still, it'd put a dent in the debt he was still paying to the werecats for taking us in after I'd been kidnapped by the Darkwatch. Or give me individual funds to live off of while we settled in wherever we were going.

The biggest part, though, was that I—we—didn't have a choice. Leaving the Triangle in September had necessitated an agreement to be on Callista's payroll.

I just couldn't seem to climb out of debt here.

Rather than objecting, I said, "You have evidence for us? A starting point?"

"Yes. I have Watchers pulling together the likely locations. All you need to do is go in for the kill," she said, and I could hear the venomous smile in her voice. "I thought you'd enjoy eliminating this particular threat."

Something nasty curled through my gut as vengeance smothered fear. "I appreciate that."

"Good girl. I expect you here before midnight to collect the intel."

The call ended.

Snarling at the patronizing tone, I exited the bathroom to find the table set with food and Cade lounging on the sofa. There was a stiffness to the posture I didn't think was that of an unfed undead. Not with the tightness of his jaw and that twitching pinky finger.

"Two hundred K." I sat at the chair he'd left pulled out for me, my attention on the smells making my mouth water. I lifted the reflective lid from one plate and shivered with pleasure. This was going to be a good meal, doubly so given how much my stomach twisted with hunger. "She has a starting point for us, and it sounds like her Watchers are doing the heavy lifting on the investigation, which makes the pittance of a paycheck slightly more agreeable." I hated the research part. I'd gotten good at it because being informed kept me alive, but I massively preferred the action. "We're expected by midnight to pick up what they've got so far."

"Good," he said, dark savagery in his tone.

That pulled my attention from the steak I was cutting into, and I found it echoed on his face before he realized I was looking and blanked his features. In the expression was a hint of who he might have been a century or two ago.

"Ask." His voice was a taut whisper.

Suddenly, I was hesitant.

What, and how much, did I really need to know? Nobody in Otherside got a nickname like the Butcher of the Bayou because they served cold cuts and cheese. Was it fear that kept me focused on my food? Cowardice? Or was I finally getting smart, now that I had an idea of what was behind the curtain of that gorgeous face? All vampires were deadly dangerous. Most at least pretended to be constrained by modern sensibilities. Cade certainly did. Nowadays. If I found out the whole truth and he'd been something worse than a simple predator, would it distract me from getting this job done?

Probably.

I hated choosing between safety and focus.

Hoping I wouldn't regret it, I finished my food and leaned back in my chair.

He hadn't moved in that time, nor had his attention shifted from me. He seemed balanced on the edge of something. I couldn't tell what. He wouldn't hurt me. But my heart quickened in anticipation nonetheless.

Especially when the change in my scent hit him and his eyes went vampire black.

Chapter 9: Cade

Cade watched Lya wrestle with the questions she'd been so adamant in wanting to ask. First was avoidance—she focused on eating. Then came doubt, seeping into her until she started fidgeting. Next came indecision, in the cautious flicks of her gaze to his face and posture.

He wished she'd just ask already. But he was an old hunter and a patient one. He didn't move. Barely breathed. If anything, that agitated her more.

Good. Not that he wanted to intimidate her, but he did want her to think. She might still break from him, and if she did, he wanted it to be now. The last twelve hours had told him he couldn't bear the tension anymore. Either she cleaved to him entirely, or they needed to part ways before the solidaire bond deepened further.

Before it could hurt more than it already would to lose her.

Burying his anguish at the thought required him to draw on that old part of himself though, and from the spike in her heartbeat and the sharp edge to her scent, she saw it.

That's right, love. I only play one of the good ones, no matter how much I wish it was true.

She leaned away from her empty plates, going for casual but too stiff in it. After a long silence, she said, "What do I need to know to be safe?"

Cade frowned. That hadn't been what he was expecting. She was an all-or-nothing kind of woman. He'd been preparing to go into detail. This was…

Was it a compromise?

He considered his options. A little more than he thought she was asking but maybe not the fullness of the gory details.

"I killed Morris—attempted to, rather—in 1750, after two hundred years of torture and abuse. Over the next few months, I made my way from Tortuga to Florida and then to a newly founded New Orleans. I wanted nothing to do with the British territories on the East Coast. The journey back across the Atlantic, back home, would have been too much for me with the state I was in. I'd have drained the entire crew before we got a night's sail from port. So. With barely enough sense to keep myself hidden and maintain the Détente, I made my way west."

She blinked rapidly, her eyes widening.

"I mean it when I say I lacked sense. I was barely sane. Maybe I made my attempt on Morris sound reasoned. If it had been, I wouldn't have botched it so badly. He fed on me even as he kept me starved, unless I participated in some depravity or other. Then, I was rewarded with as much as I could drink. Eventually, I learned to shut off my conscience. To survive."

He had to look away then because the expression on her face pained him. Somewhere between pity and anguish. He didn't want it, but she had a good heart.

Agitated, he rose to pace.

"That's no excuse for what I became when I got to New Orleans. But it is the basis for it, so I'm telling you." He forced a smile that even he could feel was sickly. "I suppose in the vain hope you'll… Well, never mind. I was nearly discovered somewhere in modern-day Mississippi and made the rest of the journey without feeding. I'd already been malnourished by two centuries of deprivation and torture. The long journey and the stress of staying hidden for the first time in my life as a *moroi* tipped me into full-on madness."

Cade clenched and unclenched his fists as he remembered that. The cold seeping into him, despite the humid heat of the Gulf Coast. The fear that drove him as much as the hunger he denied. The aching pain of every movement, unsmoothed by blood.

"I'm missing pieces of the journey and my arrival. What I do remember is Donatien leaning over me. Slapping me. Morris had been fond of slapping me awake. I thought Donatien was him and attacked." He snorted. "Donatien's younger than me, but I was in such a wasted state that he easily overpowered me. I should have died my second death that night. But he was lonely and bored, and I soon learned that, when Donatien is lonely and bored, bad things happen. But that night, he was kind. Gentle, even. After centuries of pain, he seemed like an improvement. Anyway. I've told you what happened from there."

She nodded when he glanced at her then grimaced. "Cade, you don't have to—"

"The moniker comes from my time with Donatien."

Lya pressed her lips together at his interruption and subsided.

"I could show you. Mind to mind. We can't talk like master and fledgling yet, but I think you've had enough of my blood now that I could push a memory to you if we were touching."

Blood drained from her face so quickly she swayed. "I— No. I don't need to know that much."

Good. "So. You have the rough sketch," he said. "This is the part of it you need to know: Donatien and I specialized in hunting down Othersiders. Prostitutes and orphans and other forgotten humans, yes. But that was an appetizer. For the entirety of our time together, we co-ruled as the Masters of New Orleans, despite being centuries too young for it. Savagery and cooperation go a long way, even in Otherside, especially in uncertain territory. And not only were we jealous in defending the territory, we also went out of our way to hunt powerful blood."

"Shit." She scrubbed her hands over her face. "That's why you're so…modern. With the driving and the sexting. You had to stay ahead of stronger Othersiders. And it's got to be why Donatien felt so strong."

"Felt?"

She shrugged. "I realized when I was sitting with him that I could kind of get a feel for his power level. I assumed it meant he was as old as you."

"Interesting. But no. I have a century on him. He's just been feeding on more Otherside blood."

"And I let him into our *home*." Her eyes flashed, and her rage seared his nose.

"That's what you're upset about? I've just told you I spent decades making enemies of a good chunk of Otherside in the most brutal ways I could conceive of, and you're mad he was in our nest?"

From the glare she leveled at him, that was exactly her problem. "I let my guard down. I made myself prey."

Cade started to deny it then decided not to lie to her.

"He's very charming," he said instead.

She bounced up from her seat and took up the pacing he'd left off with. "That's why he thought you'd share me."

"Yes. We used to share all of our prey. We weren't lovers, but that kind of sharing can be nearly as intimate."

"Got it. So why is Maria—why is *Torsten*—allowing you anywhere near their territory?"

He shrugged and stared at the floor, still uncomfortable with the details. "The Master of New York had an old second, Giuliano's predecessor. Hector. He and Luz, Santiago's second, were dispatched to get Donatien and me under control when we were on the verge of breaking the Détente. Donatien doesn't know, but I…gave up."

"Gave up? Like surrendered?"

Cade nodded, the shame of it burning all over again. "I was already looking for an out. Donatien just wanted more blood, more pain, more chaos, and hang the cost. I… Something happened that made it clear I was turning into Morris. I thought about— Anyway. I abased myself to Hector. Let him take me out of the territory in chains. Offered my blood in exchange for a pardon. He was more than happy to take it and steal some of the strength I'd acquired."

He rubbed his wrists, still remembering the chafing of the silver-lined irons. "So after swearing I'd never be someone else's meat again, I spent a decade owned by Hector. When the bastard got himself killed in a dominance battle, Giuliano moved up. I refused to submit to further bondage without a fight, and Giuliano couldn't be bothered with forcibly taking control of another *moroi* of my strength. The coterie and the unsettled politics of the colonies—states, by then—took too much of his attention. He gave me a choice. I could leave or die. I left. I've been wandering ever since, both because I couldn't bear trying to belong anywhere again and because, after what I'd done in New Orleans, there was no safety in staying still."

"Oh, Cade." Far from the censure or disgust he'd feared, her voice carried compassion and a hint of sadness.

He still couldn't help flinching when she came to him and stretched out a hand. When she pulled it back, he caught it and kissed her palm. "I never bothered Torsten or his people, and he finds it amusing that, having once been a city master myself, I gave it up or was defeated and driven from my seat. He thinks me weak. And that, love, is why you should have been safe. And also why he attacked you. Because normally, I'm beneath his notice. But last night, he was reminded that I have a reputation.

One that might well be a threat. And in you, he saw the means to shut it down before it could be reborn."

Lya sank down next to him on the bed. "Let me make sure I have this. You have enemies crawling out of the woodwork because, once upon a time, you were in a fucked-up headspace at a fucked-up time in history and did some fucked-up things. You got mixed in with some even more fucked-up people—Donatien and, later, Alejandro."

"That's one colorful way to summarize it."

"Anyone else?"

"No. I was too heartsick, and then I learned my lesson for good when Alejandro stuck silver in my back. After that, I laid low." He glanced at her. "Always kept my eye out for opportunities to take stronger blood but never expected to fall in love. At all, let alone with someone who is so evenly balanced between accessible, capable, and vulnerable."

"So the biggest risks to my safety are Donatien, Alejandro, and the people of anyone you hurt?"

"Yes."

"There lots of those around?"

"There used to be. Even Othersiders die. Some did when they came for me later. Others simply reached the end of their lives."

"And staying with you means I'll need to look over my shoulder for any of those people who are still living or their descendants."

Fear clenched Cade's guts and sent his glamour spilling free. He reined it in with effort. "Yes. And me, I suppose. I don't know how easily I could let you go now."

"Okay." Lya bumped his shoulder with hers. "Thank you. I don't love the situation, but at least I know now to be wary of anyone who says they know you. I can be more careful."

"You're not going to ask if I'm sane? Safe? You're not worried I'd keep you against your will?"

Lya snorted. "I think we've established that, safe or not, I can't seem to bring myself to have more than a healthy appreciation for your deadliness that crosses into the sexual. Sane? We've been together eight months, and you haven't so much as forgotten an item on the grocery list when you don't even eat food. You've never gotten lost in the past, although you clearly remember it well enough, and you've never forgotten you are here and now, no matter how many times I've startled you out of your sleep." She grimaced. "I might not push you like that now that I know your history with being awakened suddenly, but I feel more safe now, not less." She sobered. "I'm a little worried about what would happen if I tried to leave, but deep down, I like the illusion of being able to leave more than I actually want to. I like that you need me. I like that *somebody* cares about me that much."

That made Cade shift on the bed until he was half-facing her. "I'm beginning to wonder if *you're* entirely sane."

She laughed.

The bright sound shocked him so badly he froze. He'd recounted horrors, and she could still find it in her to laugh? Not *at* him but in a shared joke?

"Does that mean you're not leaving?" he whispered.

The firm look she gave him almost made him flinch. "I told you on Ocracoke. I won't punish you for honesty. I can't demand you tell me the details and then use them against you. Or I won't, anyway. I just need to feel safe, Cade. Ignorance makes me feel *un*safe. And it means I can't ask other important questions."

Relief shuddered over him, and cautiously, he reached out an arm, hovering it over her shoulders. Regardless of her words, he was still surprised when she cuddled against him. He was a fiend.

A devil of the worst sort. And she accepted him. Accepted his truths and the remorse and regret he felt over who he'd been and what he'd done. Accepted that his wandering was as much about safety as it was a penance. It wasn't until that moment that he realized he hadn't completely accepted that himself or forgiven himself for becoming another Morris, however briefly. He'd told himself he had, but the strain of trying to keep all of it separated, of keeping the past walled off, had been weighing him down.

"What questions?" he asked.

"You've already said you don't think Alejandro and Donatien know each other. Are you certain about that?"

He frowned. "Not to my knowledge."

"In that case, why is Donatien coming out of whatever hellhole he's been hiding in now? What does he gain? And is he going to be satisfied with one quick encounter with you?"

Apprehension bit Cade with icy teeth. "Those are very good questions indeed, love."

Questions he hadn't thought to ask because he'd been so caught up in getting out, getting away and on the move again, that it hadn't even occurred to him that there might be more to Donatien's visit than whispers and happenstance.

"He said he'd heard rumors in Miami and thought to investigate," Cade said. "It could be nothing."

"Neither of us is lucky enough for it to be nothing," she said flatly. With a light grip, she turned his wrist so his watch faced her. "We have a few hours before we have to meet Callista. Do you need to hunt?"

"No. I'll do for another night." He winced when she arched an eyebrow at him. "But I shouldn't see her on an empty stomach, so to speak. She's difficult on a good day."

"Difficult is one way of putting it."

"You'll be okay for an hour?"

"Yeah. I don't love being back in Raleigh, but I can stay in the room and get some more rest." She slapped her belly. "Do something about the imminent food coma. And don't worry. I'll be here when you get back. If I'm not, then I was taken."

His relief at her answering the question he hadn't wanted to ask cut off at the last part, and he scowled. "Don't even joke about it. I nearly lost myself the last time. I would do *anything* to get you back." In a quieter voice, he said, "Losing you means I lose myself, I think. I love you too much."

"I know. I love you just as much." She kissed his cheek. "Thank you for talking to me. Go eat. If you make it quick, we'll have time for another cuddle before we go see the head bitch in charge."

Chapter 10: Lya

I threw myself back on the pillows and scrubbed my hands over my face as the door swung shut behind Cade. It wasn't just the food coma making me sleepy. It was the emotional intensity of the last twenty-four hours.

I dealt with shit in two ways. I got mad and fought, or I got away. There was no fighting a five-hundred-year-old vampire directly. Especially when he didn't want to fight. I'd tried once. I couldn't even remember what had set me off, but I'd jumped Cade and it had gone about as well as our first fight. He'd simply held me immobile, just on the edge of pain, until I'd worn myself out. It also tripped my masochistic streak and turned into a consensual mid-month bite and fucking, which itself led to the bondage conversation.

Maybe I *was* the crazy one in the relationship.

Snorting a laugh at that memory, I set it aside. No wonder he put up with me.

No, that wasn't fair to either of us. For all the shit in his past, he genuinely loved me and had been busting his ass to make sure I was both comfortable and unaware of who he'd been. Because now that I had all the pieces, I suspected it was guilt that had kept him silent. That and shame, maybe. I hadn't told him yet that I was starting to get echoes of what he was feeling if he was feeling it strongly enough, and the shame and guilt and self-hatred had been strong enough for me to catch it from more than his posture and tone.

He wanted to be a good person. I think he saw the path forward in me, even as my presence highlighted all the evil he'd done in the past and deepened his fear that I'd find out about it and leave him.

Goddess, what a mess. I had to do better. I'd been honest when I told him I wanted the illusion of being able to leave. He indulged me in it, letting me take off when I got heated, but that was probably what had fed into his not telling me all of this before I had a full-on meltdown about it.

Now it was me feeling ashamed. I was thirty-one years old. Yeah, that was still pretty young for an elf or half-elf. The elf-blooded weren't considered to be in our majority until twenty-five. We could live to be two hundred or older, if we were careful. Even a half-elf would push a hundred, easy, and stay both sharp and fit for most of that time.

But even if I was young for an Othersider, I was more than old enough not to act like this with someone I loved.

My phone rang, interrupting my self-recrimination. I reached for it and frowned at the number. The same French number as before. I genuinely did not want to take the call. I'd meant what I'd said to Cade in the car. I was exiled. There was no reason for anyone to be calling me, and I didn't give a shit what they wanted.

Hell. Why not tell them so?

I answered in French. "What?"

"You know better than to answer the phone like that, Lydia."

Sick surprise washed through me at the low, melodious tones of my mother's knight, also speaking French. "Samarre."

"Why didn't you pick up before?"

"I was driving." Then, because I was mad as hell at my automatic, defensive response, I snapped, "Should you even be calling me? The queens were pretty thorough in their declaration that I was on my own and indentured to House Monteague."

She ignored my question, as she did anything and everything that wasn't to her plan or liking. "We're arriving in the States tomorrow."

"Good for you."

"Apparently your time there hasn't improved your manners or your sense. What a shame."

I held my tongue, ready to burst with anger. It would make no difference if I did, but it would prove her point.

She sighed. "It would be well if you made yourself available. We have news."

"Tell me now then."

"No. This is news best told in person."

That got me up and pacing. "What business could any of you possibly have with the exiled, bastard low-blood that *none of you* could be bothered to stand up in court for?"

My hot accusations had absolutely no effect on her solid steadiness. "Don't lash me with your temper, girl. You knew better. Prices must be paid."

"Yeah, yeah. By some of us more than others."

Her silence then might have said I'd struck a nerve. It also might simply have meant that she was waiting me out.

"Goodbye, Samarre."

"I mean it, girl. We will expect to meet with you while we're in town."

I hung up on her. A thrill of forbidden satisfaction raced over me as I did, and goosebumps prickled over me. I'd never have dared to do such a thing before.

Samarre had scared the living daylights out of me as a child. She'd followed my mother into disgrace rather than give up her charge as a royal knight, and she'd had the early part of my combat and Aetheric training before I was given over to the

Darkwatch for a brief time. She was stern, commanding, and utterly implacable. Whatever she felt for me, I never knew because she'd treated me with the same indifference she did a chair. But she was like that with everyone, so it wasn't just a me thing.

I stopped in the middle of the room as a thought struck me. She'd said "we" and "in town." There were multiple people coming Stateside. Coming *here*.

Did that include my mother? Samarre would never leave her side.

My father? My mum would never leave him open to attack from the Houses. My grandmother in particular blamed him for Mum's fall and would relish the opportunity to remedy the problem she considered him to be. Me, Mum had left hanging out to dry rather than fight for. Him, though, she'd do anything for.

What could possibly be so important for any of them to come here? And demand to see *me*?

I didn't like this. Any contingent made up of royals would take some serious negotiation. I assumed they'd stay at the Monteague family mansion with Queen Keithia and her high-blood heir-apparent. That was the typical arrangement, staying with cousin-Houses. But the typical arrangement didn't include royals, even fallen ones. With the exception of eligible princes, elven royals stayed close to home. It was part of why exile was such a grave punishment, aside from being messed up by our social hormones being thrown out of order.

This trip might have been months in the making on House Desmarais's side, and I had no idea *why*. What the hell couldn't she tell me over the phone?

Suddenly, I wished I hadn't been so quick to lash out with my hurt feelings, but it was too late. I'd thrown my tantrum, and

Samarre wouldn't acknowledge me again until it was time to command my presence.

I was still pacing in agitated frustration when Cade came back, looking calmer—at least until the scent in the room hit him.

He shut the door behind him and threw the security lock.

"Ly?" His voice was heavy with concern that sent goosebumps rippling down my arms as it slithered over me, and his pupils went a little too wide. "What happened, love? I thought you were going to rest."

I slid my fingers between my curls and clenched them, inhaling sharply and blowing out in an effort to calm myself. Cade might have just fed, but the scent of me in any state of high emotion always whetted his hunger anew.

"Sorry," I muttered. "I'm fine. I— You remember in the car when I got that call?"

"From France."

"They called back." I'd debated not telling him but that was exactly what all the problems between us had stemmed from: hiding things in an effort to keep one another safe.

"And?" He ghosted a few steps closer, looming until he pulled me into an embrace.

"It was Samarre, my mother's knight, the one who held to her oath after my mum was disowned."

Cade was silent while I gathered my thoughts.

"She said they're coming here."

"They who? Here where?"

I flushed and buried my face against his chest, embarrassed. "I got mad and hung up on her before I thought to ask."

"But it's to do with you?"

"So I gather. She insisted I make myself available when they arrive tomorrow."

"They're coming here?" His hand rubbed soothingly along my spine. "Do they know about the power sharing arrangement?"

"I don't know. Callista wasn't on anyone's radar when I was exiled, as far as I know. Or if she was, they were less interested in her than the local Houses. They're all continually spying on each other. Sometimes to get better marriage arrangements, sometimes for blackmail or assassination. I know I said I'd be nothing if I'd stayed there, but I can't say that'd be entirely a bad thing given the House politics."

"Hmm." The sound rumbled in his chest, and I let myself be eased by his attention and consideration. Then he peeled me away from him. "How do we handle this?"

I scowled. "I want nothing to do with them."

"Want isn't relevant. They're coming. They might have Keithia's permission. But if they expect to see you, will you go to Chapel Hill?"

"No." I pulled away and started pacing, agitated all over again as I remembered Leith Sequoyah's twisted nature. "Fuck no. Sequoyah territory is closer to Jordan Lake, but the whole Greater Chapel Hill area is elven. The Monteague princess is rumored to be a real piece of work as well. And no way am I risking being pulled in for treason charges again."

He winced. "I hadn't realized those would still be active. I thought Callista overruled them."

"She did. But Keithia's the sort who'd rather ask forgiveness than permission. There's a reason Farand went as far as he did with me."

Cade's fanged snarl made me feel better. He cared, and it made my heart swell. It twisted when he tilted his head and asked, "So you won't go there. If they insist on seeing you?"

"They can go to hell."

"You wouldn't go to RTP?"

"No. Nowhere they could get to me easily."

His gaze weighed on me. "And if they tracked you here?"

"What, to The Umstead?"

He nodded.

I started to say they could fuck themselves again then frowned. "What are you getting at, babe?"

"This is vampire territory. The edge of it, but the hotel is owned by the coterie."

It took me a moment, but then I got it. My pacing stopped, and I stood almost as still as Cade could as I processed that. "You're asking me if I'd turn them over to Torsten."

"Maria would be the smarter choice."

I stared at him. If what I'd done in September had been treason, I didn't even know what it would be to turn over elves—even foreign ones—to the vampires. Blood drained from my face, and my heart raced as I grasped the full import of what it meant for me to be a solidaire in a way I'd never considered before.

I'd rejected my own people myself in choosing Cade. I knew that.

But rejection wasn't the same as…this.

He nodded. "You understand the predicament this creates."

I didn't answer that. I couldn't. I didn't know what it meant yet.

"Why Maria?" I whispered.

Again the head tilt. "I don't want another night like last night, so I will tell you. Are you sure you want to know?"

"Why wouldn't I?"

"Because it's my life and yours if the wrong ears hear it."

Cold fingers of apprehension gripped me. "Shit, Cade. What did you two do?"

"Nothing. Yet. I only promised her my support in the event she needs it, in exchange for her keeping you safe, should I die. But this elven arrival creates opportunities to go beyond that."

"What opportunities?" I could barely get the words out.

"The kind that topple city masters."

I sat down, hard, right on the floor, then popped back up again and got in his space. "It's not enough that *I* committed treason? You want to jump right up on the gallows alongside me?"

Far from being intimidated, Cade just blinked too rapidly and tipped his head back. I backed off, mentally cursing myself. I was pushing every single button that would make him want to bite me, and we didn't have time for it if we were going to see Callista tonight.

He cleared his throat. "Maria needs to replace Aron. The sooner the better. That means powerful blood. In-territory elves are off limits."

"But out-of-territory elves trespassing on vampire territory are fair game. Just like I was."

He nodded, not even bothering to deny that was how he'd thought of it.

"Why the sooner the better?"

"I told you. He's going rakshasa."

"Okay, so how long do we have?"

"I don't know. He's never been that aggressive before, not with me, and he had no interest in you, despite knowing of you. We had—I'd thought—a good working relationship." He grimaced. "My extensions of residence in the territory went through him. He allowed it because I hinted I'd take you from Maria if I had the chance, and he's scared of her potential."

I reeled at the fact that vampire politics had included me.

"There's no pattern to becoming a rakshasa?" That seemed like a good thing to know for my own safety, not just this situation.

Cade shrugged. "Could be months. Could be a decade. Depends on how much Otherside blood he's had up to now and how much he gets. Aron's always been more of a homebody than most, so he hasn't made the connections Maria has in Otherside, nor has he been as bold in seeking powerful blood. She always beats him to it, and she had decent ties to House Monteague even before your arrival." He shook his head. "Torsten has to know, but Aron is his favorite."

"And Maria wants to move up?"

He nodded.

I hugged myself. "So I have a choice as to who I belong to."

"You belong to me."

The grouchy dominance of the statement broke through my mood and made me grin. "There is that."

Cade moved in that too-fast vampire motion, and I was suddenly in his arms again.

"I won't make the choice for you," he said. "But you said you needed information to ask the right questions. That's everything I know that might be relevant."

"Thank you for telling me." I wrapped my arms around him and squeezed until he grunted. It took some doing—all my strength—but I got the noise out of him. "I like this. Being partners in a decision, even if it's a tough one I really hate."

"I see that." His tone was dry but pleased, and he hugged me back until I grunted. "We shouldn't keep Callista waiting."

"Ugh." I resisted pulling away from him for another minute but eventually let my embrace slip away. "You gonna be okay?"

"Me?"

I waved my hand around the suite. "I kind of upped the scent load in here."

"You did." His eyes flashed glamour black for a heartbeat. "And I'll address that when we return."

A thrill of anticipation raced over me. I really liked when he played the big bad vampire.

With a last cheeky grin, I set about changing my clothes and getting my weapons sorted. He watched me with a fierce gaze that said he'd be damned if anything at all happened to me.

I just prayed Callista wasn't in the mood to put it to the test.

Chapter 11: Lya

For once, my prayers were answered.

Callista radiated fury as she glared at us from behind her desk in the private office off the main bar, but it was nothing to do with me this time. If anything, I'd earned points for coming when called and arriving early.

Her green eyes sparked with rage. "A blood witch in my territory is intolerable. I won't have it. You two will remove him."

"Of course," Cade said smoothly. "Lya mentioned you were offering two hundred?"

"That's right."

"Each, of course."

Her rage cooled to something harder and meaner. "Excuse me?"

"Two hundred. Each. You and I both know a five-hundred-year-old blood witch with shapeshifting abilities is worth at least that much."

Callista sneered. "You rate your solidaire as your equal? The Butcher of the Bayou on the level of a low-blood elf?"

Cade's shrug was stiff with fury, but his tone was even enough. "I'm rusty. She's not."

I kept my face blank as Callista looked at me to see how the moniker had landed. At my lack of reaction, she arched an eyebrow. "The girl knows?"

"She does."

I wanted to jump in and say, "You're damn right I do," but in this case I was playing a role, and that role said Cade spoke for us both.

Callista looked me up and down. Annoyance and something like respect flickered in her gaze before it was gone. "So, girl, you've tamed the Butcher."

"Would you call me in for this job if I wasn't at least that good?" I snapped, no longer able to hold my tongue and irritated she kept throwing it in our faces.

Her reaction suggested she'd been doing some digging into Cade and had been hoping to blindside me with it, which was probably why it hadn't come up before. I imagined the Raleigh coterie simply hadn't seen a point in bringing it up.

She just smirked, probably thinking I wasn't comfortable with it when the truth was I just couldn't stand her.

"Business, Callista," Cade said. "Two hundred each, plus expenses. You cover our stay at The Umstead, since we'd only planned to be here a day and have no other reason to stay in town."

"The Umstead? No."

"Yes," Cade insisted.

I did my best to stand impassively with a blank face. Personally, I wouldn't have dared push the bitch, but I also didn't have Cade's standing in the community except as his solidaire. This was what I'd wanted from the arrangement—enough power to at least advocate for better treatment from the rest of Otherside. Getting it made last night's fight with Cade worth it.

Callista snarled, and I stiffened as shadows edged the room, seeping in at the corners.

"You've grown rather bold," she said. "You both agreed to be on my payroll."

"Indeed," he said. "And to come when you called, which we have, and early no less. Nothing was agreed about the rate of pay or the manner of negotiation, so we're within our rights."

"Your rights are what I say they are." The malevolent hag rose from her chair. She was smaller than me and shouldn't have been able to cow either of us, but I suddenly got the feeling that somehow she was much bigger and more dangerous than she looked. "You dare to defy me?"

"Of course not, my lady," Cade said with icy courtesy. "We will do the job. When we come to a fair price for it." He tilted his head. "Or has the Triangle fallen on hard times? That's a shame. I keep seeing news reports of the explosion in mundane relocations to this area. I would have thought business was booming. Alas, if you cannot pay…"

"Don't think I don't know what you're doing, *moroi*." Callista glared hard enough that Cade must have hit a sore spot. I didn't know how Arbiters made their income, but there had to be some kind of racket involved.

Cade didn't answer, just tilted his head and looked patient.

"One fifty each plus expenses," Callista finally said.

"One hundred fifty thousand US dollars each, plus full expenses associated with the job, including our stay at The Umstead from this night until the job is completed. Done." Cade bit his palm and extended his hand as blood beaded on it.

With a nasty sneer, Callista dug a knife from her drawer, nicked her own palm, and clasped Cade's. "And done."

Magic burst as the deal became binding. Cade had just insulted her by insisting it be bound in blood, but inside, I was cheering. Callista had screwed us both out of too much already, and my heart exulted at seeing her put in a position where she would be forced to honor our agreement. A blood oath wasn't as serious as a geas—it didn't come with an automatic death curse if it was broken, for one—but there'd be some pretty nasty consequences if it wasn't honored. Callista must have really wanted Alejandro brought in.

The look she gave me said that maybe she could smell my satisfaction, so I dropped my eyes and bowed my head like a good little solidaire among my betters. That must have shifted my scent or body language or whatever she was reading to something that satisfied her better.

She returned her attention to Cade.

"Here," she said.

A scrape of paper across her desk had me glancing up. She must have pulled the stack of manilla folders out of her desk drawer because it hadn't been there when we walked in.

"Everything my Watchers have discovered or overheard and everything the cleanup crew documented before they disappeared the evidence. I want this done quick and quiet, or it's your heads if the Détente is broken."

"Excuse me?" Cade's voice had gone from icy to glacial.

"It's your problem now. Fix it. Fast."

My stomach dropped. Of course there'd be a price for defying her wishes on the bounty price. Callista never lost. I didn't know how exactly she'd foist responsibility for the problem off on us, but I knew she'd find a way. I didn't even know who, if anyone, the Arbiters answered to in Otherside or if they were wholly independent rulers of their own demesnes. Either way, we'd gained some to risk more.

Cade glared at her then bowed his head. "As my lady commands."

I followed his lead and bowed slightly lower.

"Good," Callista said. "Now get out and don't come back without proof of death."

With another, shallower bow, Cade extended an arm to gather me in and propel me ahead of him out the door.

I held my temper until we were in the car and on the road.

"What the *fuck*?" I slammed the heel of my hand on the steering wheel. "Who the hell does she think she is? This is *her* fucking territory, she has all these Goddess-burned Watchers we're all running scared of, and she's gonna pin it on us if her failure isn't cleaned up?"

Cade just rolled down the window and stuck his head out despite the cold night and the drizzle that'd started. Vampires hated cold and damp—hence the fire in Torsten's throne room—but I'd pushed Cade too much this night and last for him not to be struggling with his control. He'd fed, but when I was agitated, I was a steak in front of a starving man where he was concerned, especially after the strain of dealing with Callista.

I managed to hold my tongue for the rest of the drive but was still steaming when we got back to The Umstead and blew into the lobby a little too fast. Cade caught my arm, also too fast, but fortunately it was late and the doorman just blinked, frowned, and shook his head.

For good measure, Cade glamoured the man and handed him a bill. "Thanks for catching my girlfriend."

I was too sure-footed to slip even on the rain-slicked marble, but I summoned an embarrassed smile and squeezed his arm. "I'm so clumsy!"

"Of course, ma'am. Please accept my apologies. We'll have someone mop this up."

Cade pushed again with glamour. "Truly not a problem. It happens."

"Of course, sir. Thank you."

I slipped my arm in Cade's, still playing the clumsy mundane, and shot him a grateful look as I took a breath and blew it out to calm down. Breaking the Détente over Callista was exactly what I didn't need.

As we passed the lounge on our way to the lifts, a man's voice called out, "Lya?"

I missed a step, and this time, I really did need Cade's arm. I knew that voice.

Henri.

I only glanced, but it was definitely him. Average height and build. Brown hair. Brown eyes. Light brown skin, almost olive. Not much more magic in him than myself, especially now that I'd had vampire blood and was getting stronger overall.

Cade had slowed and was looking for the source of the hail, which meant I couldn't just pretend I hadn't heard him.

Didn't matter. I kept moving. Cade went along with me, though his arm went rock-solid under my hand and the scent of ash and iron spiked as he took in my reaction and responded as though it was a threat. Fortunately, he waited until we were in the lift before looking at me and cocking an eyebrow.

I shook my head. "In the room."

As soon as we were through the door with it shut and locked behind us, I closed my eyes and rubbed my temples then swallowed against the bile rising into my throat. I was never supposed to see Henri again. What the fuck was he doing here?

"Ly?"

"That was Henri. He must have gotten an earlier flight or something." I could barely get the words out around the lump in my throat. I don't even know what I was feeling—dread, fear, shame, rage, all of it in an ugly ball that demanded retribution.

When Cade didn't answer, I forced myself to look at him.

He was completely blank and deathly still. Then, "Henri. Your—"

"Yes," I said, before he could say "lover" or whatever other word he was going to use because whatever that word was, it didn't fit between me and Henri anymore. That word—those words—were only for Cade and me now.

Again, the iron-and-ash vampire scent spiked.

I shook my head. "I don't know what he's doing here. I didn't tell anyone where we were. I don't want to see him. I want nothing to do with him. He—"

I made myself stop talking, pressing my lips together and crossing my arms. I was babbling, and it was a bad look. I just…the memory of my court hearing flashed to mind all over again, the abandonment, and then I was hugging myself hard to stop the shaking, and I couldn't breathe, and—

Cade pulled me into a tight embrace. I pressed my face into his chest and let the lack of oxygen stop me from continuing to hyperventilate.

"Shh, sh. Easy, love. It's all right. Look at me."

I hunched closer.

"Lydia."

I jumped at the command in his tone and leaned back just enough to look at him.

His eyes were full black. "Do you want a glamour?"

"No," I whispered.

"Okay. Then I need you to breathe." He rested his forehead against mine and rubbed his hands along my arms. "What do you smell?"

The unexpected question refocused me. "You. Vampire. Iron. Ash. Granite. Cold."

He grunted in surprise. "I smell cold?"

"Not alive. But not in a bad way. Just is." I shrugged shakily. "Cold. But overlaid with borrowed warmth, some of it mine."

"That's fair. What else?"

"Damp cotton. Rain. Nasty synthetic room freshener." As I listed more things off, I calmed. With a last shuddering inhale, I pulled back and shook myself before hugging him again. "Thank you."

His arms wrapped around me and rubbed my back, keeping me grounded. "For what?"

"Not judging me."

"I imagine it was a shock. I know what those are like. Talk to me?"

He could have phrased it as a command. I might have shut down if he had, but this was an invitation. He stiffened when I pulled free, as though worried I was about to run, then relaxed when I tugged my boots off, then my weapons and clothes.

When I was naked, I took another breath then dropped all my walls. Mental, metaphysical, everything. I was too shaken by my past chasing me into my present and calling my name. "Hold me. In bed. Please."

Cade's eyes lit with interest then faded to careful neutrality. "My pleasure."

I slid into the bed, my back to him, aching for him to touch me until he switched off the lights, stripped in a quiet rustle of clothing, and was curled around me, enveloping me.

"I flashed back to the courtroom," I said when I was calmer. "That feeling like nobody cared about me or wanted me. Like I was alone and would be forever."

"And the elf-blooded suffer when they're alone." His voice rumbled in his chest against my back, soothing me further as much as his understanding did.

"Yes." The word came out smaller than I'd meant it to.

"Fortunately, I might well live forever if I keep getting Otherside blood. And as long as I'm alive, you won't be alone."

The last tension went out of me, and he held me tighter.

We laid in silence for a while before a thought occurred to me. "Last night was a trial."

Cade hummed. "Actually…yes, in a way."

"You could have handed me over."

"No," he snarled. "I bloody well could not have."

I turned in his arms. "That's the response I should have gotten from my parents. From anyone who claimed to care about me."

A low growl emanated from his chest. Vampires didn't often make the noise, but they were as capable of it as werewolves and it was a good sign that blood was about to be in someone's mouth.

"Do you remember when I said I hoped I never met one of your people?" he asked.

"Yes."

"They had better hope they never meet me."

Heat curled through me, slow at first, like a fire trying to take hold of kindling under damp wood before it caught. I'd had a mild freak-out before, when he'd pointed out that I would have to make a decision soon about my birth faction versus my chosen faction. In that moment, conscious choice was like a knife finding the heart through ribs: hard to line up but so much easier than a random stab. I could see what had happened clearly for the first time, freed from the emotion of it by Cade's own wrathful commitment.

Whatever their reasons had been, my people hadn't been about what I needed as a daughter or scion of the House so much as what they needed to save themselves.

And that meant there was no conflict.

My way forward was clear. I needed to save myself.

I kissed Cade, deeply and passionately, hard enough to roll him to his back with me straddling him. I knew exactly what I needed to do, and Henri, Samarre—all of them—could go to the ninth circle of hell.

Chapter 12: Cade

Cade watched Lya from the corner of his eye as she drove to the location she'd noted as the geographic center of all the kill sites the Watchers had found. She seemed much better tonight than she had the last few nights. Calm in a way he couldn't remember from her before. Streetlights striped her face in bright orange at regular intervals—she was keeping the speed steady for once, rather than speeding up when a thought came to mind to piss her off. She wasn't boiling over with energy.

There was just the focused intensity of a huntress with a scent.

It was strange, but it let him relax. He might be the so-called master in the solidaire relationship, but he exercised his role based on her cues. A well cared-for solidaire was one who wouldn't have to be replaced, one way or the other, and she was too valuable to him to replace.

Or to lose to some unworthy prince from a European elven House.

He'd mentally marked the elf who'd called Lya's name from the hotel lounge the previous night, as much for his seeming to know her as for the sudden spike of panic in her scent and her uncharacteristic response in the room.

That man was a dead man.

Not out of jealousy. Cade had plenty of that and knew how to keep it under control. No. He was dead because all the compassion left in Cade after five hundred years was invested in Lya now, and that man had hurt her. Badly.

Some hurts could be forgiven or at least forgotten. Cade didn't think Lya had done either. So. A more permanent solution.

Lya shifted. "I can feel you looking at me, creeper."

"Of course I am. You're a delight to look at."

She snorted. "You're thinking about murder, not sex."

He froze before he could catch himself.

"Thought so. I can sort of…feel a vibe, I guess."

"Already?"

Glancing at him, she frowned. "Was that sooner than expected?"

"Much. Even with the amount and frequency of blood I've been giving you."

"Glamour and Aether?"

"Maybe." Cade reached over and squeezed her thigh. "I won't tell if you don't."

She laughed, and the sound eased his mood.

"I still think it'll be a trap if we do find Alejandro in the area," he said, not wanting to let her in on his thoughts just yet. Not when she was focusing on a job, at the very least. They'd need to be at their best against the witch.

"I don't disagree." She flexed her hands on the steering wheel, and the car sped up before she eased off and let the cruise control set their speed. 540 still had traffic at this time of night but not so much that she couldn't use the setting. "But I had an idea just now."

"What's that?"

"Rather than sniffing around the area, we have a date."

"A date? I thought we were hunting."

"We are. Think about it though. He left the construction site with my blood smeared all over a bunch of treasure. Metal holds blood nicely." She lifted her left hand and waggled the pinky finger, the one with the ring that told him where she was. "My tracking tag wore off and broke months ago. But blood magic?"

"He knows where you are. You've escaped him once. Or twice, even, if we count you leaving the beach with me and then bargaining your way out of the Darkwatch trap. That will have become an obsession." The thought sent Cade into fight mode, and Lya cracked a window. Usually it was him doing that when her scent got to be too much. That his scent affected her this strongly was another sign of the tightening solidaire bond between them. He really was fucked if he lost her.

"Exactly," she said. "And he stayed in the area, in a part of the Triangle that's neutral territory. He could have gone farther out, to Falls Lake or Occoneechee or Raven Rock. But he stayed in the Triangle. Briar Creek, even, which is safe, in that it's neutral for Otherside but heavily populated by mundanes and therefore difficult to get the privacy or secrecy he'd need for major works. That tells me he's less interested in sacrifices and more interested in knowing if I return to the area. So why try hunting him down on terrain he knows? Why not see if he comes to us? There's loads of good bars and restaurants at the shopping center over this way."

"And if he follows us home?"

She shrugged, although the tension in her shoulders told him she wasn't as nonchalant as she was trying to appear. "Let him. It's not a real home. Even if it was, we're on the move now, right? Because Donatien? And if there's an elven prince at the hotel, there'll be at least one knight and an entourage. It's Torsten's territory, so if Alejandro is obsessed enough to follow us there, that's two whole factions pissed off. I'll be the least of anyone's worries but yours."

Cade considered the idea, annoyed that it required this Henri to stay alive until Alejandro was brought in. But, feelings aside, it was a good plan.

"Sneaky little thing," he muttered, teasing her. Really it was quite clever.

"Damn straight. I don't have the magical chops to stand up to the rest of you." She grinned. "You have no idea how sneaky I can be."

"I have some idea."

"You think you do."

With a snort and a shake of his head to signal his concession, Cade gripped the back of her neck.

The car swerved.

"Lya!"

Her laugh and the easy way the vehicle found the center of the lane told him she'd been playing with him.

"Brat," he muttered.

"Punish me later."

"Oh, I will. I most certainly will." Once upon a time, Cade had been able to go weeks without blood and years without sex if he had to. Now? He wanted Lya—all of her—every night. That she was increasingly open to bondage and other more serious play only stoked his appetites.

"First," she said, glancing at him with a grin, "you buy me dinner. A nice one. At the steakhouse."

"Of course, love."

"The *Brazilian* steakhouse."

He frowned. "Is there a difference?"

"All-you-can-eat steak?"

Cade shook his head, still confused. "You say that like there's a limit to what I'd spend on your nourishment or pleasure. You're elf-blooded. You need the protein. And you're mine, so you'll have anything you wish."

Lya darted a sideways glance at him, the look she got when she was inexplicably confused about some detail about her role as his girlfriend and solidaire and the attendant benefits.

He tried another tack. "Call it a business meal."

She was, annoyingly, more comfortable with that. "Do you think Alejandro would be able to find us inside a building?"

"Of course. It'd mostly be a matter of not spooking the other guests."

"Can your glamour manage that?"

"Yes." He grinned at her. "How else do you think we've been out in public without anyone freaking out about a gorgeous young woman being accompanied by a walking corpse?"

Lya laughed, that burst of sound that was equally joyful and sexual. It turned heads when they were out together. In the car, it was his alone to enjoy. That she was amused by his undead state rather than disgusted was a constant relief. Not all the living Othersiders were so openminded. Especially when it came to sex with a vampire.

"Order whatever you want," he said. "Let your shields down though, to make sure we have the best chance of drawing Alejandro in if he's around."

"Good idea."

Cade studied her as she took the Lumley Road offramp. "You trust me to ensure he can't bespell you?"

She looked at him like he was addled. "If I didn't, we wouldn't be here."

He held her hand the rest of the way to the restaurant, too overcome by emotion at her faith to answer.

***

Lya had made it through more skewers of fire-roasted meat than the men at the adjoining table, despite her having eaten a snack on waking at sunset. They eyed her almost enough that Cade considered using a glamour to make them forget. But Lya was having too much fun goading them with a wide smile, even as Cade was happy to recline and watch, plate empty except for smears of food she'd snatched from it when nobody else was looking—much to the consternation of everyone around them. His glamour kept it from being commented on too much, but he was relieved that the restaurant was closing soon, even if Alejandro hadn't turned up.

Of course, he'd thought their plan a failure too soon.

The turnskin was waiting for them in front of the restaurant, leaning against one of the red phone boxes dotting the square. Lya had wistfully explained that they were meant to be replicas of British ones before ignoring them the way she did most hurts.

Hunger sparked in Alejandro's eyes as he spotted them and straightened, and Lya stiffened at Cade's side.

"Told you," she muttered.

Cade didn't bother responding. All his attention was on the blood witch.

The witch in question looked Lya up and down with a desire that made Cade snarl. She'd been right. Alejandro hadn't been satisfied with the blood she'd left on the gold.

"Look who it is." Lya's voice was tight enough that Cade knew she was trying to keep it from shaking, and it didn't.

"Look who it is," Alejandro echoed back. When they were close enough that their overlapping magics would prevent mundanes from noticing or overhearing them, he smirked at Cade. "I'm deeply surprised you're here, my friend. Especially with her."

Cade glanced around the fancy strip mall. Too many mundanes to try taking their bounty here and having it turn into the kind of fight that'd break the Détente, and Alejandro knew it or he wouldn't have dared coming out in the open. Assuming, of course, that he even knew he was being hunted. "Imagine seeing you here."

Alejandro's eyes stayed on Cade, the way one kept their attention on a wolf when both the wolf and a feral dog were in front of them. Both were dangerous, but one was a certain, known kind of dangerous. "I thought you ran back to St. Augustine."

Lya laced her fingers in Cade's to stop him answering. "We took a vacation. Now we're back. For the night, that is. We'll be on our way tomorrow."

It was all Cade could do to keep his face straight. They had absolutely no intention of— Ah, this was her sneakiness coming through. He'd had enough power to not need guile for long enough that it was now a secondary response for him.

Alejandro stiffened. "Leaving? Tomorrow?"

Lya nodded and leaned against Cade, looking up at him like a lovestruck fool. "We're going on a road trip. And you know? I never got a chance to thank you, Alejandro."

Both men stared at her like she'd lost her mind.

"That deal you made me." She released Cade's hand so she could pull up her sleeve and show her forearm, the one Alejandro had sliced to pieces, under the overhead lamp.

Cade glanced around and boosted his glamour. He didn't need any mundanes taking notice of the scar that looked like tally marks on Lya's left forearm. Usually there was a knife hidden there. She must have taken it off when she'd gone to the bathroom.

"What of it?" Alejandro's voice was soft with hunger and a want so deep Cade nearly hit him.

"I mean, without you, I might be dead." Her eyes widened dramatically. "Can you imagine what the Darkwatch would have done to me? What *Leith* would have done to me?" She shuddered. "He has a reputation, you know. But now I get to be Cade's."

She leaned on Cade's arm and looked up at him so adoringly that all he could do was stare some more. Lya was *never* the fawning type, but here she was—

It's an act, you fool. A lure with herself as bait.

As the realization broke through, Cade slipped into his role in the charade. He tilted her chin up for a quick kiss then turned his own satisfied smirk on Alejandro. "I suppose I owe you thanks as well, my friend. I was on my way but too far behind to have done much good if you hadn't been there."

Lya's death grip on his hand eased. Good. He was playing his part correctly.

Fury tightened Alejandro's expression for all of an eyeblink before he bowed in the old fashion they'd both known when they were young. "Of course. It was my pleasure to be of service." His sharp gaze skewered them as surely as the little sticks had Lya's meat this evening. "Are you sure you must leave next sundown?"

"Afraid so," Lya said. "The Umstead is nice, but—"

"Lydia," Cade snapped, as though she'd given away too much. It wasn't all charade. He didn't like that she'd gone so far in their game, even if she was setting a trap.

She flinched and tucked herself slightly behind him. "Apologies, Master. I was just—"

"Enough." The behavior was so unlike her that he didn't have to pretend to be unsettled, especially at Alejandro's quick interest and equally quick attitude of boredom at the exchange.

"So harsh with your woman, Cade?" Alejandro's smirk was back. He thought he had them. "You seemed more flexible before."

"After the disaster in the Outer Banks, she needed to learn her place," Cade said softly. What he meant was, *You would be wise to know yours, and that it is far away from us*, but he knew all Alejandro would see was a five-century vampire controlling his modern woman. It was how the blood witch wanted to see the world, it was how he wanted to see *Lya*, and so he would.

Alejandro studied Lya, taking in her downturned eyes and submissive posture before smiling. "So she does. Look at you, Cade, breaking in a half-elf."

And with those words, the witch's plans were confirmed. He still wanted Lya, much as Aron had wanted her. Both parties were hoping Cade taking her as a solidaire meant she'd had the fight beaten out of her, but neither of them understood the nature of the dynamic between Cade and Lya. Neither of them saw, or would ever see, a half-elf as the equal of a full Othersider.

Which was why Aron hadn't seen her full potential until she'd fought back and why Alejandro was standing there like he could see Lya naked and bleeding, rather than seeing the rage leaking off of her for what it was—a readiness to kill the witch, rather than resentment for her so-called master's sharp rebuke.

Cade pulled Lya in against him, hugging her close and kissing the crown of her head even as he kept his eyes on Alejandro. "It's not hard, once you know what they crave. And once you make them crave blood most of all, of course."

Lya's grip tightened painfully around his waist.

But Alejandro just threw back his head and laughed. "Ah Cade, I was afraid you'd lost your touch on our last little engagement. But I think all you needed was a challenge." He eyed Lya hungrily again for half a heartbeat before blanking his expression. "Well. Safe travels, my friends."

"And you," Cade said.

With a last, greedy look at Lya, Alejandro took a few steps backward. "Don't come after me."

"Why would I?" Cade shifted his grip to the nape of Lya's neck, threading his fingers through her hair to tilt her head back and expose her throat in a calculated risk that screamed danger. "I have everything I need."

"So you do." And with that, Alejandro turned his back to them and was gone.

Cade waited until they were in the car to speak again. "Are you okay?"

Lya started to answer then stopped short and shuddered before trying again. "Yes. I hate how that conversation went, and I'm pissed that we couldn't kill him right there without breaking the Détente. But it answered a question. He must've had only enough blood to track me, not compel me. And in any case, I'm glad you took the ball and ran with it."

"Then that is what you intended me to do?"

"Yes. Exactly that." She reached for him, hand shaking, and he took it. "I'm not used to hunting with a partner. It bothered me to call you…" She trailed off and grimaced before continuing. "And I know it had to have bothered you to use me as bait like that. But you sold it, Cade. Now we don't have to hunt him down. We just need our fake time limit to draw him to us and let him create a situation he thinks will separate us so he can take me."

"We need to warn Maria," Cade said. "If there's a potential breaking of the Détente at The Umstead—"

"No. Not yet. Not until I confirm whether Henri is staying at The Umstead alone or if Samarre and whoever else are stupid enough to join him." Lya got the car started and didn't speak again until they were on the freeway. "This is like Ocracoke. We bring all the parties involved to us. And then we spring the trap."

Chapter 13: Lya

I half expected to be accosted by Henri again as we returned to our rooms, but Cade steered us around to the road down to the spa level. The steep incline was slick with yet more drizzle trying to turn into freezing rain, but it was better than risking Henri camping out in the lobby. Yeah, if he really wanted to find us, he could track us by scent or mindmaze a member of the hotel staff, but that would demonstrate a level of desperation that'd be too much for his pride. He'd never live down following a half-elf around like a lost dog. Bad enough that he'd made the trip to begin with.

"Do you need to hunt?" I asked when we were back in the room.

He shrugged. "Technically not."

I just looked at him.

Cade scowled then scrubbed a hand through his hair to ruffle it. "I honestly don't *need* to feed as much as I have been. Powerful blood sharpens the hunger is all. It's like…" A frown pinched his brow. "Eating because it tastes good?"

"Got it."

His expression turned wicked. "And because I like bedding you."

I laughed then went to kiss him. "Does that mean you can hold off until we can do some planning?"

"If I must." The put-upon tone was laced with teasing.

I kissed him again before toeing my boots off and getting the documents out of the room's safe. We couldn't leave those out where housekeeping could find them. My weapons—the ones I wasn't wearing—were locked in the new car safe for the same reason.

Cade snagged me around the waist as I passed him, awkwardly matching his much longer steps to mine and nibbling my neck as I towed us to the couch. Fangs grazed my skin, sending goosebumps racing over me.

"Later," I insisted, groaning.

"It's not the new moon."

"I don't care. I'll survive a little bite."

His hum of pleasure told me we'd revisit that idea as he released me to collapse onto the couch.

I spread out the photos and papers on the coffee table as Cade dropped down next to me and leaned forward to rest his elbows on his knees. When I had everything laid out the way it was when we left off last night, I recapped. "Okay. So we've confirmed Alejandro is in the RTP or Briar Creek area. That's high risk for him because it's so densely populated, but high reward because once he decides to move on from animals he can take victims without much interference from the rest of Otherside. Plus with all the business travelers coming in and out of RDU, he has some more flexibility while he waits for a shot at me. How does he get to me?"

Cade reached for the paper map we'd grabbed at the petrol station. "He needs to get you isolated." The playfulness from earlier was gone, replaced by a cold, leashed rage. "The state park on the other side of the freeway or this smaller one—Lake Crabtree?—are possibilities. He'll want room to use magic, since you're not a mundane and he has to assume you're stronger now with me hinting you're addicted to vampire blood."

"Is that a possibility?" I blurted out.

I'd never even thought about it. I mean, it was damn good and I wanted some if it was on offer, but now I worried it was more than just the high I was chasing. Like maybe it was a need rather than just a distraction.

He started to shake his head no then tilted it. "It's not exactly an addiction for the blood itself. It's more like a link between us that gets stronger as we pass blood back and forth. That's what Noah meant the other night when he said we were one flesh." He glanced at me. "I think it's another evolutionary survival mechanism, to be honest. Does that bother you?"

It should have. But I'd already committed.

I blew my breath out between my lips. "No, I guess not. I just hadn't thought about it. Anyway. Alejandro needs me alone. Preferably at one of these wooded areas. They usually close at sundown." A quick look at Google Street View gave me the answer to my other questions. "Umstead State Park is technically in Raleigh, so vampire territory. Lake Crabtree is Morrisville. Is that vamp held?"

"Arguable. I think it's contested between the elves and the vampires, although neither actually have people living there, from what I recall of one of Maria's little rants. If there was a dividing line between the airport and the state park, Morrisville would fall on the RTP side of it, Cary on the Raleigh side."

"Okay. There's minimal security. A little gatehouse that's closed after hours and some light swing gates that I can get us through. Which begs a question: how does he lure me out without you, or alternatively, how does he separate us if we happen to be there already?"

"Hmm." Cade leaned back, gathering me under one arm as he did. "I don't know yet."

"Wait." I stiffened as an idea came to me.

He tilted his head to watch me, a small smile tugging at the corners of his lips.

I elbowed him—he always got amused when I really put my thinking cap on instead of just going after something with knives flashing and guns blazing—and went through the idea again. "Remember how I said we need to get everyone in one place?"

He was quick. "You want to confront the Lyon elves."

"Yep."

"Which is more bait for Alejandro."

"Exactly. Even if he can't get at me, he'll have even stronger consolation prizes."

"I'm surprised at you, love. You weren't as easy with the idea of treason last year."

Despite the neutral tone, guilt and something a little like shame curdled in my stomach and tightened my chest. "Yeah, well, last year I hadn't been captured by the Darkwatch and beaten to hell. Exile as a punishment didn't fit the crime, especially when there was no crime, and all I've ever tried to do is survive in the situations my people have put me in. Fuck. That. Shit."

Cade pulled me close again and kissed the top of my head. "I'm proud of you."

"For what?" I snapped.

"Going your own way. It's hard. Especially, I think, for an elf."

"Good thing I'm only half."

"Hey." He leaned back and turned my face toward him with a finger. "Enough with the bitterness. You're everything you need to be. And you're everything I could ever ask for. All I'm saying is that you have been up against culture, conditioning, training, and your own nature, but here you are."

I couldn't let it go. "With your help."

"Is that really so bad? To have someone who cares enough to help?"

Squirming, I snuggled closer and rested my head on his chest. "You have a point."

"Okay then."

We sat in a silence that grew more comfortable as I relaxed.

"Thanks," I said.

"For?"

"Helping. But also all the little ways you check that I'm okay with whatever it is we're doing. And putting my head back on straight."

He kissed me again then chuckled. "It's a much better alternative than begging your forgiveness later if I don't check."

I climbed onto his lap, straddling him and deepening the kiss. Seeing Henri again had brought back so many feelings of worthlessness and doubt.

With a few words, Cade dispelled them.

We'd hooked up fast, moved in together fast, committed to this solidaire arrangement fast. Yeah, we got shit wrong together. But being with him always felt *right*. Not just physically, although as he gripped my hips and pulled me tighter against him, that definitely felt right. It was the way we kept getting better. Or at least kept trying.

Cade tilted his head back and spoke to the ceiling when I ground against him playfully. "Please tell me we're done planning."

Smiling, I nibbled the skin of his throat.

His fingers pinched as he groaned.

I kept my lips against his neck as I spoke. "We have the broad strokes. We can take a break. And get the ball rolling."

"I'll give you broad strokes if you don't stop with my neck."

I stopped nibbling—and then, without warning, bit him hard where his shoulder met his neck. Before I could figure out how he'd managed it, I was on the floor pinned beneath him, each wrist trapped alongside my ears in a firm grip as his body weighed on mine.

This time it was his teeth at my throat. "You always enjoy playing dangerous games with me, Lya. I should repay that. With interest."

Swallowing past the lump the adrenaline rush had pushed into my throat, I gasped, "Later."

"Why later?" The coolness of his breath raised goosebumps on me as much as the points of his fangs did.

"Take me down to the bar for a drink first."

"A drink. To what purpose?"

I hissed as the hint of fang became a pinch, not quite breaking the skin. He must have been thirstier than I thought, but it didn't scare me. It turned me on—a lot.

Adrenaline junkie.

"Reconnaissance," I whispered. "See how many Lyon elves are here. Give them a reason to think I might go along with what they want. If Alejandro followed us, let him see the buffet available if he sticks around."

Cade growled in frustration. "More work."

"And then play. Samarre wanted to meet me. That's how we get them to one of the parks."

"Which?"

"Definitely Crabtree. Aside from the territory questions, it's easier to get rid of a body if we don't have to hike it out on rough terrain."

At the word "body," his fangs pinched tighter before he pulled away. "Fine. But I'm biting you later."

"Good."

He kissed me roughly enough that I was surprised I hadn't been bitten. Whatever he'd been or done in centuries past, the man had learned self-control. I kissed him back, tempting him again by nipping his lip, which he put a stop to with a firm grip on my jaw and a warning look. Despite the fact that it almost mirrored the time he'd threatened me in his bed, I laughed.

"Up," I said.

After arching an eyebrow to warn me I was on thin ice, he stood with vampire quickness. I took the hand he extended and got to my feet then kept going toward the closet where I'd hung a few things after seeing Callista last night and realizing we'd be here a while.

"Give me a few minutes to freshen up, okay?" I said.

"A few minutes, she says. Well, I suppose I should as well then." He eyed the red dress I pulled out of the closet. "Definitely need to freshen up."

Watching each other get changed from the casual clothes we'd worn to dinner into something fancier for the five-star hotel's bar was foreplay in and of itself. By the time we left our room, both of us were running hot enough that any human would be able to sense the sexual tension—and any Othersider would smell our mutual desire for each other. As far as I was concerned, we were potentially going into battle, and this was both our armor and our way of demoralizing the enemy.

Realizing I thought of the Lyon elves, my own people, as the enemy as much as I did the local elves who'd physically hurt me should have set me aback.

It didn't. It rekindled the fire in me.

I was going to get justice for myself. If it meant putting on a slinky dress and heels instead of strapping on weapons, so be it. Some people might have called it petty. I called it using my assets and connections to their best advantage to get a job done.

I'd been in Alejandro's hands twice. No way was I going to walk into them again with just Cade if the blood witch had been leveling up. And no way was I letting the people who'd exiled me think they were going to walk back into my life like nothing had happened.

We found seats at the bar, on the side where it'd be harder to see the basketball game most of the bar patrons were watching. I let Cade order for me—I drank just about anything, and he'd be drinking from me later—and to my surprise, he ordered a whiskey neat for himself as well.

"Making a point?" I asked.

Older vampires could drink alcohol, but most avoided it as a general rule because it contributed to cellular degeneration and made it harder for the vamp virus to repair their undead cells.

He smirked. "I might be." His gaze slid down my body and back up. "Much like you are in that dress, love. You look good enough to eat."

I laughed. I didn't know why, but that was one of my favorite jokes. Maybe because it was true. I covered my mouth when it drew attention, but Cade took the hand and kissed it.

"Never hide your joy with me," he said. "It gives me a reason to—"

A woman's voice, one I recognized, interrupted from behind us. "Well, this is unexpected."

Cade and I managed to turn on our stools at the same time, somehow not knocking our knees together.

"Samarre," I said, all joy fleeing.

The tall, dark-skinned elfess stared down at me, even though her stance said she was paying more attention to Cade. Something like disapproval flashed in her brown gaze, and I steeled my spine.

I'd done enough flinching as a child; she wouldn't get more from me.

Tilting his head, Cade returned the look. "I don't believe we've met. Samarre, is it?"

My mum's knight gave a tight nod before answering in French. "And you are?"

"Cade." He rested a possessive hand on the back of my neck and squeezed in a massaging grip that screamed ownership, then replied in the same language. "How are you and my Lya acquainted?"

Samarre's disapproval went from tentative to icy. "*Lydia* is the daughter of my employer. I did some of her training, years ago." Her eyes narrowed. "Apparently not well."

The clink of glasses on the bar counter gave me a reason to spin away from the judgment in her eyes. I handed Cade his drink, taking a moment to clink our glasses. "Salut."

"Salut, mon amour."

That sent Samarre from ice to subzero. "Excuse me?"

I sipped my cocktail, something with mezcal and stone fruit, and leaned against Cade. "I've made new connections."

"With his people?" Samarre's voice was as emotional as I'd ever heard it.

"Considering what my cousins did to me in my time here, it was a wise choice." I couldn't help the snarl in my own voice. "Ever been lead poisoned, Samarre?"

She blinked rapidly. "How—"

I raised my free hand and, under the cover of Cade's body, mimed a gun firing.

"The Monteagues?"

I nodded.

"And on that unpleasant note," Cade said, "I'll thank you to leave us to enjoy the rest of our evening in peace. Your people don't seem fond of my Lya, so you'll understand if I'm a mite protective of her."

Stubbornly, Samarre gritted her teeth, making the muscles in her jaw bunch. "We need to talk, girl."

"We did talk. My master asked you to leave."

That took her aback more than anything else. "Your—" she whispered. "What have you done?"

"What I had to." I turned and kissed Cade's cheek to cover the roil in my stomach at calling him "master" twice in a night as he continued giving Samarre a smugly superior look I'd never seen on him before. "And what I wanted to. Cade takes excellent care of me."

"Because he—" Samarre broke off, her teeth grinding audibly.

I'd never seen her so discomposed.

"Because she's my solidaire and I take care of what's mine," Cade said, cold as the grave. "Now if there's nothing else?"

Samarre fixed me with an angry look. "You will want to reconsider this, girl. You are to be offered terms to come back home."

That hit me like a slap. "What?"

"Pick up your damned phone the next time I call you. Enjoy your evening."

With that, Samarre stalked away, as soundless as all high-blood elves were even when furious.

Chapter 14: Lya

I could tell Cade wanted to ask questions, but his self-control extended to his tongue as well as everything else. I was determined to act like my mind wasn't racing, whirling like a tornado on the question of what the fuck it meant that I might be offered terms.

"That went well," I said as brightly as I could while keeping my voice below the level of the bar's general buzz. There was an itchy feeling between my shoulder blades, like I was being watched, but Samarre and any others of my mother's House would be keeping an eye on me now.

This wasn't at all what I'd expected them to be here for. I pushed aside the ache in my heart as the thought of where my mum was crossed my mind. Not here. Not now.

"If you say so." When Cade sipped his whiskey, he actually swallowed some of it, though whether he was making a point or just agitated, I didn't know. "Gods, I miss whiskey."

I leaned into his arm, glad for him to be playing along. "Does it make any difference when I drink it?"

"No. I don't get a taste, just the effect."

"Huh." Maybe I should have been grossed out by the discussion of whether my blood took on flavors, but I really was curious about how it worked for him. "The effect as in…"

"Intoxication. Different than usual and shorter-lived." He swirled his glass and took another sip. "I can't truly get drunk off alcohol anymore. Only power. Everything else processes too quickly."

"You know, it just occurred to me that I haven't actually seen you power drunk."

"That's because you usually pass out in sated exhaustion, and I, being a sleepy drunk, join you for a nap."

I laughed. "Is *that* why you're always dozing after?"

He nodded, and if he'd had any blood tonight, I thought he might have blushed from the chagrined expression and the way he rubbed the back of his head. "If intoxication shows who you truly are, apparently all I want is to take a nap with the woman I love in my arms."

Laughter burbled out of me again. What he'd said was sweet, but I couldn't help it.

Cade just eyed me with a rueful smile. "Yeah. Big, scary reputation. Just want to have a lie down and a cuddle. I'm buzzing when I come out of it, but that first twenty minutes or so is like everything's right with the world and I can finally rest."

"I'm sorry. I don't know why that's so funny. It's actually quite sweet."

He shrugged. "It's worth it to hear you laugh."

I started to lean in to kiss him then froze when I spotted a figure over his shoulder, standing in the rain on the patio outside.

"What?" He twisted to follow my line of sight.

"Donatien."

"Here?" Cade frowned. "I don't see or smell him."

"I swear to the Goddess, he was there. On the patio, watching us." Maybe the itch between my shoulder blades hadn't been Samarre but Donatien. I waited for Cade to ask if I was sure of what I'd seen, but he didn't.

"If he's here, he followed us," Cade snarled.

I grimaced, spotting another angle. "Or he knew we'd come here."

"What?"

"Think about it. The last time too many of the community came together in one place was because Alejandro got a whiff of something and engineered it. What are the odds we just happen to be put on a case involving him the day after Donatien turns up for the first time in, what, a—"

I cut off before I could say "hundred years" because we were in public and while we were speaking quietly, bartenders always heard more than you thought and were exceedingly good at putting pieces together.

"In longer than is reasonable, yes. Especially if he really was visiting Santiago and Luz in Miami long enough to hear rumors of us and waited until now to pay us a visit despite our being there for, what, eight months?" He frowned then shook his head. "No. Part of the reason I kept moving was because I didn't want him to find me. I'd been in Raleigh eighteen months when I met you. Long enough that Morris struck but nobody else. He could have come to me then and didn't. So why now?"

I finished my drink and signaled for another while Cade pondered something. Leaving now would look like either Samarre had cowed me or Donatien had spooked me. Part of this whole trap relied on everyone thinking I was the same impulsive fool I had been in Lyon or too drunk on love and vampire blood to know better now.

"I think you're right," Cade finally said. "Donatien could have either evaded Torsten and Aron as easily as Morris did or followed the proper procedures as I did and, assuming he told the truth, as he did in Miami."

"Are things that bad in Raleigh? I wouldn't have thought anyone would—or even could—circumvent the proper procedures. Not a vampire, at least."

Cade frowned into his whiskey. "A year ago, I would have said no, that everything is fine. Aron seemed to have everything well in hand. But Maria wouldn't be making the moves she is, or seeking my support, if that was the case. She's… Well, let's just say the only reason I had my former position in New Orleans was a partnership with someone close in strength and stronger in motivation, and she's proposing to do it alone quite a bit earlier than should be possible. If she does succeed…" He grimaced. "That's why she wants my support."

I couldn't follow most of this, being too new to vampire politics and society. "Why?"

"Raleigh is pinched by New York and Miami. Aside from the coterie in Charlotte there's one in Atlanta, but they keep their numbers low and their politics neutral to avoid Santiago's ire. Philadelphia is practically a vassal to New York, and the rest of the stretch between Miami and here is claimed by the furries and the shadows."

Weres of some description and elves. I knew there were conclaves in Charleston and Richmond, semi-independent holdings with no Arbiter, although Callista liked to think she owned Charleston, at the very least, given she claimed all of the Carolinas. But if she was calling Cade and me in to deal with something in her own demesne, I strongly suspected that, whatever she'd once held, she'd slowly lost control of as the mundane population exploded in the last century. It was a story playing out all over Otherside.

Another of my mother's House Guard crossed my vision on the way back from the bathrooms, and I blinked a little too fast as he glared at me. I'd gotten so focused on the question of Donatien I'd practically forgotten my other problem.

One thing at a time.

"Okay." I took a big swallow of my drink then shook my head and grinned at the bartender. He smiled back. At Cade's confused look, I said, "He put an extra shot of mezcal in this one."

"Apparently he can read his patrons."

I kissed his cheek, since he sounded amused rather than upset or jealous. Yeah, he smelled jealous sometimes, and he played the controlling asshole real well, but if I was happy, Cade was happy.

"Love you," I said.

He caught my head and turned the kiss into one that lingered. "Don't think I didn't see the look that other one gave you. Someone you know?"

"One of my mother's people," I grumbled.

"She's not here?"

"As far as I can tell, no. She has a siggy, unless she mutes it." Not all elves developed power signatures, but my mum had by the time I'd left.

Cade grunted. "That explains your strength."

"Yeah. And why her marrying my father was such a problem and why they sent me here rather than…finding a more permanent solution."

"Fortunately for us both." He kissed my temple and then finished his whiskey, shaking his head when the bartender started over with the bottle. "What was your relationship with her like?"

"I— Don't take this the wrong way, babe, but I don't want to talk about it right now. I'll tell you anything you want to know, but after it's done."

He studied me like he was trying to decide whether my emotional state would be a problem for our hunt then spun his empty glass. "Back to the business at hand then. Donatien is here. He might be in league with Alejandro. In which case, we were driven out of St. Augustine intentionally."

I nodded. "That's my read. Reps from Desmarais and Lavigne being at this hotel is a coincidence but one we can use." I swirled my cocktail before drinking some more. "Donatien screws with our original plan though."

"How so?"

"You'd know better than me, but Alejandro was bold as fuck when he thought he had allies on Ocracoke. Or tools, I guess. Assuming he's working with Donatien, that means two things. First, there's an agreement for something." I shuddered. "Maybe me? Probably, um, in their hands." The word "dead" tended to draw attention, and that bartender was attentive. A benefit of being in a classy establishment, but for Othersiders, potential trouble if too much of what we were saying was overheard.

Cade knew what I meant though. His snarl nearly showed fang before I elbowed him and his expression blanked. I swayed before I could catch myself as he loosed a bit of glamour, enough that if he slipped again nobody would notice.

"Second," I continued, "we can't afford to risk at least three of my mum's people plus three of House Lavigne on one side, Alejandro and Donatien allied on another, with us trying to cover them all. We're good, but that's too much of a gamble."

"Even for you?"

I snorted a laugh. "Even for me, now that I have something to lose."

Cade frowned. "What, me?"

Nodding, I leaned against him.

He shifted to drag my stool closer then wrapped his arm around my shoulder to pull me into him. "You know, in all the years I've lived, I never thought I'd be that person for someone. Especially not after New Orleans."

"I'm not naive enough to believe everyone can be redeemed," I said in a near-whisper. "But you? I've staked my life on it."

"So you have."

As always, the emotion in his voice spurred heat in me.

Most of the old Othersiders—anyone over a few centuries—had either lost the knack of emotion or learned to bury it. Cade was perfectly capable of either burying his feelings or putting on a convincing façade that showed whatever he wished, as he'd demonstrated first with Alejandro then with Samarre.

He played the master vampire to keep me safe. But his domination of me was entirely based on my consent and the limits I set.

To anyone watching us, his half-embrace might look loving, but it might look possessive as well. That was up to the viewer and their expectation of a well-dressed, mixed-race couple or, if they were Othersiders, what they thought a half-elf was doing with a vampire.

Only I knew the depths of what he felt for me.

Only I knew that he'd broken multiple formal rules and informal taboos to do everything he could to strengthen and protect me, simply because he loved and needed me.

"I love you," I blurted out. "I never want to be with anyone but you. Ever. If there was a way…"

To turn me, I wanted to say, but I swallowed the words.

It wasn't done. I knew it wasn't done, and I knew the reasons. Being together gained us both a few more decades—me of life, him of sanity—but he couldn't share immortality with me.

I leaned my head against his jaw, willing the thought to him anyway. He'd explained that fledglings and their sires could communicate mind to mind and that a similar telepathic link eventually developed with a solidaire, although to a lesser extent.

"Please don't tempt me," he murmured back. His grip on me tightened. "Because I don't know that I could let you…"

Die was the word he didn't say.

I loved him. I knew.

So I kept the wish he might break that law secret in my heart.

Then his lips were on mine, a claiming he stopped as quickly as he started it, given how fancy the venue was and the eyes on us, despite the ongoing basketball game.

"Finish your drink," he ordered in a low growl. "We've done what we came down here for, and we got more information than we bargained for. I'm taking what I almost got earlier. And then we'll discuss what to do about this three-way clusterfuck."

A bite. And, presumably, a fuck as well. I obeyed, happy to take orders when they benefited me, as Cade paid in cash.

"I'll have your change right out," the bartender said.

Cade shook his head and made a negating motion with his hand as we rose. "No need."

"Sir, this is—"

"You made my lady smile. It's exactly what is owed."

"Thank you very much, sir."

I winked at the man as he cheerfully stuffed the change for the hundred Cade had paid on fifty dollars' worth of drinks in the tip jar. Charm and money bought allies, and if we had both, this bartender would tell his colleagues. Any questions we had later would be answered a bit more readily, especially since a lot of rich folks at fancy venues tended to be stingy tippers. Cade had more money than he knew what to do with in the modern age, even with inflation jacking prices up to a level he found outrageous, given what things had cost when he'd died, and anything or anyone that drew a smile or a laugh from me saw the benefit.

I kept my composure as we made our way back to the lift and our room, but as soon as the lift doors shut, I was on him. We had one floor to go, and I didn't care. Drinking vampire blood made it harder to get drunk on alcohol, and I was nowhere near close.

I just wanted him.

We'd barely gotten started when the ding signaled we were on our floor. I let him back me out of the lift, trusting him to be my eyes as I kept mine on him.

The moment the door to our room shut behind us, I pounced, jumping to wrap my arms around his neck and my legs around his hips. He caught me, pulling me tightly to him even as he pressed me against the wall with a thud. When I broke for air, he nibbled his way down my neck.

"Bite me," I panted. "Please, Cade."

For once, he didn't question. He pulled away just long enough to submerge me in a light glamour then did what we both wanted, sinking fangs in my throat just long enough to take a few quick swallows of blood before pulling away. Then he shifted me over his shoulder to carry me back to the bed before throwing me down and dragging the side zipper of my dress down.

I wiggled to help him get the damn thing off then tried to help with his buttons. He caught my wrists and held them in one hand as he did the work himself with the other, his eyes never leaving mine.

"You're mine. Say it," he commanded when he was as naked as I was.

"I'm yours." I used my legs to pull him closer, since he still held my hands captive. Come hell or high water, come ex-boyfriends or blood-thirsty enemies, that would always be true. He'd shown me the truth of it over and over again.

This time, I hoped our play would hurt at least a little, to ground me for the days to come.

Chapter 15: Cade

Cade resisted taking Lya as long as he could, although he freed her wrists long enough to get his shirt, trousers, and briefs off. She slid from the bed to kneel in front of him and help get the blood flowing to his cock faster.

He couldn't help a growl of pleasure at that. As much as he repressed his natural dominance to keep her from getting scared and running, she responded well to it when eased in, especially when it came to sex. He made a mental note to take more control in bed going forward, given that she consistently yielded to him happily and readily when he did.

As a test, he tangled his fingers in her curls to guide her then held her nose to his belly as the blood he'd taken flowed with increasing speed to the crucial area.

Her nails dug into his hips as he thickened, but she didn't resist.

He liked when she did though. He liked dominating her. Taming her, over and over again. It wasn't everything he could take from her, but it was everything he dared dream of. When her throat spasmed around him, he pulled her head back so she could breathe.

"Who do you belong to?" The words sprang from him before he could stop them.

He hadn't thought he was that bothered by all the people from her past turning up at their hotel or Donatien and his charm being both in St. Augustine and here, but apparently he was. So be it. He'd work it out in bed.

"You," she gasped. Her chest heaved, more as he kept pulling her head back just to see her arch. He kept going until she hissed. "You, Cade. I'm yours."

"That's right." He released her. "Show me."

She worked him with mouth and fingers as though she understood exactly where his head was at, and maybe she did. He didn't take any particular care to shield from her, and she'd become sensitized to his moods much more quickly than he'd anticipated. He'd have to account for that in their interactions before it tempted her to run, but for now, she seemed inclined to suck rather than flee and he was happy to let her.

Naughty as she was, she grazed him with her teeth, equal parts tease and threat from the vague sensation he was getting from her.

"Up," he commanded.

Lya obeyed with enthusiasm, letting out a surprised sound when he spun her, grasped the back of her neck, held her hip steady, and forced her forward to bend over the edge of the bed. The angle was slightly awkward, but the position still reminded him of the first time he'd fucked her in his nest in Raleigh, bent over the granite countertops and panting with need for him.

Just like then, he leaned over her, blanketing and claiming her with his whole body as he pulled her head by the hair to bring her neck to a bitable angle.

"What are you?" he whispered.

"Your solidaire," she answered in a breathy pant.

"And what does that mean?"

"My body and blood are yours." That was the correct answer, the one he'd explained was typical, in case any other *moroi* had cause to question them publicly.

Then she added, "My heart and soul are yours. Please, Cade, please—"

He never could resist her when she begged. Especially when she did it so completely.

Cade freed her hip to grasp his cock and guide himself into her, going deep but not as roughly as he wanted, even if giving her more force than usual. At the first hint of sound from her, he covered her mouth with one hand while keeping her hips steady with the other.

"Tonight is for me," he warned her.

Lya nodded, fast and sharp, even as her cries were muffled against his palm as he picked up the pace of his thrusts and plunged deep.

The last thought he had before losing himself to taking her was that this was part of why he loved her so much. She gave him what he needed and didn't stop at not making him feel like a monster. She made him feel wanted, desired, whole.

No matter how hard he took her.

***

Sunset.

The weight of the sun slipping below the horizon dragged Cade to consciousness. To life, really, given he technically died again a little at each sunrise. He inhaled harshly, and his heart thudded, the living functions circulating the vampire virus anew so he could continue the semblance of life another night.

Lya stirred in his arms, tucking closer against him with a murmured protest at his movement.

Every time he woke and she was still here, he considered it a gift of Hekate and whoever the elves worshipped as primary among the gods. Cade frowned as he realized that was a thing he should know and didn't. Did Lya even have any particular beliefs? It could wait. For the moment, he set theology aside and submersed himself in the physical.

A mundane could only give a full blood donation every six to eight weeks. They'd figured out that someone with half Otherside blood could reasonably sustain a vampire of Cade's age every four weeks with no noticeable effects, setting aside his increased hunger. But part of the reason vampires fed their solidaires was to boost their healing and reduce the recovery time so that they could feed from them more often.

This was the first time he'd fed from Lya, even a little, in a matter of days.

He maybe shouldn't have, and guilt crawled through him. She hadn't taken quite that much blood from him—he thought—so while her healing had accelerated, it wasn't quick enough for him to live off of her alone just yet. But her color was good, and her breathing, pulse, and heart rate were even. She was sleeping easily, untroubled by nightmares. And then there was that burst of power she'd shown against Aron.

That was interesting. Maybe they could manage twice monthly or even weekly? He'd been feeding her much more than was usual.

Don't get greedy. Taking more means feeding more, and Torsten has already noticed.

Half-elves were prone to becoming maenads, but Lya hadn't tried to kill him yet. Not seriously anyway. Or not since Callista had set her to hunting him, at least.

Good signs, even if they'd have to be careful.

Cade tucked in closer at Lya's back, burying his nose at the spot where the nape of her neck met the middle of her shoulders. Usually she was awake before him, but he didn't usually drink from her at this cadence. If she could manage it—

"Babe?" She stirred in his arms in the oddly systematic way she did, like she was testing every muscle in her body to make sure everything was working when she woke up.

He kissed the back of her neck and tightened his embrace. "Evening, love."

"Hi."

As she decided whether she was ready to be awake, Cade revisited their conversation from last night. "Lya?"

"Mm?"

"What do you think of calling Maria before we lure everyone to Lake Crabtree?"

"Yes."

Still not quite awake. Cade grazed his fangs along the back of her neck.

Lya jolted, her body stiffening against his and his metaphysical sense of her crackling like lightning.

Now she's awake.

She rolled in his arms and kissed him, heedless of the fact that the last thing he'd ingested was her blood.

"You read my mind," she said. "I meant to ask you about Maria last night, but I got distracted."

Cade hadn't taken enough blood from Lya to have a proper good morning, but he kissed her like he had anyway. "Distracted?"

She groaned and writhed against him. "Bastard."

He grinned, enjoying the effect he had on her.

"If we give Maria a heads-up, we gain her good graces with a tip on accessible elven blood," Lya said. She looked half-asleep with her eyes nearly closed, but her mind was working, so Cade let her talk. "They'll owe her a forfeit. If they still want to talk to me, we make everyone go to the park. The elves are distracted and thus a better target for Alejandro and Donatien. If we have to, we convince the Houses we're on their side for my sake then turn on them. Otherwise, we let those two parties fight, and we mop up the pieces, using Callista's team for a cleanup to deliver the bounty before getting the fuck out of this state."

"Have I mentioned you're fucking devious?" Cade said.

"Mm-hmm. But it still makes me happy to hear it."

"Good." He kissed her forehead. "I refuse to lose you. That's not an option. Whatever we do, it has to involve us walking away. Together. None of what happened on Ocracoke where we tried to be self-sacrificing for each other."

"Deal."

Cade sealed it with a kiss, surprised and pleased when Lya nicked her tongue on one of his fangs and gave him a quick taste before pulling away.

"I'll call Maria," she said.

He arched his brows, surprised she'd insist on it.

"They're my people." She glanced down, and bitter shame tinged her scent before rage chased it away. "They *were* my people. They threw me away. Now I have to make a deal. I need Maria to know I'd back her if something happened to you."

"Are you afraid she wouldn't take you in?"

Lya's cringe hurt his heart. She nodded.

"I won't tell you your fears are unfounded. You have history enough for them." He stroked her cheek before pulling her in to kiss her forehead and then studied her. This vicious pragmatism was new. He liked it very much, but he was still concerned. "Maybe I should—"

Something shifted in her face. "No. It has to be me, or she won't trust that I'd put the vampires first. I'm done, Cade. I'm closing the chapter on the Houses." She hugged herself. "I'm committing to you and to the *moroi*. All the way."

"Okay, love. I approve, of course, but I don't want you doing something you'll regret later."

Her expression became fierce. "My only regret is letting any of them think they'd have a chance to drag me back. There's nothing they could offer me that would make me walk away from you."

"What if they let me come with you?"

She snorted, and her lip curled as she shook her head. "I guarantee you part of the agreement would be leaving you behind with no further contact and detoxing from vampire blood. Forever."

Cade didn't say anything. If he opened his mouth, he was afraid that either desperation would pour out in an embarrassing flood of *don't leave me* or that an order he had no right to give would. If this was what she wanted, he'd get out of her way. He rose from the bed and fetched her purse from where she'd dropped it the night before.

"Thank you." She fished out her phone, grimacing at something on the screen—the battery, probably—and dialed.

He started to go to the bathroom to give her some privacy, but her hand shot out and caught his wrist in a surprisingly strong grip. Her expression pleaded for him to stay, and he sank back down on the bed.

Lya would do this but wanted him near. There was something...not quite satisfying or comforting but reassuring about that. She'd been so upset the other night. He couldn't think of any other time when she'd outright said she couldn't bear the sight of him. It hurt, still, although the pain eased now.

"Maria!" she said in the fake-bright tone she adopted when uncertainty had won out over anger. "Got a minute?"

The other vampire's voice came through faintly but loud enough Cade could hear it. "You're the last one I expected to hear from anytime soon. Cade tells me you're on a job for Callista now?"

"Yes. We are."

"Is that what this is about?"

"No. I might have a tip for you."

"A moment." The faint sound of footsteps was followed by a door closing. "Talk to me, doll."

For a moment, Cade thought Lya would change her mind. The pulse in her throat thudded hard enough that the sight of it jumping beneath her skin made him hungry.

Then she sat up straight, expression firming. "Were you aware of out-of-territory elves staying at The Umstead?"

"Excuse the fuck me?"

"I take that as a no."

"That's correct." Silence stretched. "Why are you telling me this, little Lydia?"

"Because when Aron went for Cade, Noah stopped me from acting too early and told me you promised you'd look after me if anything happened to Cade." Lya's dark gaze flicked to his, and she released his wrist to cup his jaw. "I'm impulsive, not stupid, Maria. The bounty we're hunting is big. We drew him out and laid a trap the other night, but now we think he has help. Cade, bless him, loses his reason if someone comes after me, so if it gets him killed, I need a plan. I won't be able to go back to my family now. Not ever." Her voice dropped. "And I've had enough of Cade's blood that I don't think going cold turkey will go well for me."

Cade's stomach twisted. She was right, of course. On all counts. She was so much a woman of action that it was easy to overlook or forget her intelligence.

Maria didn't respond for long seconds.

"Well?" Lya said.

"How many elves?"

"I don't know. At least three from each of two European Houses. My bet is nine, a triple triad, given a prince and a knight are included in that number."

"European Houses. Your kin?"

"Does it matter?"

Another silence from Maria. As chatty as she was, she knew how to wield silence.

"Fine. Yes. Some of them, from my mother's side."

"You're really going all-in on the *moroi*?"

This time, it was Lya who refused to answer. Cade shifted so he could pull her in close and wrap his arms around her, offering her as much physical reassurance as he could. What she was doing humbled him. He'd never given up so much in his life. Walking away from the Mastery of New Orleans didn't count. That hadn't been something he loved. It'd just been a means to an end, a way to exorcise his demons.

This took a level of courage and commitment he prayed Hekate would never make him dig deep enough to find.

"Answer me, Lydia. You're making a bargain. I won't hear later that you feel it a poor one."

Cade winced at Maria's no-nonsense business tone and use of Lya's full name. All the flirtation and pet names were gone. This was a turning point for both of them. Cade as well, but the deal was between the two women. He just benefited from it, both in Maria's goodwill and in knowing Lya would be safe if he was gone.

A shudder ran over Lya. "Yes, I am committing to the *moroi* by betraying my mother's House and that of a former lover so you can get the blood you need to make sure that fucker Aron doesn't win. Happy?"

Lya's rage was usually a scorching hot one. This coldness was something she'd learned from him, and it scared Cade more than the other. This was a woman who had the steel of ages.

He'd never wanted to turn someone as badly as he did Lya. And even when he'd sought escape from Morris or the sweet release of his second death, he'd never been so frustrated by something he couldn't have.

Maria's purred words were nearly as frightening. "Oh yes, doll. I'm pleased as punch. Give me a night to figure out people."

"People?" Lya said.

"I do have a prodigious thirst for elf blood, but even I can't take a proper forfeit from nine high-bloods. Cade? I know you can hear me, muffin."

He jumped, not having expected to be addressed. "I'm here."

"I'm assuming you're in?"

His head spun, and he glanced at Lya.

She shrugged, and the sense he got was along the lines of *In for a penny, in for a pound.*

"If you're extending an invitation…" he started.

Maria laughed. "Normally I'd keep it all in-house, but you heard Torsten. I'm at the center of too much mischief."

Or you don't have enough people you trust, and if Lya is pissed about this later, you'd rather her ire is targeted at me. Fine.

"Then I accept," he said, "with deepest thanks."

"Good. I'll be in touch in a day or two. Call me if anything changes before then. Happy hunting, my lovelies."

The call ended, and Lya slumped.

"Every time I think I've done the hardest thing I've ever had to do, I'm proven wrong." Her face was a blank mask, but the tension in her body said she was at a breaking point—and Cade didn't have the faintest idea of how to fix it.

Chapter 16: Lya

Just because I was ready to cut ties with my past didn't mean it was easy to do.

I finally gave in to my feelings and buried my face in my hands. I wouldn't cry over this. I refused. It was entirely my choice.

No, it wasn't at all who I was raised to be or who I wanted to be.

But Goddess burn me, I was doing what I could to protect myself in a system that was set up to exclude and actively harm people like me. Virtues and morals and honor were all pretty concepts—and I couldn't afford them. Not right now. I had been pushed and prodded to the very margins of elven society and Otherside for shit that wasn't my fault. I'd been shot, stalked, kidnapped, beaten, lead poisoned, cut up, and generally used and abused by elves on both sides of the Atlantic, a blood witch, and Aron. I'd been denied opportunities, compensation, and justice, over and over again.

Shonda, the human I'd struck up a brief friendship with, had said something once that didn't quite apply to elves but still stuck with me: skinfolk ain't kinfolk.

Not everyone who was like me had my same needs and interests. The high-bloods would always choose themselves first, even if we were all elves. They always had. And the royals among them would be even tighter in their allegiance to each other, bent on keeping the caste and class systems in place to maintain their stranglehold on absolute power within our faction in Otherside. So whatever it was Samarre was here in bloody person to talk about would benefit them somehow, first and foremost.

The queens were calculating and ruthless. They traded family members like livestock for breeding programs and political advantage. Their power had no limits within the holdings of House and conclave, and they did whatever the fuck they wanted, up to and including breaching the Détente when they could get away with it. There would need to be a reckoning, and if my tattling to Maria to force the Lyon contingent to pay a forfeit was a small part of it, then I'd bloody well deal with the blow to my honor.

"Lya?"

Cade's whisper and his hand rubbing up and down my spine brought me out of the spiral of my thoughts.

I lifted my head and sniffled then darted in for a kiss before getting off the bed. "I need to hurt something."

"Shall we investigate the situation at Lake Crabtree?"

"Yeah. That's smart." I glanced out the window. At this time of year, sunset came early, and it was barely past six. "Let's give it another two hours to make sure park staff or whoever have gone home. Meantime, I'll eat something."

"And I'll hunt. I don't want to be caught hungry if we run into someone." He grimaced at the admission that his control of his appetite and instincts wasn't quite what it usually was.

I rubbed his arm. "Don't worry about it, babe. We've had a really rough trip."

I bit my lip, wondering if he was still worried about our big fight the other night, and leaned in to hug him just in case.

"I still trust you, and I'm glad you're taking care of your needs. And I'm always glad when you're up for action." I waggled my eyebrows so he knew I didn't only mean fighting.

The hint of tension that'd been thrumming through him eased. "Thanks, love."

My stomach chose that moment to complain, and we both laughed.

"You wash up or whatever you're doing, I'll order, and we'll be ready at eight."

"Deal."

While he was out and I ate, I took another look at my Maps app and planned out our night. A thrill ran through me to be hunting again. This was what I loved, and while my work in St. Augustine was important, I wasn't a manager, if I was honest with myself. I was good at logistics and organization—necessary skills to be a good bounty hunter—but I wasn't a natural carer.

Guiltily, I took a few minutes to check in with Izzy, the property manager we'd left in charge. Our supernatural guests had moved on, we had new mundane guests on a short-let contract, Cade's house was fine, and everything was quiet.

Was that a sign? That while this work was needed, it wasn't mine to do? Or was I just looking for a way to assuage my guilt?

I set it aside, spinning the ring that told me where Cade was as I refocused on my plans. He was in the garden, somewhere along the footpath loop that surrounded the manmade lake.

That gave me an idea, and I pulled up the Street View map of the other side of Lake Crabtree from the main entrance, where…

Bingo.

There was a narrow, poorly maintained road with a gravel pull-off running past the opposite side of the park from the main gate. A chain-link fence topped with barbed wire marked the edges of the park, but that too was poorly maintained, with ivy or kudzu, some kind of vine, growing over it in multiple places. It was low enough that any Othersider could jump over it, in any case. I didn't see any cameras, but that would be part of the recon. I'd need to do something about any cameras in advance, just in case we had to get a body out. This was a much better access plan.

Pleased with myself, I put the tray with my now-finished dinner outside the room and went to wash up. Cade was still in the same place he'd been earlier when I got out, and I frowned.

That was odd. It'd been almost twenty minutes. He was quick with his feeds and didn't stay too long in one place.

Something wasn't right.

I dressed quickly, pulling on jeans, a black T-shirt, knives on my left forearm and at the small of my back under a black hoodie, my combat boots, and my leather biker jacket. I didn't look quite elegant enough to be staying at this hotel, but that was fine. I pulled on Aether and muttered a quick "don't see me" spell before slipping out of the room.

The rings weren't an exact science, just a vague mental nudge that the holder was "over there" somewhere. I followed it, adjusting as the feeling grew stronger, keeping my hood up and my head down to help the spell along. Most elven magic was supported and strengthened by physical action, hence the spoken spells where most of Otherside just magicked or whatever. A powerful high-blood could draw shadows without a word and might be able to subvocalize a spell. But not me.

Cade didn't move in the time it took me to get outside, and I hustled, breaking into a near-silent trot. I followed the feeling to a little grove of winter-bare trees, slowing as I scented the wet ash and hot iron scent of a pissed-off vampire. The hint of granite was Cade, but there was something else in the mix.

I frowned, torn between trying to figure it out and barging in.

A compromise. I crept closer, one hand on the hilt of the knife in my sleeve, until I could hear the whispered words clearly despite the distortion of a heavy glamour.

"—told you, Donatien, no. A thousand times no," Cade said. "Now release the mundane before you force us into breaking the Détente."

I froze. Donatien was back? Or had he never left? Was he staying at the hotel? Did he have permission?

"I thought you were only staying the night, but here you are. Methinks the gentleman doth protest too much." Definitely Donatien.

Feeling like a snitching child all over again, I sent a quick text to Maria. *You know a four-cent vamp named Donatien is here as well?*

Her response came back almost immediately. *No. He's not authorized.* Another text followed it. *Unless Aron is shirking again. Or setting me up. Leave it with me, doll.*

I put the phone away and refocused on the conversation.

"—the mundane comes with me." Donatien sounded delighted by whatever situation he was putting Cade in. "Tick tock, my friend. The glamour is wearing off. If you don't—"

My phone buzzed, and I winced as Donatien cut off.

"Who's being a naughty little spy?" he said. "Come out, come out wherever you are."

A push of glamour accompanied his words, one I shrugged off easily. Donatien was weaker than Cade, and I was close enough that Cade's own glamour helped shield me. The rustle of clothes was followed by Cade's growl. That drew me into the clearing where the glamour hadn't.

Donatien held a human woman by the throat with her back to his front.

A set of bite marks decorated either side of her neck, and I figured out what must have happened. Cade had lured her and fed then been set upon by Donatien, who must have followed through on whatever his sharing kink was. The poor woman was shaking from what had to be a combination of cold and, from the scent in the air, terror.

"Help me," she whimpered.

"Fuck," I muttered. This was a clear breaking of the Détente. The woman either had to be glamoured or spelled to hell and back, turned, or killed. "Donatien—"

He ignored me and addressed Cade. "You summoned her? She can hear your call already?"

"That's neither here nor there," Cade said. "This one has seen too much now, thanks to you."

A low moan of fear slid from the woman, and her knees gave out. Cade focused on her and must have caught her eye because more glamour rolled out and she slumped, dead weight Donatien could easily manage but looked annoyed at having to.

"All you had to do was come with me," Donatien hissed. "Now look at this mess."

"Leave the woman and go." Cade's voice was cold and hard. "I'll fix this."

"No, I don't think so." All-black eyes flicked to me, and I turned my head, checking the path behind me rather than meet Donatien's gaze. "Alejandro wants a human to play with now. This one will do."

"No," I whispered.

I knew what would happen to that woman if Alejandro and Donatien had her. Not a trip to the Raleigh coterie or the clean death Cade or I would have given her if forced to maintain the Détente, but something uglier, messier, and far more painful.

Something that would have Alejandro powered up ahead of the trap we'd been trying to set.

Donatien grinned. "A trade then. Offer yourself in her place."

"No!" Cade growled before I could say anything. "She is *mine.*"

I couldn't pull my eyes away from the woman slumped on the ground. She was wearing black spandex exercise pants and one of those heat-tek breathable tops. With the running shoes, she'd probably been out for a jog. Women should be as able to exercise when and where they wanted as men, and she should have been safe here. But she wasn't. Because of me.

Stop that, I scolded myself. *Donatien did this. Alejandro did this. Not you.*

Still, it was hard to stand firm and keep my mouth shut. If I went with Donatien, worse would happen than the last time Alejandro had me. Not only that, but my going with them wouldn't save this woman.

The rules of the Détente were clear. She was dead already, one way or another.

Donatien watched my internal struggle with a gleeful light in his eyes. "Are you sure about that, Cade? I think your lady has other ideas."

"No," I said before Cade could do more than shift to glance at me.

That distracted movement gave Donatien an opening. He dropped the woman and lunged at Cade.

I exploded forward, drawing my knife.

My interference checked Donatien's swipe, giving Cade time to dodge and me just enough reach to cut Donatien.

"Bitch!" he hissed.

This time, it was me he leapt for and Cade who got between us.

With an ugly, wrathful expression, Donatien fell back.

"Fine." He moved, again, vampire fast, to snatch the woman and throw her over his shoulder. "This one dies in pain because of you."

He held up his arm to show the blood dripping from it and his lips twisted in disgust. Before we could do anything else, Donatien pulled a heavy glamour to cloak him from mundane eyes and fled into the bushes.

"Shit." Cade knelt and sniffed then scooped up a double handful of the dirt Donatien had bled on. "Get the rest. Throw it in the lake. Someone will investigate that woman's disappearance, and vampire blood can't be present here."

I hurried to do as he said, heart pounding and acid burning in my throat. I hated the choice I'd made. But all of my choices tonight were driven by survival.

Not that it made me feel any better about following the letter of the law.

We did our best to obscure all the evidence that anything had happened there. This was the part of being an Othersider I didn't like. The secrecy. The way good people—or at least uninvolved people—got caught up in the twisted games of more powerful supernaturals. I was half human. If I had any less magic than I did, that could've been me. I'd have drawn every predatory Othersider I encountered and been able to do even less about it than I could now. And if I'd been any less lucky than I had been in meeting Cade, it might have been me anyway.

For a brief moment I wanted to be mad at the vampires. Of all the Othersiders, they were the only ones who regularly preyed on humans. Wereanimals were forbidden from increasing their numbers by biting humans. Elves would fuck them and create offspring which would, in a few more generations of breeding with humans, have nothing more than a little magical sensitivity and maybe be necromancers or psychics. The fae stayed in the Summerlands these days or stayed hidden here on the earthly plane.

Nope, it was just the vampires—the faction I'd adopted—who continually risked breaking the Détente just by existing.

With a heavy sigh, I shook off the unfair thought. If they didn't prey on humans, they'd have to prey on the rest of us. That couldn't be allowed, or the balance of power that kept us all safe would be fucked.

"Talk to me, love."

I glanced at Cade then finished surveying the crime scene. It was as clean as we could make it, and I walked to the edge of the boardwalk around the lake, knelt, and cleaned my knife before plunging my hands into the icy water and scrubbing so that nobody would ask why they were dirty if we were caught walking out here. Fortunately, the bitterly cold evening had encouraged everyone else to stay indoors.

Cade rinsed his hands, and then we both stuck our hands in our pockets to dry and warm them.

"We need to do a walk around the loop," I said in a voice low enough that even another Othersider would struggle to hear me if they were farther away than Cade. "If we're questioned, we can throw off the timeline by saying we hadn't seen her."

He fell into step beside me. "I thought you'd be more upset."

"I am upset. I feel like I'm going to throw up the very expensive dinner I just ate. But that won't save her. Getting myself killed for being involved in a breach of the Détente won't save her. Nothing I do will save her." I swallowed hard at that, fighting back tears. That really could have been me. "I hate that. But the only way I have a chance at fixing it is if we hurry up on this walk and then go and scope out our trap grounds. Maybe if we find her alive, Maria will take her in as a pet or something."

"Maybe." He sounded like he was humoring me rather than like it was a real possibility. After another few steps, he said, "Thank you. For your help. And for not blaming me."

I shook my head. "It was nothing you did. It was Donatien and Alejandro. Just promise me we'll try to help her. If nothing else, that we'll ease her passing."

"I promise."

I tilted my head to rest against his arm then straightened when my phone buzzed again. I pulled it out, expecting it to be another follow-up text from Maria. I did have two of those—

Donatien was definitely a rogue in the territory—but the phone kept buzzing, and the caller ID showed Samarre's number.

"Shit," I said with feeling. "I have a feeling this is about to get much more complicated."

Chapter 17: Lya

I didn't want to answer, but I did. "Yes, Samarre?"

"We need to talk."

"We're talking."

"Insolent brat." The words were harsh but the tone was tired. "Fine. Are you alone?"

"Yep." I glanced at Cade.

"You're lying."

"What does it matter?"

"On your head be it. Your mother sent us here with a message."

That confirmed she hadn't come. "Can't be that important if she couldn't be bothered to call herself. Or you know, come see her only daughter."

"She's dying, girl. Have some respect."

"What?" I stopped on the path and swayed so hard Cade steadied me with a hand on the arm.

"Shit. I hadn't meant to say it like that." Samarre sighed. "She's dying. There was an assassination attempt. Poison. I just got word they don't expect her to last the night."

"And you're not there?" I hissed the words to stop from screaming them. "Protecting her is your *one fucking job*, although frankly, I don't know why I care, given how she cast me out." Too much emotion roiled through me, and I choked on it before I could say more.

"She's with as much security as we could spare. I'm here for you."

"For me." I felt stupid, repeating words after her, but my brain wasn't working.

"She's named you her heir, girl. You can come home now."

Cade's grip on my biceps was suddenly the only thing keeping me on my feet.

"No," I said. "That's impossible. The exile was twenty to life. It's been—"

"All that matters is that it's been lifted, and given your mother's condition, I'm now authorized to tell you all this."

"I'm not a high-blood." I looked around, afraid someone would have heard the whispered shout, but Cade was keeping an eye on the surroundings and had loosened his glamour to flow around us in a warm pool.

I pulled us into motion. We had to get away from the scene of the kidnapping and go do our recon, or nothing that'd happened tonight mattered. I had to be moving before I collapsed or did something extremely impulsive.

"Low-blood or not, your mother's will was read. You're named. There are to be trials to judge your fitness."

I knew it. I fucking knew it.

"Trials. Is that why they sent Henri?" I snarled.

"Yes."

The simple word took me aback. "Excuse me?"

"Should you pass the trials, you'll be allowed to resume your relationship with him. The House needs legitimacy and your grandmother is running out of heirs. He's the only high-blood who'll have you." She paused. "Giving up your vampire will be a condition. He will not be allowed to set foot in Lyon. Ever."

I shook with rage. This was *exactly* what I'd said would happen. Being right was somehow the worst part. Remembering my previous mistake of putting the phone down on her, I swallowed hard and found my manners. "I beg two nights to consider."

"Fine. Consider well." She ended the call.

Cade snatched my phone before I could do something stupid like throw it on the ground or into the lake. "Look at me."

I closed my eyes and tilted my head down. I didn't want comfort right now. I had been pushed into too many choices I hadn't wanted to make. Choices I shouldn't have had to make. And just this second, I wanted to wallow in feeling angry and betrayed.

"Lydia." Cade tilted my chin up.

My eyes flashed open, and I started to swing at him. But he caught my wrist easily and raised an eyebrow at me before kissing my knuckles.

"We will sort this out," he said. When I finally met his gaze, he didn't try to pull me under, despite the glamour still flowing to divert any mundanes who might also have fancied a night walk in the cold. "But if you want to call off Maria, it has to be now. Before she gets too many of her people involved and is undermined."

I swallowed hard against the burn of acid in my throat, then again when it sloshed back up a second time. "No. I made this bed. I'll lie in it. Everyone else might change their mind and do what suits their convenience, but I'll stick to what I've said. And what I've done."

The hand under my chin shifted to caress my face. "Not just you, love. Not just you."

I leaned forward, falling against his chest to bury my face against it and just breathe. It was stupid—I should have been paying attention to my surroundings. Donatien might be gone, but Alejandro would be out there somewhere. The Lyon elves were here. Callista might have her bloody Watchers surrounding the hotel to make sure we were working on her damn bounty.

But for once in my life, I could trust someone to have my back.

That brought me back to myself, and I pulled away, rolling my neck to crack it. "Let's go. We've got work to do."

Cade fell in beside me, and we said nothing else as we made our way to the car.

***

The lake was just as deserted as I'd hoped it would be. No cameras. Not even any kids fucking around in the park after hours. It was too cold for that, and a weather front was bringing freezing rain by sunrise. Cade and I stood shoulder to shoulder, arms crossed, as we stood on the wrong side of the fence at the lake's edge.

"Cade?"

"Mm?"

"Why wait?"

"In what way?"

"Why wait until tomorrow night? Let's get this over with. There's enough moonlight left."

He frowned, keeping his attention on the water. "That wasn't the plan."

"Fuck the plan. Donatien got bold enough to kidnap a woman. We know he's working with Alejandro now, and if I can't get the Lyon elves here tonight, we'll take care of them tomorrow night when Maria's ready. All my gear is locked in the trunk. You've fed. I've recovered from the last few nights. Let's fucking do this."

This time, he glanced down at me, nostrils flaring as he took in my scent and tried to figure out how serious I was.

"Okay," he said. "I want the Sawback."

"All yours, Long John Silver."

161

He spluttered as we turned back to the Escape. "I am *not* anything like that rogue."

At the absurdity of it, I started laughing so hard I had to stop and bend over to catch my breath. "I forgot you might have lived through that time. Sorry, babe."

"Long John Silver." He scoffed, shaking his head. "The bloody cheek."

Still grinning, I got my phone out and dialed Samarre.

She picked up after one ring. "What now? Don't tell me you've come to your senses already."

"I need more details. I want to talk face to face. There's a lake near the hotel where we can speak freely."

"Absolutely not," she said. "We can speak freely enough under a soundproofing spell here."

"Fine. Eight PM. Two nights from now. If I have to come to you and you won't tell me anything, then I want time to prepare."

Samarre sighed, likely tired of my inconsistency. "Very well. Two nights from now at eight. Someone will meet you in the lobby and take you to our rooms."

"Fine." I hung up and shook my head.

"Not a surprise," Cade said lightly. "I suspect Alejandro will be easier to bait."

He called the blood witch, and we sat on the rear bumper of my SUV while we waited for the answer.

It went to voicemail.

"Shit." I rose and started pacing. So much for my amazing last-minute plan.

Before Cade could answer me, his phone rang. With a grin wide enough to show fangs, he answered. "Alejandro."

I hurried to his side so I could hear both sides of the conversation.

"Cade. To what do I owe the pleasure?"

"I know you're working with Donatien."

Alejandro's rich chuckle made my skin crawl. "Finally figured that out, did you? What can I say, I had to get you to leave St. Augustine somehow. But are you still in the area? I thought you were leaving. Donatien tells me you were still at the hotel."

A scream echoed in the background, and guilt collided with fear in my gut to twist in an unpleasant mélange.

Raising his voice to be heard over it, Alejandro said, "As you might be able to tell, I'm afraid you've caught me at a bad time, my friend. Was this important?"

I snatched the phone from Cade. "Let her go."

"The lovely lady solidaire. How are you, bonita?"

"Alejandro, let the woman go."

He chuckled. "You know I can't do that. Nor do I have to. It would be a breach of the Détente now."

Cade plucked the phone back, giving me a hard look before answering the witch. "One you and your friend precipitated. Don't let this get ugly. We have knowledge of the crime, so we're duty bound to report it to Callista."

I blinked.

Of course. Alejandro wouldn't know that Cade and I had been contracted by Callista already.

The blood witch growled, sounding more like an angry wolf than anything else. A red wolf was one of his stolen forms, so he might well have part-shifted for whatever they were doing to their victim. Unlike all but the strongest—and, ironically, the weakest—weres, he could do that.

"Why bring that bitch into it?" he snarled. "I thought we were *friends*, Cade. We had such a nice chat the other evening."

"You cut up my solidaire." The anger in Cade's voice was real. No playacting now.

"Ha! So I did. Although I did walk her out of that building, as promised."

Another scream rang out in the background, and I nudged Cade to hurry up.

"So you did." He paused, like he was considering something. "I suppose I don't need to insert myself in a deal she made. Fine. I'll keep what I know to myself, but Donatien reminded me of a few things. A few simple pleasures I haven't sampled in far too long."

"Oh? And what does that mean?"

"I've had a think and I want to meet. Bring the woman. We can't have a breaking of the Détente, and you never did learn how to hide a body properly. We've heard rumors of strange animal deaths just in the short time we've been here." Cade's tone shifted, as did his expression, both becoming harder and uglier. "Besides, my solidaire is much more…resilient now. After the shit you pulled, I had to accelerate the work to break her in. You saw her the other night. A little glamour and she'll beg for it."

I flinched, and he grimaced, shaking his head. He wouldn't do it. He didn't mean it. But we had to bait the trap somehow, and I'd said it should be me. It was just awful to see what had to be the Butcher of the Bayou slinking into his face and features.

"You could simply come here. We could have two wenches to play with between the three of us." Excitement tinged Alejandro's tone.

"No. Silver in my back taught me I can't trust you. Show me you're willing to be a team player first. Then we'll come play."

Silence hung on the line long enough that I was afraid Alejandro would decline.

"That's fair," the witch finally said. "Given the prize is your woman. First, though, why would you share? You started this conversation threatening me with Callista."

"Ask Donatien."

Heavy breathing was the first hint that the other vampire had left off whatever he was doing to the woman he'd taken and was listening in. "You mean it, Cade?" Donatien asked. "The three of us with your solidaire?"

"Only if you both meet us here and let me get rid of the woman. We can't play safely if the authorities are looking for a brutal kidnapper."

"That's true," Donatien said. "Hm. I don't know how much I trust this change of heart, but I agree. Tell me when and where."

Cade squeezed my hand. "Alejandro?"

"Fine, fine, I agree. You can have the woman and sort out her disposal this evening. Tomorrow night, you come to us, and we make merry."

"Tonight, one AM," Cade said. How he managed to push predatory excitement into his voice when he was gripping my hand like he'd die if he didn't was beyond me. "Lake Crabtree, the Old Reedy Creek Road entrance. You'll need to take the Harrison Road exit from I-40."

"Lake Crabtree, Old Reedy Creek Road," Alejandro muttered. "See you soon, my friend."

The call ended.

Cade rose and pulled me into him, crushing me against his body. "I'm sorry. I would never—"

"I know." I squeezed him back just as tightly. "You had to sell it. It's a good trap."

"You know they're going to bring the woman's body, right? She's already dead."

I forced myself to just breathe and not scream. "I know."

Alejandro's phrasing had been too strange for that not to be his plan, and he was a blood witch partnered with a vampire. Donatien would glut himself, and Alejandro would take what was left. I just prayed we'd made the end faster by offering me as an option, rather than leaving them to drag it out over days.

Shitty. It was shitty.

Sometimes Otherside was too awful to bear. But this was the world we lived in, and all I could do was try my damnedest to stay alive and minimize the harm done to others along the way.

Chapter 18: Cade

While Lya pulled gear out of the lockbox bolted to the cargo hatch in the back of her vehicle and became a walking arsenal, Cade leaned against the fence and looked out over the lake. It was nothing like the ocean, but bodies of water always soothed him at least a little.

Not that anything could really soothe him right now, nor could he afford the luxury if he had to become the Butcher of the Bayou again for the evening.

There was no hiding what he really was from Lya now. To sell the subterfuge, he'd have to fully tap into the darkness he'd only sipped from when she'd been kidnapped last September. He'd also have to have a damn good explanation for changing his mind after being so firm in turning Donatien down earlier—and for letting Lya attack him. If either of their adversaries hadn't wanted her as much as they did, they wouldn't have stepped into this trap.

Cade didn't turn when Lya's barely-there footsteps paced to him, nor did he acknowledge her when she leaned against his arm.

"Talk to me." Her voice was tight, controlled, almost empty.

They were both getting in the zone. Good. Well. Not *good*, but it was necessary.

"I can't be your lover tonight. I have to be your master."

"I understand."

He tilted his head just enough to look down at her. "Do you?"

"Maybe not. I guess I mean I won't hold it against you."

"We'll see."

"Come on, Cade. I know I haven't always been fair with how I react to things, but haven't I earned a little faith this week?"

Sighing, he slipped an arm around her and kissed the top of her head, breaking character for just a moment before wrapping the Butcher around himself like the coat he wasn't wearing. "We'll need to strike a delicate balance. I need to be domineering and cold to the point of cruelty. You need to be a barely leashed rabid dog, happy to cringe for me if it means more glamour and blood but eager to bite them should I drop the leash. Attacking Donatien at the hotel, showing him the anger under whatever he saw of us at the bar the other night, was a good start. It's not just blood they want from you. It's domination. The thrill of breaking another person. That will tempt them to abandon sense."

She shivered but nodded. "Okay."

"I mean it, Lya. I need you to follow my lead. No matter how awful."

"And with these two, it'll get pretty awful. Fine. Point made. Let's get inside the fence before someone drives past and sees us."

"They'll see the car."

"Not with the 'don't look' spell I wove over the turnoff."

That got Cade's attention, and he glanced down at her again. "I thought that was a high-blood spell."

"It is. Low-level though." She shrugged, lips pressed together as though fighting a grin. "Turns out faster healing and blood regeneration isn't the only side benefit to drinking ridiculous amounts of vampire blood in a short span of time." A frown pinched her brow. "I just wonder if I lose the power if you scale back on feeding me."

Cade frowned. That was good for him, certainly. But it was exactly the reason what they were doing was forbidden. "Don't use it again unless it's an emergency. And don't let Maria talk you into going back to the coterie's nest. If someone realizes a half-elf can do a high-blood spell—"

"We'll have to kill someone. I know."

He snorted, finding a dark humor in her confidence. "Good."

After hiding his machete, they stood at the lakeshore, angled to watch the road, listening to the wind whip through the trees as they waited for their guests. Shortly before one, Alejandro's red Nissan drove past the turnoff, braked hard, and backed up, nearly hitting Lya's truck.

"If that asshole puts so much as a dent—" she started.

"Quiet now. Remember what I said."

She pressed her lips together and nodded.

Better, although he didn't like it. He couldn't comfort her now though.

Alejandro and Donatien were getting out of the car. They both leapt the fence, clearing it easily, and approached with the air of two men joining a party. Jovial and ready for mischief. Cade sank deeper into who he'd once been, finding the old coldness, the violent assurance that he was owed and nobody could stop him from claiming whatever he wanted in compensation for what'd been done to him.

Donatien smiled widely as he approached, his attention on Lya and the hungry look in his eyes making Cade want to behead him more than ever.

At his side, Lya trembled. Rage lifted from her, blended with a little fear and more than a little desire—almost certainly a wish to kill the two herself, not fuck them. Alejandro's eyes reflected the light of the streetlamp like a cat's as the scent hit him, and Donatien bared fangs outright.

Lya's hand shifted to rest on the Beretta holstered on her hip.

"Down," Cade murmured.

He'd only meant for her to take her hand off the gun, but she knelt at his side and bowed her head. Cade went with it and caressed her hair like one would a dog, willing the mien of the Butcher over him so he could keep his expression bored, arrogant, and hungry.

Alejandro laughed, although it was more the cough of a puma. His animal forms were too close to the surface for him to be fully trusting of them.

"So you really did tame the bitch," he said. "I had my doubts the other night. You'll have to share your methods later. I would have sworn that one had too much fire and steel in her to be retrained that quickly, especially when our friend here came home with a scratch. A bare five months ago and she was making arrangements behind your back."

"For which she was soundly punished." Cade gripped Lya's hair and shook her head lightly. "Weren't you?"

"Yes, sir," she said, breath short.

Donatien smelled of excitement. "I told you he was good enough to manage it. You didn't know him like I did."

"Apparently not. I would have sworn he didn't have it in him. You should have seen them fawning over each other." Alejandro eyed Lya. "You're sure she'll play? Donatien says you were doting on her at the hotel bar last night. And she did cut him."

Cade shifted to stand behind Lya, cupped her chin, and tilted her head back to look up at him. Baring her throat like that made her tense, but she didn't move, although she panted with the effort to restrain herself.

"I treat her now and then to spoil her and keep her sweet. She went after Donatien earlier because he'd angered me and then moved in a threatening manner. But she'll do whatever I tell her to do, with a little glamour and a little pain," he said. "You're right, Alejandro. I was too lenient with her before. Partly to draw her in." He let a twisted, celebratory grin curl his lips. "And it worked."

Lya shuddered, tightly restrained fear edging out the rage in her scent, and Cade released her as Donatien took a creeping step closer.

"Why wouldn't you let me join you in St. Augustine?" the other vampire asked. "You were rather rude, brother. And you let her draw a blade on me then too."

"You'd come to my hunting grounds unannounced, walked into my nest, and were trying to seduce my solidaire. She was doing her job. It would be bad for my health to discourage that." Cade shook his head and *tsk*ed. "Boundaries, Donatien. Boundaries."

"I don't recall you having those before."

"And look what happened." Cade's snarl was genuine. Being captured and held a second time had been intolerable. He'd survived it but nearly at the cost of his sanity. "I won't have it again."

Donatien raised his hands, smiling as his gaze flicked to the still-kneeling Lya. "Fine."

Cade shifted his attention to Alejandro. "The woman he took from the hotel?"

"In the trunk." The blood witch narrowed his eyes. "I want assurances before I turn her over to you."

"What assurances?"

"That your woman is truly under your control."

Cade sneered. "My word isn't good enough? I'm not the one with a history of stabbing allies in the back."

Alejandro waved his hand as though it didn't matter. "That was over a century ago. Let it go. Especially if we're to be playmates."

Lya shifted to one knee and looked up at Cade.

"What is it, pet?" he asked.

"If it pleases you, I'll offer whatever assurances they need."

Alejandro narrowed his eyes at her. "I want blood."

Lya bowed her head. "It is my master's to give."

The witch's eyebrows shot up. "Well then. Cade? Shall we make the bargain and get out of this cold? If I'm to be denied warmer pursuits this evening, I don't care to linger."

Cade studied Lya, trying to figure out what her play was.

She was still following his lead, but he knew the woman. There was a plot hiding behind the rage in her dark eyes.

"Very well," he said.

She rose and slowly approached Alejandro and Donatien, eyes lowered. Cade tensed as she got close enough for them to grab. His heart pounded like he'd never died. She was skilled and faster than ever, but this was her first hunt for something more dangerous than a fire sprite since September.

When she was close, Alejandro's hand shot out, too fast, and caught her by the wrist.

Lya gasped, and the scent of her fear almost made Cade step in physically.

When she lifted her head defiantly and offered the blood witch a wordless snarl, Cade said, "Easy on the goods, Ale."

"Omelets and broken eggs, my friend." He shoved Lya's left sleeve back.

Cade barely managed not to frown when it was bare rather than wrapped in the knife sheathe she usually wore on that arm.

Arching an eyebrow, Alejandro said, "Trained her indeed, to get her out here with just that silly gun."

"A small punishment for attacking Donatien without orders when we were just talking." Cade crossed his arms, more to keep himself from intervening than anything else, as Donatien nodded in approval. Cade had had to remind Lya to take that damn knife off before coming to bed at least twice.

What game are you playing, Lydia?

Silence and tension stretched as Alejandro just stood there, making no move, watching as Lya trembled with unspent adrenaline, waiting for her to disobey.

Shit. He doesn't trust she'll behave.

Cade sighed as though bored. "You're not the only one who wanted warmer pleasures this evening, Ale. She's offering what you asked for. It's rude to keep us all waiting."

"So it is." Slowly, deliberately, Alejandro lifted his free hand. It shifted to a puma's paw, and with a flex, wickedly sharp claws extended. "A little foreplay, bonita. You understand."

Lya tensed and jerked her wrist then stood terribly still.

"Good girl." Alejandro set his claws against her skin, watching her pant, savoring the spike of fear at the first few beads of blood—

Which almost covered the renewed burst of adrenaline that presaged Lya reaching behind her back.

At the first hint of adrenaline and the start of the motion, Cade moved, scooping up the Sawback from where he'd hidden it in a winter-browned stand of lake weeds. He had to trust she could take care of Alejandro, which left Donatien for him. In his peripheral vision, he caught the graceful swing of Lya's arm and the flash of the silver-edged tanto she was so partial to.

Alejandro blocked her with an upraised arm then shouted in enraged pain.

Cade let his glamour spill out to muffle sound and turn eyes and then fell on Donatien.

They fought like vampires. Soundless and ruthlessly violent.

The fighting skills they'd carried over from their human lives, or picked up after death, had been improved by accelerated reflexes and speed. Cade had been a pirate, but Donatien had been a soldier. A deserter really, a coward.

"What is this?" Donatien hissed. "Betrayal?"

"You broke the Détente. It's what needs doing," Cade snarled back.

The other vampire was unarmed, but he was trying to retreat, not attack. Cade slipped between Donatien and the fence. Donatien turned tail—and attacked Lya from behind.

"No!" Cade pulled the machete swing that would have taken Donatien's head, and Lya's along with it, as the other vampire pulled her in front of him. Cade flashed back to Morris using him this same way against Lya and froze.

Lya, though, wasn't a fledgling addled by her master's glamour. She fought Donatien with the tight control of a trained commando.

"Get him!" she yelled. "Get Ale—"

Donatien wrapped an arm around her neck, cutting off the rest of her words, and bared his fangs.

Again, Cade froze, until movement in the corner of his eye drew his attention to Alejandro drawing sigils on the frozen ground with his own blood. Pure fear sent Cade barreling into the witch, knocking him off balance and interrupting his spell.

Lya's scream pulled everyone's attention.

With the scream and the scent of blood, the Butcher took over Cade, and there was only the enemy in front of him. Dangerous. Powerful blood. A worthy prize. One he'd have to take if he was going to be safe—and a new thought, keep *her* safe.

The world narrowed to the tunnel vision of his fight with Alejandro. He lost track of what was happening around him. The witch did something that made the nearby plants wither and die, casting a spell at Cade that made him stop in his tracks until an enraged shout from Lya broke it.

"Goddess burn you," Alejandro said.

Then he switched to ancient Greek. A necromancy spell. One that Cade would have sworn would only work for a lich lord and not a blood witch.

Unless that witch had leveled up and become a sorcerer.

Had there been another artifact in the haul, one Lya had missed in the gems she'd given Callista? Or was he getting outside help? Was this the djinn's work?

Fuck.

Cade pushed harder.

Alejandro slashed with a knife, his free hand turned to a claw-tipped paw, moving almost as fast—just fast enough to block Cade's machete swings.

"You found a mentor," Cade said.

The witch didn't answer, picking up the spell again.

Another sharp cry from Lya pushed Cade into near madness. The next time Alejandro blocked a machete swing, Cade dropped it and let the witch's knife pass over his shoulder.

The sudden lack of resistance threw Alejandro off balance and straight into Cade's embrace—and his fangs.

Cade struck, deep, hard, and savage.

He missed the artery in the throat, but he had control of the witch's neck with his fangs and one hand. Making a hard blade of his other hand, Cade drove it deep into the flesh alongside Alejandro's spine, hooked his fingers, and ripped.

The witch dropped, in too much pain to even cry out, one kidney ruptured and part of his spine torn out.

Cade rode him down, biting again to slash fangs over the arteries and veins in both sides of Alejandro's neck before pulling back, jabbing a crippling blow to his throat to stop him from voicing any more damn spells and falling on him to feed.

This one had hurt Lya.

He'd wanted to do worse than hurt her. He'd wanted to break her, like Cade had been broken. He'd forced Cade to be someone he hadn't wanted to be ever again and forced a situation where Lya had seen and endured too much.

It was only fair that he paid in blood.

Chapter 19: Lya

Alejandro had blocked my first swing with a knife he pulled from under his coat, though I got a good slash in on his arm at the cost of a few pinpricks to my own. I hadn't been sure they'd fall for that trick and had been counting on their desire to hurt me to override common sense. The old Othersiders got arrogant, especially when it came to half-human people like me, even when they should have known better.

Cade, bless the man, let me fight the battle I'd started and went after the other target, hence my surprise when that target grabbed me to use as a shield.

I should have been paying better attention. My situational awareness was usually better. But every time I tried to keep a mental tab on Cade, I got distracted by wanting to help him. Our playacting turned my stomach, but I'd known it was coming. I loved him. I wanted to fight at his side, and the only way to do that was to keep Alejandro off him while he finished Donatien. So I shut him—shut *them*—out.

It was the only way to keep Alejandro occupied.

"Not so tame after all, eh wench?" Alejandro said. "Good. It'll be more fun to break you."

I ignored the taunt and kept fighting. I got small bites in with my knife, but he scored a few hits with his claws. My leather jacket took the worst of it.

"Cade as well," he said. "He's clearly not what Donatien thought he was."

I dodged a swipe of his claws, coming back with a punch to his short ribs that barely fazed him. I was too close to try using the Beretta. At best, I'd miss. At worst, he'd take the damn thing and use it on me.

It had to be knives. I edged sideways, looking for an opening.

"In fact, I know just the spells to use. One to control the undead. One that requires a defiling by three to taint the victim so the blood can be used for greater things. Shall we have a go?" He started a spell, something in old Greek, I think.

I nearly kicked myself. I used my magic for smaller tricks and still didn't think of using it first in a fight. Alejandro's magic required drawing on the energy of plants and whatever small animals were in the vicinity.

His auratic shields were open.

Pulling on Aether, I sent a lash of it at his mind and snapped, "Shut the fuck up."

The spell cut off abruptly, and he frowned as his mouth kept moving but nothing came out.

It wouldn't last long if he had spells that would work against the undead. Corpses were easy for a witch of Alejandro's strength to turn into zombies. But the higher-level undead, like vampires? That was heavy shit. Anxiety jolted in amongst the adrenaline of a fight, and I shut it out like I had the fear for Cade.

All I could think when Donatien jumped me was what a cowardly move it was.

As we whirled, I had half a second to see Cade swinging the Sawback before he pulled it short. For all his ugly cruelty earlier, he was still him. That gave me hope.

Alejandro started muttering off to the side. My spell had worn off.

"Get him!" I shouted. "Get Ale—"

Donatien strangled me, flexing his arm to cut off my air and my shout. I lost track of Cade then. All that mattered was surviving, and the immediate impediment to that was the fucker trying to asphyxiate me or stop me from voicing a spell or both.

Scratch that. Drain me.

A scream leapt from me as Donatien shifted his arm and sank his fangs into the curve of my neck.

Without a glamour, it hurt like hell. Every nerve in my body was on fire. My blood burned like acid. Cade must have scored a hit to Donatien's face, enough to bleed, and that must have seeped into the wound because I couldn't figure out what else would make me feel like the time Leith Sequoyah had hit me with an enervation spell.

A pull on the wound infuriated me. Nobody drank from me, *nobody*, except Cade.

I still had my knife. With a furious shout, I stabbed behind me. Donatien and I were close enough together that I bloody well could have stabbed myself, but if I didn't get him off me, it wouldn't matter.

Soundlessly, Donatien tore away from me, taking the knife with him.

I let him have it. I had more.

As he stumbled back, I took advantage of the distance between us, drew my gun, and flipped the safety off. Why get up close and personal with a vampire when I had silver bullets? The silencer ate most of the sound as I emptied the clip into the asshole, but we'd still need to get the fuck out of here as quickly as we could.

When I counted all twenty bullets in the Beretta's mag, half in his heart, the other half in his head, I stopped and holstered the gun, feeling like I was moving in slow motion.

Cade was bent over a downed Alejandro, feeding messily from the sound of it. No way was I coming between a vampire and his prey, especially when that prey was a blood witch. I sure as hell wouldn't have wanted to eat the fucker, but I reckoned there was a lot of power in his blood.

The machete I'd loaned Cade lay abandoned in the grass nearby. I staggered over to pick it up, wincing at the pain in my right shoulder from Donatien's bite. Stumbled back over to the downed vampire, lined up my strike, and swung the blade. His head fell away as easily as Morris's had, bouncing down the gentle slope to the lake's edge before stopping.

Just because he'd pissed me off, I gave the rest of Donatien's twice-dead corpse a solid kick before wobbling a few steps away from it.

My blood was still burning in my veins. I didn't know what that meant. I assumed it was bad. I'd never thought to ask Cade what would happen if another vampire got blood into me.

With a gasp that sounded like it hurt, Cade arched away from Alejandro then wrenched the witch's head off with pure, brute savagery.

I stood very still. Dismembering a body like that took an incredible amount of strength. Most human-shaped things couldn't manage it. A strong enough Othersider though? Yeah. Totally possible. And Cade was more than strong enough. Usually that was hot. But usually, he was in control of himself and not drenched with blood or ripping people's heads off.

Then he stilled, like he was trying to remember something.

"Lya!" He scented the air.

"I'm here." I stayed where I was though.

Cade snapped around to look at me. Fast. Too fast, with barely enough movement for me to track. Then he wavered, falling forward onto his hands.

Shit. I was messed up and bleeding, and I had a five-hundred-year-old vampire blood drunk on the death of a powerful witch the same age.

I stayed as still as I could as Cade monkey-walked to me, looking like a demented parkourist in designer jeans before he popped up directly in front of me. One moment, he was on all fours. The next, he was just standing there, looking down at me with eyes so dark they drank the light of the moon and stars from a mask of fresh blood.

"You're alive." His voice wasn't quite his.

I wondered if I was talking to the Butcher of the Bayou rather than my lover, but I didn't dare ask. If he'd snapped and gotten lost between past and present, addressing the past wouldn't help anything.

"Yeah. Well. I got bit, but—"

I cut off with an involuntary hiss as Cade grabbed my arm and dragged me closer to sniff my neck. The growl that followed sent chills over me. He was definitely not himself as he cleaned the wound with long licks.

"Cade," I whispered. I swallowed hard, trying to keep my voice steady. "Babe."

"He bled on you. In you."

"I mean, if that's why my blood feels like it's on fire—"

Another growl made me shut my mouth.

For a good minute, we stood there, both of us trying to control natural reactions and instincts. If I fought him now—or worse, if I ran—I didn't know that he would be able to stop himself.

The freezing rain that'd been promised arrived, dousing us in biting pinpricks of icy moisture, and with a shudder, Cade shut his eyes tight and bowed his head. His grip on my arm tightened painfully as his other hand fisted.

"Lydia."

"I'm here."

"Help."

My heart thudded. He never asked for help. Tentatively, I put my free hand on his arm and squeezed. It took me two tries to find my voice. "Whatever you need, I'm here."

"Talk."

I didn't ask useless questions about what. He was lost somewhere—in bloodlust or his instincts or his long past—and needed a thread back to himself or back to now. From the shaking grip on me, that thread could be words, or it could be blood. Blood, he could have, but I had to protect myself as well. I couldn't pour from an empty cup, and the fight had taken a lot out of me.

That and I remembered what had happened the last time I'd offered him blood when he wasn't entirely in his right mind.

"When I first met you," I said, "I couldn't believe my good luck. I needed a connection. Any connection. And there you were, looking hungry and fuckable."

I kept talking, rambling really, and each word loosened the unearthly tension in him. I told him how much of my running was fear of myself, of more change and what it meant, and not him. How much better my life was, not only because I wasn't alone, but because he brought joy to it. Because he made me feel valued and wanted and useful in a way nobody had before. Not just because of my skills as a bounty hunter or my looks or whatever passed for charm, but because he liked *me*. Saw *me*.

He just stared at me though, unblinking, restrained murder in the back of his eyes.

The rain kept coming, and the bodies at our feet didn't get any less damning. But I kept talking, even as I started shivering. I'd dressed for a fight, not exposure to the elements. And it was damn hard to be this vulnerable. At all. But with no feedback? No response?

I swallowed my fear that it wasn't enough, that *I* wasn't enough, and kept going.

Finally, he shuddered and squeezed his eyes shut. When he opened them again, his face had eased from the stiff lines that'd distorted it to cruelty during our earlier roleplay, and his grip on me eased.

I stopped talking as he bent toward me, cradling the back of my head and tilting it forward to kiss my forehead with lips far warmer than usual.

"Thank you, love," he said. "I—don't know that I would have found my way back without you this time."

I wrapped my arms around him and squeezed as hard as I could. "Does that mean we can get out of here?"

He pulled away, looking around. "I suppose we should. What do you want to do for cleanup?"

"I don't."

"You…don't?"

I snorted. "Hell no, I'm not doing cleanup. It's going to be enough of a pain in the ass getting back into the hotel all cut up and covered in blood. Callista wanted a bounty, and she wanted proof. We call in her cleanup crew and let her have both."

Cade frowned. "I suppose that does make sense." Then his eyes flicked over me. "I smell your blood. Where are you hurt?"

"Everywhere." I couldn't keep the miserable note out of my tone. I didn't mind rain normally, but this was cold and all my adrenaline was spent. That would be enough to give me the shakes on its own, except that in all the words I'd poured out to be Cade's anchor, I'd realized something.

I never wanted to be without him.

Like, really never.

Yeah, we fought and hid things from each other, and he had a really fucked-up past. I'd almost walked out a few days ago.

Almost.

If I'd really wanted to, I would have. But what I'd wanted was for him to stop me. I ran from him because I wanted to see if he'd chase me. Fight for me. Do whatever it took to keep me.

And tonight, he'd become something he clearly hated because I'd been threatened. So I was shaking not just from cold and exhaustion but from the fact that I couldn't keep testing him.

I had to accept that he really would be there for me. Always.

And that scared me more than fighting a blood witch and a centuries-old vampire in an icy field in February.

"Love?" he said.

I jumped. "Sorry. What?"

"I'll call Callista. You go get warmed up in the car. If you still have those spare clothes, get changed." Worry pinched his brow.

"Right. Yeah. Thanks."

I stumbled off in the direction of the car, crouching in place as another vehicle crossed the bridge, headlights flashing. It kept going though, the driver apparently not having seen my car or Alejandro's under the spell I'd laid at the edge of the turnoff.

Rising, I stumbled into a running start and jumped the fence. I staggered on the landing, distracted by the ongoing burn in my veins and the whirl of thoughts in my head.

At the cars, I pushed through the dregs of what remained of my energy and wrangled enough Aether to refresh the spell before hopping into the back seat of mine and clicking the overhead light off. Turning the car on would be nice, but lights, a running engine, and the steam it would've created would've ruined the effect of the spell.

Tiredly, I leaned over the back seat and grabbed the duffel of spare clothes I kept in here for exactly this reason. Dragging my wet clothes off was a challenge as much for the slices and bites decorating me as for shivering and being damp. The first aid kit was in the same duffel, and I cracked it open after I'd dried off with the towel in there as well, blinking at finding some of the smaller wounds already closing.

Cool.

Cade would have done something about them, but I had a feeling he'd sent me to the car more to get the scent of my blood away from him than anything else. I might trust his control, but he clearly didn't. Or maybe he just didn't want me seeing what he'd done to Alejandro. For his sake, not mine—I would have gotten some satisfaction out of seeing that wanker torn to shreds.

As I patched myself up and shimmied into clean, dry clothes, I turned an idea over in my mind. I still had the little knife I'd given Cade for his birthday. We'd used it a couple of times but quickly and briefly, despite the hunger on Cade's face. I'd thought it was just for drinking from me, but what if it was more? What if it was something he'd been pushing away and hiding because deep down, there was still something of this Butcher in him? Would accepting that side of him get him to finally stop being afraid to tell me things?

A knock on the window made me jump.

"It's open," I called.

Cade got into the back seat as quickly as I had, bringing a fresh burst of cold air with him, and slumped, eyes drooping. "Callista's sending a cleanup crew. Fae, from the sound of it, so stay in the car."

I shivered, noting that he didn't, despite the weather and the time he'd been standing in it. Vampires hated being cold and wet. I laid the back of my hand against his cheek and found him burning hot.

He jumped, suddenly wide awake, and lurched away, hitting the door hard enough to rock the car. "Don't. It's all I can do not to pin you to the seat and—" He tilted his head back and breathed. "Fuck."

"Sorry." I stayed where I was though. "Fae?"

"Yes." He shuddered.

"I brought a kelpie in once."

Cade glanced at me sideways through slitted lids. "Oh?"

"Yeah. Pain in the ass. Had to get special knives. Iron and silver."

"Still have them?"

"No. Had to turn them in with the bounty so they could keep him."

"Definitely stay in the car then. They'll find you as delicious as I do." As though that was too much to think about, he shuddered and got out of the car, leaning against the door in a tired slouch while we waited.

And yet with all that, my mind kept turning on what he might do with that knife if I gave him free rein.

That, and whether whatever he did would be enough to get Samarre and Henri to back off with this offer that wasn't one. My mum being poisoned sucked. It was a bad way to go, especially for an elf, because it took a pretty brutal poison to work on a high-blood. And it wasn't that I didn't care. It was that I'd shut that door. She'd had more than a year to reach out to me before now, and it was only when she wouldn't have to bear the consequences that I heard anything at all. It was me who'd deal with the fallout, and I was done. No more.

I'd meant what I said to Cade after the call, and talking it through to his face, his gaze locked on mine, only solidified the feeling and sent it deeper.

He was my home and my family now.

There was no going back to what I'd had. I didn't want it. I wanted him. I wanted the power that came with being his, and I wasn't ashamed to use him to get it when he was using me to gain power of his own.

We both benefited—but only if I tied him to me.

I'd been avoiding thinking about the coming confrontation with my past while we focused on the job that was the only reason I'd been in town long enough to cross paths with the Lyon elves, but they'd be looking for my answer the night after tomorrow.

I'd have to move fast. But would Cade be up to it?

Chapter 20: Lya

We didn't have time for me to answer the question before sunrise, which was probably for the best. Cade was still strung out—not helped at all by the mischief and taunts of the fae cleanup crew—and we both needed rest. He passed out hard when I got him down to the room and cleaned up. A sleepy drunk, as he'd said, at least once the adrenaline from the fight crashed and we were safely locked in our room.

I woke as the sun slipped below the horizon, wrapped tightly in Cade's arms. A risk he'd have scolded me for taking if he'd been in his right mind, but he'd been dreaming, eyes moving rapidly behind his lids and with the occasional small sound. Unusual for him, given he usually slept like the dead. Or maybe actually was dead during the day, at least in part. I'd watched his tortured sleep until I'd given up trying to make the couch comfortable and joined him. The moment I was on the bed, his subconscious reflexes had him reaching for me.

Not to bite. To hold tight. Possessive. Protective.

He'd dragged me in almost too fast for me to control my tumble into his arms then settled immediately, dropping into the unmoving, dreamless, undead sleep that was more typical for him.

If I hadn't been decided before, I was now.

Still, I laid there, thinking over my choice once more. I didn't know what exactly it'd entail, but I did know he'd been holding some things back. Afraid the pressure or the control would make me run.

Fair. It hurt, but it was fair. I could own who I'd been up to that point.

There was also my strengthening Aetheric power to contend with. If this—whatever it was—went wrong, he might be put in a position where he'd have to put me down like a dog who'd bitten a child. Loyal and faithful but too unpredictable and dangerous to keep among the rest of society.

But if he wasn't prepared for that, he wouldn't have been giving me so much blood up to now. If I wasn't prepared, I wouldn't have accepted it.

I'd been offered a place in House Desmarais, a real place that'd come with a title and incomes. And yeah, I wanted power. I wanted strength. But I wanted them on my own terms, with no expectations for serving a power structure that had cast me out for daring to reach for more to begin with.

Cade wanted power and strength too. Our goals were aligned. And we were both willing to pay the price if it meant the chance of a few more decades gaining both side by side.

As I worked through every angle, I had to admit another thing to myself: I liked when he took control, at least in our sex play. I liked submitting to him. I didn't have to be defensive or strong or anything at all, except his. I could trust him to take care of my needs, even the ones I wasn't aware of. Whether it was by physical senses or something more ethereal, he could read me and draw out pleasures I couldn't conceive of.

So what might he do if I offered more? If I offered the deeper connection I knew he craved, one sealed with the trust behind the gesture of the ceremonial knife? How might this make it easier for him to tell me things that would keep me safe?

I managed to wrestle free of his embrace, called Maria to check in, and was eating some snacks and drinking Gatorade on the couch when he woke.

"Hey," I called softly to ease the panic in his eyes when I wasn't on the bed.

His gaze snapped to me. "You're still here. I dreamed I was…" He trailed off and shuddered. "It doesn't matter."

"Maybe it does." I rose and moved to stand at his side of the bed, my pace slow and deliberate and my gaze never leaving him.

He stiffened. "Lya? What's going on, love?"

After spending so much time thinking about it, I was tired of the usual dance. This needed to be straight to the point. "Make me yours. I know you want something more from me than what you've been getting. Take it."

Cade stared at me, utterly expressionless, then was on his feet and in my space without a hint of clockwork motion in his vampiric swiftness. "Be very explicit in what you mean now, Lydia, because that deeper connection? That has a specific context in *moroi* society. One that will make it very hard if not impossible for you to leave me and will reduce the likelihood of other vampires taking you in if something happens to me."

I stared up at him, falling into the dark depths of his eyes. They were technically brown, but it was by a shade only. I'd always found it an odd contrast, given how pale his skin was. Odd and striking.

But just now it wasn't just the color that spoke of darkness. It was something hovering behind them, in his mind or maybe driven down into his soul.

I was making myself prey, giving him permission to see me as such, rather than with the careful equality we'd established. And something about it was pinging on the parts of him I'd only just learned about. Parts that could probably very easily kill me…but that I trusted would not, even after what I'd seen last night. Maybe especially because of last night. He'd held onto control despite the bloodbath the fight had become.

Still, I thought carefully before elaborating. Reconfirming to myself that what he'd said aligned with what I'd been thinking earlier. "I want every Othersider we encounter to know that I belong to you. I don't want people calling the police when we go down to meet the elves tomorrow, and I want to be able to get down there on my own. So nothing that maims, disfigures, or kills." I wrinkled my nose. "Don't like, shave my head or anything either."

He stared at me for long moments, not breathing until he asked, "Marks?"

"Yes."

"Bites? Bruising? Scratches? Cuts? Tell me exactly what you'll allow without being upset tomorrow, Lydia, because there are things a vampire would usually do to demonstrate a desirable solidaire has been claimed. Things I haven't dared to think about before now."

A chill ran over me.

It was so easy to forget what he was: an apex predator. Consent and self-control mattered to him, but I'd seen enough of him last night and heard enough about his past to know he'd once walked a different path.

I ran a finger over his chest as I reflected again about why I was asking this. Was it to make a point to Henri and the rest of the Lyon elves? Or was it for me?

I thought again of the small ceremonial knife I'd gotten for Cade's birthday. Imagined him drawing it over my skin—and gasped at how hot I found the idea. To completely give myself over, glamoured and riding waves of ecstasy on the point of a knife.

His hand closed around my wrist, firmer than usual. "Lydia."

I flattened my hand against his chest.

His heart, usually almost still, was racing. I liked that. I liked that my choices could elicit this much response from him. That after almost five hundred years of undead life, *I* excited him. Me. The half-elf nobody wanted. Who'd had to make her own way in the world. It felt powerful.

Was that twisted? Yeah.

But I wasn't in the habit of second-guessing what I liked. I'd done enough of that while I waited for him to wake up.

I pulled away, and he let me go, although his attention weighed on me as I went to my suitcase and dug around until I found the small box. It might have been a gift for him, but he'd left it in my keeping. Probably for this very reason.

"What would you do with this?" I balanced the knife across my hands, holding it like an offering.

His pupils flashed wide, pushing into the sclera as he fixed on it. "Anything and everything you consented to."

"Give me an idea."

"Vagabonds take a personal sigil, much like city-level master vampires, since there are so few of us." His gaze flicked from the knife to me and back before holding mine solidly. "Traditionally, one's solidaire would be marked with it. While under a full glamour, of course, for the pain. Tattoos are a more modern alternative though."

"Where?"

"Anywhere."

I twisted sideways and lifted my shirt, tapping my left flank with the point of the knife. "Here?"

"That will hurt. A lot."

"I didn't ask if it would hurt. I asked if you'd do it here."

Cade's eyes went fully black, and he swallowed hard enough for me to hear it. "Love, I will put it wherever you like if you're consenting to it."

"I consent. To the rest as well. Bite, bruise, scratch, or cut. Just not too deep and nothing disfiguring, maiming, or killing. Nothing that will be visible in my usual clothes or make people think you've abused me and they need to call the cops."

He practically vibrated with what had to be restrained desire. He'd been so fucking careful for long months. Never leaving the tiniest mark or the faintest bruise to show others that I was truly, deeply his.

"Why are you offering this now?" His voice was hoarse, and he clenched his fists. "I don't want to be a tool for revenge in some spat with your ex or your family."

"You're not. I'm offering it because I'm the kind of fool who has to be pushed to see what she really wants, even when the best option has been in front of her for months. I've been thinking about our fight a few days ago. I keep pushing you and pushing you, thinking that if my family let me go then you would too. But you haven't. And you won't. I finally get it." I extended the knife to him. "If you don't want to—"

My words cut off as his hand moved too quickly for me to see and closed around my throat. I hissed in surprise, but all I felt was arousal, not fear.

He grunted in surprise and studied me as he squeezed then eased his grip. "There's no retracting consent when you're under a full glamour. You won't be able to speak. I might have given you enough blood by now that you could blink, and I'll get a sense of your mood. But the paralytic effect will be heavy. You're fully trusting me to know your body, heart, and mind. To know when you will enjoy what I might do and when it'd hurt. When it'd bring you to orgasm and when it'd break you. You're consenting to being physically unable to withdraw that consent later."

"The fact that you're looking at me with black eyes and a hand around my throat and still making sure that I know what

I'm signing up for rather than sinking fang tells me that it's safe to trust you. You had a big feed last night. Our enemies are dead. You can maintain control now. *I trust you.*"

With a shudder, he released me and turned away. "You have no idea what you're agreeing to, and yet you trust me."

"I do know."

He snapped back around to look at me.

"It wouldn't be the first time you've held my life in your hands." On a flash of instinct, I knelt, raising the knife as an offering. "Make me yours." Doubt flickered as he squeezed his eyes shut. "Unless…you don't want to? Did I—"

"I do want to." His eyes flashed open, and the blank mask he'd made of his face shattered.

Pure need painted his expression. Hunger. Desire.

One big hand smoothed over my head, curling around my face to tilt my chin up. "I just… This was territory I told myself was off limits, and you offer it on your knees with upraised blade. Hekate preserve us both. If you offer yourself freely and using the traditional forms, I accept and agree to be held to the limits you've set."

My heart pounded. "I offer myself."

He took the knife and made a swift cut along the vein in his wrist. "Then be strengthened in anticipation of your gift."

That sounded formal.

I tilted my head back and drank four swallows of his blood before he pulled away, twice as much as usual and way stronger with Alejandro's stolen power zinging through it. I swayed with a groan, dizzy as it sent a jolt through my system, still not used to it enough or used to having that much at once, to take it as easily as he took mine.

Cade caught me then pulled me to my feet, steadying me as he caught my gaze. "Last chance."

"I consent." I leaned forward to kiss him. "And I love you."

"I love you too. More than you can know." He kissed me back and, when he pulled away, said, "Strip now."

I did as he said, making a tease out of it. The hunger returned as he watched me, but it was deeper and darker than usual, alight with new possibility as he considered all the violent delights newly available to him.

When I was naked, he circled me once then again before stopping at my back.

One hand closed around my throat, pinning me against him as my pulse fluttered against his grip. The other trailed down the front of my body, dragging the tip of the knife carefully between my breasts and down to my belly before making its way back up.

"I'm going to use you in every way possible," he whispered in my ear. "And when you come out of the glamour, you'll know that you're mine. But you'll also be safe and cared for and loved. Food and drink will be waiting. And so will I, for anything you need. Do you believe me?"

"Yes." I quivered with eagerness, and my heart thudded as much from the zing of vampire blood making its way through my system as from want.

"Good." He released me and came back around to stand in front of me.

When I met his eyes, glamour washed over me stronger than it ever had.

I fell upward, completely lost in the euphoria of his magic. Distantly, I was aware of him catching me as the paralytic effect kicked in and my muscles went slack. There was a shift. The bed. A pause. Then I was lifted again and set down on a towel.

I was still vaguely aware of what was going on, but as he'd warned me, there was a grand total of sweet fuck all I could do about it. I was completely and utterly at a vampire's mercy, trusting this one loved me enough to have his fun, make me feel good, and leave me breathing despite the violent past that'd given him his moniker.

And in that acceptance, I found a depth of peace I'd never known before.

Spike of pleasure. He'd bitten my neck, hard.

Another spike from the other side. And again from each major pulse point in my body: the underside of each arm, the bend of my elbows, the inner thighs.

Each one built pleasure, until I was on the verge of climax.

Another shift.

My head straightened so I had a clear airway. I almost didn't feel the knife in my flank. It had a keen edge. But then my flesh caught up, and the new sensation paused as my orgasm finally ripped free.

"Good girl," Cade murmured.

The knife's point screamed through me again, building quickly to another climax.

"You make me wish I'd worked on a half-elf earlier, love. In fact…"

I was repositioned, head upside-down. Then his cock was in my mouth, pushing deep, then back, then in again repeatedly.

"Fuck." Pressure as his hand bracketed my throat. "All mine. In every way. Complete surrender. You have no idea how much I've wanted this." He pulled out and finished on my chest, and I came again as he bit into my wrist.

A moment of rest, swimming in ecstasy.

"Lya?"

I blinked, trying to focus, but all I could do was breathe and ride the wave.

"Still out. Let's finish this sigil, shall we?"

Again, I was positioned, and again, the knife drew pain transmuted into pleasure.

"That'll do." Heat as his tongue pressed against it, cleaning and stopping the bleeding.

Cade played my body like an instrument while I floated, distantly aware of what he was doing, unable to do anything beyond register it and enjoy it.

And I did enjoy it, all of it.

He took me to the very edges of pleasure but never into unbearable or unwanted pain.

When the glamour started fading, he asked, "Back with me, Lya?"

I groaned. Every nerve ending was alight.

"Look at me."

I obeyed. I should have been afraid of the naked domination in his gaze, but it just turned me on.

"I'm going to fuck your pussy now," he said. "Hard."

"Good," I managed.

Then his hand was around my throat again, and his cock was in me, the former squeezing tight as the latter plunged deep. When I came, so did he, with a last bite to my breast as he suckled a nipple.

Then his movement slowed, and he withdrew.

"All done, love. You're mine now, in every way. Rest." He turned me to my right side and adjusted me into a recovery position, curling himself around my back as he reached over me and the phone clattered.

"Room service please. Two steaks, rare. The salad. Two bottles of Gatorade as well, if you have it. Yes, charge the room. No, please leave it outside the door. Thank you."

I drifted. The glamour faded, and tingles raced over me as I came back to myself. All at once, my entire body screamed at me, and I curled in on myself, hissing in pain.

"Shh sh sh. Look at me." Cade tilted my face toward him and met my eyes. "Are you okay, or do you need another glamour?"

I took a minute to breathe and listen to my body. "I'm okay."

"You're sure? Not just being brave?"

Another minute. "Yes."

"Not trying to avoid hurting my feelings? Be honest with me, love. I need to trust that you'll tell me if you're hurting too much or need more care."

"I'm being honest. I just…ow."

He traced a light finger over me. "If you can talk and 'ow' is the extent of it, so much the better. What do you need right now?"

"Hold me."

Cade's expression softened, and he obliged. I slipped into a deep sleep until a knock came at the door. His body heat disappeared, and then there was the door opening, a rattling, the door closing again, and more rattling.

The smell of meat hit my nose, and I stirred.

"Can you eat something, love?"

I made the push to a seated position and stared blearily at the plates laid out on the room's small table. He helped, cutting up the steak and opening the Gatorade. When I'd refueled, I toppled back against the pillows and closed my eyes.

The bed dipped slightly as he lay next to me and pulled me close. "You did so well tonight, Lya. Thank you for trusting me."

"Love you," I slurred.

"And I love you. Go to sleep. You're mine, and you're safe."

I offered my last surrender for the night and obeyed.

***

The next time I woke, the angle of the sun at the bottom of the curtains said it was at least late morning, if not just after midday. A pitcher of water rested on the nightstand, and I drank straight from it rather than pouring a glass. Then it was to the bathroom to address the other urgent need.

I evaluated myself in the mirror when I was done. Twin bites decorated my neck, both surrounded by a fading hickey. Similar marks stood out on all my pulse points, all nearly healed. A bandage was taped over my flank, and I didn't remove that. More faint marks, scratches, and thin red lines that had to have been made by the knife decorated my curves. Cade had said he'd use me, and everything was sore inside and out, a good, pleasant ache that carried echoes of the pleasure I'd been lost in the night before. He'd done exactly as he'd said, to the limits I'd set. I could cover up everything, but any Othersider would be able to scent both blood and other fluids.

When I made my way back to the main room, I spotted several packets of jerky on the dresser.

"Thank the Goddess," I muttered.

My stomach rumbled as I tore open one packet and brought all of them back to the bed where Cade slept on.

Once I'd stuffed myself with a full packet and drunk some more water, I curled around his back. Knowing him, he'd freak out when he woke up, afraid I was going to change my mind or, worse, run from him.

But I didn't want to. I felt good.

Not owned, not like a possession, but like I belonged. Like we'd done something special and I'd given him something that meant as much as all he'd given me. I needed him to wake up knowing that I'd been up, seen what he'd done, and accepted it—and him.

Chapter 21: Cade

Cade's arms were empty when he woke. He inhaled sharply, panicking, mind racing. Had she seen what he'd done and left? Had he gone too far, driven by vampiric lust and jealousy and the ghosts of his past?

Warmth at his back and weight on the bed behind him made him twist.

Lya slept on, laying probably as comfortably as she could, given he'd savaged her over the course of several hours the previous night.

He couldn't help the way his blood heated at the sight of all his marks decorating her naked body, and if she was still here, she'd seen them and not objected, although it probably helped that they were nearly healed already. He checked the nightstands—she'd drunk all the water and eaten two packets of jerky. Which meant she'd definitely been up. She had to have seen how far he'd gone. Had to have felt the ache in every part of herself where he'd claimed her.

And she was still here.

Relief cut the tension in his muscles, and he slumped back to the bed, rolling to pull her front to his and embrace her. She made the small, pleased noise she always did when he gave her attention while she was sleeping and snuggled closer.

Cade's heart swelled, and his chest tightened. Struggling prey was exciting, tripping certain instincts. But the willingness to voluntarily give oneself over to the control of another was a high he'd never been offered. Lya gave him an outlet to act on his desires with none of the guilt or the grief.

He'd been lost in the pleasure of her submission last night—not so much that he'd hurt her beyond what she'd accept but enough that he'd done everything he wanted. Glamour could be a tricky magic though, especially with half-elves, and he'd trod a fine line even as he got as close to it as he dared, turned on as much by its existence as by the rainbow of colors in the marks he left on her skin.

Her eyelids fluttered, and he froze.

She groaned, face tightening, as she wiggled. Stretched. Tested her range of motion. Then her eyes opened and fell on him.

She smiled. "Hey, babe."

The clenching fist around his heart released. "You're okay?"

"Yeah. That's not an every month thing, but I enjoyed myself."

Stark disbelief made Cade stare at her.

"What?" she asked.

"You enjoyed yourself. You'd do this again?"

"I mean, not soon, but yes." She frowned. "You're acting like it's usually a thing that's forced or something."

"For some solidaires, it is." He couldn't help the grim note in his voice.

"Surprise." She smiled sleepily at him. "What time is it?"

Cade twisted and reached for his phone on the nightstand. "Just past six."

"Good. Time to get ready to meet the elves. You called Maria, right?"

"I did. Last night." There was something off in her tone. "What's wrong?"

"I don't know. I'd rather just leave with you tonight." She flicked a hand up and down her body and smiled wryly. "I've made my choice. The only people who matter are you and me. The rest just seems so tiresome at this point."

Warmth—love—curled through his chest. "I know. But once it's done, you won't have to worry about them again. Right?"

"Yeah. Or if I do, it won't be negotiations." She grinned savagely. "And we can deal with assassination attempts."

Protective rage turned the warmth in his heart to an inferno. "Let them try. Let anyone try to take you from me. You're *mine*."

"So I see." With a light kiss, she shifted toward the edge of the bed with a grunt. "And feel."

Cade caught her forearm. "Wait. Let me give those another round of healing."

"'Kay." She settled back against the pillows. The little noises she made as he ran his mouth over her, drawing healing saliva over the few cuts and bites deep enough that they hadn't entirely healed while they slept, were almost enough to tempt him to fuck her again. He wouldn't have to feed again for at least a week now, although he would if high-blood elf was still on the menu.

Later. When the damned Lyon elves aren't on her mind.

She showered after then called Maria to confirm final arrangements while he took his turn washing up. They dressed in their best—her in a slinky black dress with long sleeves, a scooped back, and a blood-red scarf to cover the remaining hints of bites and scratches, him in a three-piece suit with a shirt in the same color as her scarf—and headed downstairs to wait for Maria and the elves.

Maria found them first, breezing into the lobby as though she owned the place. She was dressed in a gunmetal grey dress with lace cap sleeves and a black fur stole, with fingerless lace gloves in the same color.

Her brows lifted when she got close enough to scent them. "Well. You've been having quite a bit of fun, haven't you Cade?"

He couldn't help his smirk at that. "My solidaire was good enough to indulge me."

"And strong enough to survive you, apparently."

Cade narrowed his eyes in warning as he loosed his glamour enough to turn mundane ears away from their low-voiced conversation. Lya might know the full extent of his past now and had indeed survived, even enjoyed, his darker desires, but there was no need to mention it in the hotel lobby.

Fortunately, Lya was imbued with a calm confidence he didn't remember seeing in her outside a fight. She just leaned on Cade's arm, smelling of contentment—and him, of course, despite her shower. That was deeply satisfying.

Maria pursed her lips. "So. You mentioned trespassers?"

Lya's scent twisted, along with her mouth. "Should be with us any minute now. A prince, a knight, and an entourage. I'd rather they all be able to walk away, if you please, Maria. I don't know why I care even that much anymore, but I don't think it was intentional."

The other *moroi* smiled. "But of course, doll. I just want my forfeit, not an international, inter-factional clusterfuck."

"Lya?" a man's voice called.

They all turned toward him, and Cade fixed him with a hard look. It was the same elf from the other day, the one who'd sent Lya into a panic before.

Henri.

He pulled up short, nostrils flaring. "I'm sorry, I wasn't aware this was a party."

His thick French accent was tinged with annoyance. Then he got another whiff. His eyes widened, and the blood drained from his face as he stared at Lya, who smiled and tucked herself under Cade's arm.

"Henri. Meet my friends," she said in French. "Maria is the local number three. Cade is—"

"I can tell very well what Cade is, thank you." The prince shifted his attention to Cade for a glare. "What the hell is the meaning of this? I thought…"

Cade couldn't help himself. He tightened the arm Lya was under then reached up to clasp her throat with the same hand. A quick brush of his finger shifted her scarf just enough to flash one of the nearly healed bite marks for a moment before he let the scarf cover it again.

The blood rushed back into Henri's face as the raw scent of unfettered jealousy spiked.

Maria shuddered, unmasked avarice shining in her expression. "Henri, is it? You're aware who owns this establishment?"

It took a moment for the prince to pull his attention away from Lya's neck. "Pardon?"

"You're on shaky ground, buttercup." Maria smiled almost wide enough to flash fang. "I understand you're not from around here, but you really should have stayed in Chapel Hill. Or anywhere in RTP."

Henri's face blanked as he figured out what she was getting at. "We didn't know. This was simply the best hotel in the area near the airport."

"I think you'll find it's the best in the state, but ignorance of the law is no excuse," she said brightly. "Will you be paying the forfeit yourself on behalf of all your people? Or shall I have my friends come in to help with collection?"

"Neither." Henri glowered. "This is absurd. Your people hold Raleigh—"

"And Cary. Which is where we are. Regardless of points on a map, we hold this property in the mundane legal system." She simpered. "So. Ass, grass, or cash, nobody sleeps for free. And we don't accept two out of the three, but we do accept… Well, you know what we'll accept."

Again, the near flash of fangs.

Henri stared at her, an intriguing blend of bewilderment and outrage tingeing his scent. Cade understood. He'd had a similar reaction to Maria's haphazard modernity the first time they'd met.

Outrage won out, and the elf snarled at Lya. "We'd heard rumors that you'd run off with a vampire, but nobody believed you'd be that stupid. Your mother is near death. I'm sure she'd be proud to see what a whore her daughter has become, should she live long enough to see you like this."

Lya flinched then went completely still.

"Maybe next time you'll take Samarre's calls." With a last sneer, Henri turned back to Maria. "Call your friends. I'm not taking the fall for this bordel on my own. I only came for her, but that was before seeing what she's become. We're in rooms 201 and 202."

Maria inclined her head. "See you up there, buttercup."

With a last expressionless look at Cade and Lya, she moved toward the main doors and the car idling outside.

Henri just left, moving almost too quickly to hide that he wasn't human.

Suddenly, Cade didn't know what to do or what to say. Henri had scored a hit. That much was clear in the hard tension of Lya's body.

"Ly?" Cade said.

"I'm fine." She relaxed.

"You're sure?"

"Yeah." Shaking her head, she moved to stand in front of him, resting her hands on his waist. "The first thing you did this evening was ask if I was okay, even though you could see I was. The first thing he did was square up with you and then call me a stupid whore, even though he could smell everything you did last night and couldn't know whether it was consensual. Hell, would have to assume it wasn't, given what they think of vampires in the Houses."

She rose on her toes to kiss him, a little too deeply and lingeringly for how nice this hotel was, but Cade didn't care. He gripped her hips and pulled her closer. This had been the final test, at least for now, and she was standing here kissing him.

When she pulled away, she smiled at him. "Don't you see? He was their bait. Their best offer. 'Forget how we treated you. Come back, and you can have what you got exiled trying to pursue before.' They thought I'd fall over myself for that chance. For scraps. But at the hint that he'd have to fight for me, I was trash again."

Cade drew her in and held her close. "Never trash. Not then, not now. You're you. You're smart and capable and stunning. And best of all, you're mine. Now and always."

"Now and always," she murmured back. Then she grinned, like it was the best thing in the world.

His heart swelled.

The footsteps of a large group preceded Maria's light, "Okay, lovebirds, break it up. Are you joining this party?"

Cade looked down at Lya, and she flushed.

"You're asking me?" Lya said.

He just lifted his eyebrows. Yes, he was supposed to be in charge, especially around other *moroi*. But this was her show.

"Oh. Um. Yes. Both of us," Lya said.

Maria smirked. "Kinky. Let's go."

Cade waved Maria's party, which included Noah, Oscar, Rani, and Lucien, into the first lift. While they waited for another, he said, "I don't have to go. And you don't have to watch. You've made your point."

"I have." She toyed with the edge of her scarf. "But I'm tired of us hiding from each other. I don't ever want you to feel like you can't show me a part of yourself again. And as for this particular meeting, I've got to own what I've done. People I grew up with are paying a price because I made a call. There will be more tough calls over the next however many decades we have together. I'm your solidaire. I'll stand with you through them. Starting now."

The lift dinged. A couple dressed as well as them stepped out, leaving it empty as they stepped in and hit the button for the second floor.

"Have I mentioned how much I love you?" Cade asked.

Her wry smile gave him life. "A few times. Tell me again."

"I love you." He leaned down and stole a kiss, scraping her lower lip with his fangs as he pulled away just to see her shudder as the enclosed space filled with the scent of her lust. "To the grave and back."

"Careful what you wish for, babe. I might just find a way to make that happen."

Epilogue: Cade

Cade expected Lya to call it a night after their business with the elves was finished. She stood in the corner, watching blank faced as the six vampires fed from nine elves in turn. Maria and Noah, as ranking members of the coterie, each got a bonus bite. Cade was surprised when Maria invited him to take the remainder, but from the look in her coffee-dark eyes, it was an acknowledgment of the debt she owed for being called in the first place.

Nice to have allies who would truly be allies.

Lya's decision had advanced Maria's timetable considerably and given her and her small cabal an advantage in whatever power games were to come in Raleigh, and Maria paid her debts.

After, Lya insisted on eating in the restaurant, a request Cade was only too happy to oblige. If she could watch him eat, he could do the same, and it gave him some time to shake off the drunken stupor of so much powerful blood. The staff were too polite to comment on the lady eating while the gentleman simply watched her with sleepy indulgence, and he kept enough of a low-level glamour going that anyone in the restaurant would have trouble remembering the details of the evening.

Probably for the best. There was a zing of tension in the air at the unsolved disappearance the woman Donatien had taken. People were extra watchful. But nobody would expect two people involved in the disappearance to sit in the dining room.

When Lya stripped on returning to the room, the evidence of his claiming was nearly healed. She was moving better as well, nearly back to her usual fluidness.

The saucy look she threw him when she headed into the bathroom lured him there, shedding clothing as he went, heedless of where it landed. When the shower hissed on, he slipped in after her to find her looking over her shoulder with a lusty smile.

"Join me," she said.

Cade almost questioned her. But he was done with that. She'd been explicit in her desire for him to do whatever he pleased with her last night. She'd been there the morning after. Had smiled at him then, with his sigil freshly etched in her flank by blade rather than the easier needle.

No more hiding, no more running. If she was inviting him to join her now, that was what he'd do. Because he desperately wanted to do something about the raging hard-on that was pulling him toward her as much as anything else.

Not just to fuck her. But to connect with her.

She caught him by the cock and led him into the hot spray after her then pushed him against the wall and knelt. A small hiss escaped her as hot water hit the shallow remainder of a knife mark, and he tugged her away by the hair.

"Are you hurting?" he asked.

Lya opened her mouth. Shut it. Revised what she was going to say. "Yeah, a little. But it's a good hurt." She grinned. "And it's not every day you've fed as well as you have lately. I want more of last night before we get paid and get the hell out of town."

"Your wish is ever my command, love." He guided her back onto his cock.

As good as she was and as aroused as the elf blood made him, he didn't last long. She gripped his thighs as he held her to his belly and finished down her throat then laughed when he hauled her up and changed their places, kneeling to lavish her with the same attention.

He'd never get enough of this, enough of her.

Never. Not in a million vampire lifetimes.

Washing each other drew a note of tenderness into their touch, one that'd been lacking the last few days.

I need this. I need her. Forever.

She'd given him a gift he'd never seen coming when she got on her knees and offered him the blade. One most master vampires usually stole, by force or by guile. One that had allowed him to bridge his past and his present in a way that'd healed the jagged vestiges of Morris's abuse and Donatien's corruption.

He didn't have to be one person or another. With her limits to guide him, he could be his full self.

They both could be. Together.

By the time they got out of the shower, he was hard again. She grinned at him in the mirror and, with a delectable languor, bent over and braced herself on the counter in clear invitation.

One Cade didn't hesitate to accept.

Trapping her against the counter, he clasped her throat with one hand, cleared the fog with the other, and made her look at herself—look at them—in the mirror.

"Who do you belong to?" he asked in a silky whisper.

Her pupils dilated wide as she flushed. "You."

"That's right." He guided himself into her, pushing slow until he was as deep as he could get. She panted as he took her with long, leisurely strokes that thudded against the counter and made the silly little bottles of shampoo and lotion topple over.

When he bared his fangs at her in the mirror, she shuddered. "Bite me."

Another invitation he wasn't going to question. She knew her body. She knew what she wanted and what would get her off.

Not breaking eye contact with her, he loosed just enough glamour to take the worst of the edge off for her and bit down.

Lya watched him do it, her breathing going ragged, and as he pulled on the wound, she came, clenching around him with a cry he muffled with a hand over her mouth.

He followed her, giving himself to her as she did to him, and then carried her to bed when her knees were too wobbly to make it on her own.

***

Cade woke the next evening still buzzing from how well he'd fed the last few days, alight with the fire of new possibility. Lya's weight on his chest comforted him, as did her warmth, even if he was just as warm for once. Unusual for her to still be asleep at this hour, but she'd had a rough week. That she was still here, an arm and a leg thrown over him with one of his arms holding her against his side, gave him the most hope he'd had in five centuries.

She hadn't just watched the previous night's blood forfeit. She'd drawn him into fucking her again afterward when he'd been afraid she'd need space to process what she'd witnessed.

They were partners.

True partners, not like a master and a fledgling or a solidaire. Not like Donatien had been the bad daimon of his troubled years.

He shifted the blankets to find a new layer of fading bruises on her thigh crease from the previous night's vigorous activities. The sigil had healed nicely, and pride flushed him with renewed warmth. Not just for the fact that he'd had her full permission to do it. That was a tricky piece of work, one made all the more difficult because she'd been trembling and climaxing through it. Keeping the blade steady and not too deep…

Lya groaned and stretched, her hand slipping lower on his body.

"We need to get you fed like this more often," she mumbled when she encountered the evidence of his pleasure in the remembrances of marking her.

"I'd neither complain nor object," he said. Then words came tumbling out even he hadn't anticipated. "Marry me."

She pushed up, blinking blearily. "What? Vampires don't—"

"I know. But elves and humans do. At least let's exchange vows or something. Mami Wata would officiate. If you don't mind going back to Ocracoke and making better memories."

Her frown and her scent were confused, not angry. "Why? You have everything I can give you."

"Exactly. And I want to balance the scales. I want you to know that, even if I have to play the master in public sometimes, for both our safety, you are and always will be my equal. My treasure and my beloved. I take only what you give. Forever."

The raw emotion that swept over her features then almost had him afraid she was going to run, but then she was straddling him, squeezing him with her thighs as she kissed him everywhere. His face, his neck, under his chin, until he cupped her jaw in both hands and captured her lips with his.

"Is that a yes?" he asked, heart racing.

"Yes. Fuck it, yes."

She was his.

Truly his, by choice and not by force or tradition or desperation.

Pure joy bubbled up in every facet of Cade's being, more than he ever thought he'd experience. Whatever else came their way, Lya would be the hell, and Cade would be the high water.

Just the way it should be when two people as broken as them healed together and turned their might on the world. And when they were the hell and the high water, nothing could come between them, and nothing could tear them down.

From the impassioned way Lya rode him, she was as enthusiastic about what came next for them as he was.

Want more?

This is the third book in a spin-off series, and there's plenty more to the world of Otherside.

You can get more Shadows of Otherside content in a few different ways:

- Read the original urban fantasy series (check out the first two chapters of *Elemental* on the next page!)
    - On Amazon: whwrites.com/soo-series
    - Elsewhere: whwrites.com/books
- Subscribe to Whitney's Patreon for bonus chapters from multiple points of view: whwrites.com/patreon
- Sign up to the Write Wherever newsletter for updates: whwrites.com/newsletter.

Lastly, if you enjoyed this book, **please consider posting a review**, recommending it on Goodreads or BookBub, or telling a friend who might also enjoy it. As always, thank you for reading, and for your support!

Keep reading to meet Arden Finch, a supernatural private investigator with a deadly secret, in *Elemental: Shadows of Otherside Book 1*.

Chapter 1

Sometimes investigating a case went off without a hitch. Other times, whatever ruse I'd adopted didn't quite work, or something outside my control screwed my setup.

"Are you sure I'm not on the list?" I adjusted the wobbling box of sandwiches on my hip, hitched the insulated beverage bag on my shoulder, and cursed both my luck and the overheated air turning the office foyer into an oven. A gust tickled my cheek and the curls sticking out of the back of my cap in a short poof of a ponytail, tempting me to call on my powers to cool it. "They must have forgotten," I added.

The security guard who'd interrupted my attempt to follow an employee into the elevator reddened. He was big and hairy enough that he might have some jötunn or giant blood way back in his lineage. I eased away a half pace despite the lack of telltale earthy scent, just to be safe. Between my upbringing and my five years as a private investigator, I'd learned caution. Either way, I needed to get into this building. This job was for Callista. She didn't take failure lightly.

Scowling despite my accommodating step back, the guard bit off each word as he said, "Nobody here ordered lunch, missy. I already checked."

"Look, man, they're paid for. If—" I looked at the receipt, pretending I didn't know the name on the order, "Joseph doesn't take delivery, they go in the trash. Isn't there a break room or somewhere I can leave them?"

He eased the clench of his fists, not quite opening them, but relaxing away from the temptation to remove me. "Oh. Well, that explains it. Mr. Cumberland is on vacation."

A fact I had already inferred, having pretended to be an interested client to get an appointment on the calendar app this start-up used. The entire week leading up to the new year had been unavailable despite the office being open. I'd wanted a backup plan in case the easiest route—following an employee when there was no security guard on duty—fell through.

The research I'd done told me the VP of business development, Joseph Cumberland, had a reputation for surprising his team with catered lunches. It was easy enough to buy a load of meal boxes and borrow a cap with the sandwich shop's name on it, so delivery driver was my disguise.

I tried my best bored face and prayed that Joseph's title would outweigh the security protocol as the guard scrutinized me. My average height and weight meant I didn't look like much of a threat. At twenty-five, I could pass for one of the younger undergrad students at the nearby university and often did. Cute enough when I smiled, but no model, although the bright red sandwich shop polo I wore complimented my sienna-brown skin nicely. In short, not much of anything to take particular notice of…unless I was trying to follow a badged employee into a secure building.

The guard pressed his lips together as he made his decision. "Normally, you should be escorted in, but I'm short-staffed on account of Christmas. You go up to the third floor, you drop them sandwiches off, and you come straight back down, you hear?"

Bingo. Always have a backup plan.

"No worries," I said, restraining my smile to a tightening of my lips and lowering my eyes. The guard's diction had slipped away from Southern hospitality and toward down-home mob as he decided he didn't like me or the situation, but didn't have much choice. "I don't get paid what these kids do. Faster I get outta here, faster I can get more tips."

He grunted and waved me toward the elevator, the grand sweep of his arm carrying more than a hint of sarcasm.

I suppressed the impulse to return the gesture with a mocking curtsy. No use pissing him off when I was getting what I wanted.

As the doors to the elevator slid shut, I blew out a breath and shook my head. Even the most suspicious people tended to fall back on assumptions based on my appearance, providing opportunities to misdirect them. I wasn't an elf or a vampire and therefore couldn't cloud minds, but I still doubted any of my marks ever considered that I might not be human. Convincing humans that you're one of them without using magic is the greatest practical joke ever, and I get paid for it.

A harried-looking, younger twenty-something met me at the next door and pointed me to the break room before rushing off. Probably an intern, busting her ass to prove herself in a culture that would chew her up and spit her out if she didn't develop a stronger sense of self. I knew the look.

Start-ups had popped up like mushrooms after a rain in the Triangle—Raleigh, Durham, and Chapel Hill—with North Carolina's latest tax restructure. The influx of people from San Francisco and New York had brought money and big-city problems to a relatively smaller trio of towns. Business was booming, even if I turned down the illegal stuff. I could have made bank on cheating spouses alone.

This particular start-up had drawn the attention of the one person I couldn't say no to, and who didn't have to tell me why she wanted me to risk my PI license to bug a bunch of self-important healthtech blowhards. Video surveillance is legal in this state. Audio surveillance needs the consent of at least one of the recorded parties, and *that* I didn't have. Not that mundane law mattered to Callista, Otherside's hard-assed premier in the Triangle, my former legal guardian, and my current boss.

I spread the sandwiches on a long table as quickly as I could and lined up two one-gallon jugs, one sweet tea and one unsweet, alongside them. I was feeling decidedly unsweet as I thunked the jugs down a little harder than necessary, having taken this job gratis on Callista's orders. She'd been asking more of me lately, a lot more, and both the unpaid asks and the lack of explanation were grating. I wasn't a child or some low-level nobody. I was a Watcher. I'd earned some respect, but I wasn't getting it.

One of these jobs would eventually turn up something I could use. If she wouldn't give me the respect I deserved, I'd find a way to take it. I could bide my time until then.

With the beverage bag empty, I took a quick look around, then flipped up the cooler's false bottom and grabbed one of the small surveillance cams I'd hidden there. I stuck one to the underside of the cabinet closest to the wall. Everyone chatted at the proverbial water cooler, which, in this case, would probably be the adjacent beer fridge.

Tugging the bill of my cap lower, I wandered out, looking for a quiet hall and another opportunity on my way back through the office. My sharper-than-human hearing picked up chatter all on one side of the office, so I went the other way. The oppressive heating system kicked on again, and I relaxed my shields enough that the eddies of a disturbance in the air would warn me of someone coming. It was a risk, given the elven bounty on elementals like me, but I couldn't go back to Callista without being certain the bugs would pick up something good.

Jackpot. A tall bookshelf stood just inside an empty office with the CEO's name on it. I paused to listen for phone calls or clacking keyboards. Nothing. Heart thundering at the risk, I stood on tiptoes and pried off one of the little plugs that hid a screw hole at the top of the shelf, replacing it with an audio-only bug. If I got caught, Callista would do nothing to save me or my career, but after watching her draw stolen blood from every pore of an errant vampire with a single word, I feared her more than the human legal system. The empty office of the head of research and development mirrored this one across the hall, so I stuck my last audio bug on a shelf in there.

On my way back to the door, I glanced down the hall before running my fingers over the top of a framed, ugly-yet-typical abstract picture hanging next to the main entry. The amount of dust reassured me that this was not a place the cleaners thought about. I blew away the bunnies I'd dislodged and stuck another micro-camera there, where it could record people coming and going.

Job done.

The security guard ignored my little wave of thanks on the way out. Fine by me. I didn't like his attitude. On the plus side, it quashed any lingering sympathy I might have had for the trouble he'd be in when the board of this start-up read my report. Not that I'd had very much sympathy to begin with.

Humans. Easiest prey there was. It was almost unfair they didn't know about the rest of us: the beings of myth and legend, collectively known as Otherside.

While all of us lived by secrets and lies, my life was more obscured than most. Not just because of my job, but also because of what I was. Where most of the magic-using species were restricted to Aether, glamour, or life force, my talents laid with one of the four pure elements. That made me an elemental; my control over the element of Air made me a sylph.

Elementals are rare enough that Callista took me under her personal protection when Duke found me in foster care as a child. That protection came with some obligations once I was old enough to fulfill them.

Nobody in Otherside knows what Callista is, and nobody smart asks. Her petite frame and plain-yet-sweet features fool the stupid into missing a frightening intellect and overwhelming magical strength. The start-up's board had invited me to test their security, but it was only supposed to be an entry attempt—not unauthorized and illegal surveillance. But if Callista wanted a favor, she got a favor, no questions. For now.

I took care of some paperwork when I got back to the tiny office I rented in the big coworking space in downtown Durham, putting off the evening's scheduled meeting. Dawdling wasn't wise when Callista wanted an update, but I figured I'd earned some leeway. I had a business to run, after all, and it wasn't all as fun as tricking my way into swanky offices. There were bills to pay, emails to answer, and reports to draft.

At least, that's what I told myself. That I had a business to run. If I was honest, I was still mad about being strong-armed into the job. It was the sort of petty rebellion I'd been indulging in more frequently, and while it provided a minor satisfaction, the curdled ball of resentment in my belly grew a little larger and a little uglier with every uncompensated demand.

Lately, the demands had been for me to start using my magic in her service rather than for my best interests. After a lifetime of schooling—threats, really—in the dangers awaiting an elemental if I was discovered, I refused to draw attention to myself by using Air in an offensive against another Othersider. That meant I had to be useful in other ways. Gathering information was easier and safer as a private investigator than as a shadow in the dark, so business it was. My life and secrets depended on it.

Callista used it against me, reminding me that I both owed her and would need her intercession if an elf ever did stumble onto my secret. Hell, if anyone did. The high-blood elven houses had enough power in local and regional human government that someone might sell me to them for a favor. My logic said it would be better to leave well enough alone, and so far, I'd won the argument.

Evening tinted the sky orange by the time I left my office. A shift of the jet stream had brought a snap of cold Canadian air down south and the temperature had dropped alarmingly, especially for this part of North Carolina.

Everyone looked like a startled turtle as they tried to huddle under knit caps and behind wool scarves, hunched under their heaviest coats with arms crossed. Given that this was the South, only the recent transplants from northern states had anything adequate. I didn't feel the cold as badly as most, but it still bit through my jacket and made me hustle on the walk over.

Callista's pub sat on its own lot, conveniently close to the cluster of breweries north of downtown Durham, yet set apart. Part of that was the use of a magic that wasn't one of the four elements or Aether; I didn't know what it was, but it discouraged casual visits from mundanes. The pub was safe, neutral ground for Othersiders, where business could be conducted without worrying about what a human might see or overhear. Despite the mix of species present, some of whom had bad blood between them, nobody looked for trouble.

Part of it was Callista's reputation. She sold love potions and told fortunes with Lenormand or Tarot cards, but she wasn't a psychic or a witch as far as I could tell. That might be what the local religious folks called her when they dared speak about her behind her back, but she was more than that. Other in a way even the rest of us weren't. I'd once seen her kill a would-be burglar with a touch and I had no interest in instigating something that might draw that side of her forward.

The bar itself was completely unassuming, a chunky brick building with a metal liftgate at the back for deliveries. Inside, it was warm woods and low lights, almost like an English-style pub, but with enlarged Tarot cards framed on the walls. If anyone else tended bar there, I'd never seen them. She was always on duty when I visited.

I slipped in past some departing patrons, elves by the faint whiff of burnt marshmallow I caught as they passed. The elves didn't even glance at me, too low-blood or too drunk to catch the telltale tingle of magic as the woman's hand brushed mine in the narrow doorway. I shoved my hand into my pocket and slammed my shields up higher, counting myself lucky. It would have raised some uncomfortable questions had they noticed, the neutrality of Callista's bar be damned. Nerves had me slipping up.

"Arden Finch. I wondered when you'd get around to keeping our appointment," Callista said when I reached the bar. Her smile didn't reach her cool green eyes.

"Ma'am," I said in a cautious greeting as I slipped onto a bar stool. She knew what I was and had had a hand in raising me, but that didn't mean we particularly liked each other. I dug in my coat pocket for the rooted smartphone I'd bought specifically for this job and slid it over the bar. The only app on it was tied to the cameras I'd set up this afternoon. "It's done."

I told myself that the blast of December air following new patrons made me shiver, not her widening smile.

"Excellent, my dear." She filled a highball glass with Coke and dropped a wedge of lime in it, knowing I didn't booze in public. My insistence on appearing to do so amused her, so she played along.

I pressed my lips together, annoyed by her mocking smile. It was a bar. People tended to get nervous when it looked like you weren't drinking. Nervous people didn't play nicely and that always made my work harder.

"Still not willing to use your powers on a job? I have one that could benefit from your…particular talents."

The change in topic was both abrupt and unwelcome. I shifted on the stool and fiddled with the pendant that was the only thing I had left of my unknown father. It was one of the few nervous tics I hadn't managed to root out and I stopped as soon as I realized what I was doing.

Callista smiled, catlike. That she'd noticed my nerves made me grouchy all over again.

"You were the one who discouraged me from using them in the first place," I said, irritated enough to snap at her, though I kept my voice down. "And we had a deal. If I use my business to serve as a Watcher, I don't have to use my *other* skills. I don't need that kind of attention." It was an old argument, one I'd thought was settled.

Callista pouted and harrumphed as she cleared a few glasses from the bar. "Times are changing and you've gotten better at hiding yourself. Your shields are so tight I'd think you were human if I didn't already know. Besides, the djinn know about you and nothing has happened."

"Fine, but the djinn aren't—" I lowered my voice further and glanced around, "the elves." Preternaturally gifted humans and supernatural beings tended to have great hearing. My presence was bad enough without our conversation being overheard. It's not that I had anything against elves, except the fact that they'd kill an elemental like me upon discovery because of some stupid elven law going back to the days of Atlantis; they were sticklers for laws. Pretty shitty, but I tried not to take it personally. They weren't like the more individualistic djinn, prone to bending the rules for personal gain or pure whim. "Why push this now?"

She pierced me with a sharp gaze, but she'd pricked the one subject I wouldn't back down on. My life wasn't worth whatever had intrigued her enough to bring it up again—I was sure of it.

Never mind that I wanted, more than anything, to be able to exercise my powers freely. Allowing Callista to use me was not the way to gain that freedom. It would be a faster way to die, or another lever she could use against me. She was a master of manipulation.

"I've heard rumors," she said when I didn't look away. "The djinn are nosier than usual. The elves are boiling like a kicked anthill. The vampires have gone underground. Even the wereanimal clans are restless. Nobody seems to know why, and yet, everyone is on edge."

"Solstice fever." I shrugged and took another sip of citrus-spiked Coke. It happened at some point every winter. Something about the longer nights got everyone jumpy. Not surprising, given that most supernatural species are moon-bound and prefer the darkness, but then again…the jump of magic from that elf had been odd. That hadn't just been me; even a low-blood elf should have better self-control. Not that I would admit the thought, or the slipup, to Callista.

She read something in my face anyway. Another not-smile dimpled her round cheeks. "Perhaps. And perhaps you'll find yourself wishing you'd listened to me."

"Is that a foretelling?"

"Would you embrace your power and do this job for me if I told you it was?"

I snorted and pushed my half-finished drink away. "A dream and a bad feeling aren't worth my life."

"That might change before spring."

The cryptic words made me frown at her. Callista looked back at me with a bland expression that didn't match the charged history of our conversation.

"I'd say it's been a pleasure, but…well. You know where to find me." I gave a short wave and turned to leave.

"I certainly do."

I didn't look back, not wanting to see what might be in those cat-green eyes.

My walk back downtown was brisker than my walk over had been. A rabbit hopped away as I passed a vacant lot overgrown with grass and weeds, looking a little too big with ears a little too long, making my skin tingle in a way that was a little too close to magic. As a Watcher, I probably should have investigated whether it was a trickster hare rather than just a plain old rabbit, but I didn't care. Unlike everyone else, it wasn't bothering me, or asking me to do shit that would get me killed. I left Brer Rabbit to his evening and kept going for my car, parked in the garage across the street from the coworking space.

A freezing rain had started falling by the time I made it back to my place. Not very conducive to New Year's Eve fireworks, which was fine by me. The pops and sparkles were pretty, but only after I'd gotten over the wave of fear that someone had figured out what I was and fired a spell at me.

My lot was down a narrow gravel road and backed onto Eno River State Park, outside town, with lots of land on all sides. It wasn't convenient to anything except the woods, and that was how I wanted it. Good fences made good neighbors, but some things couldn't be hidden behind a fence. I liked being able to slip out the back gate and walk in the woods at night, or sit by the firepit I'd dug out of the backyard and listen to the music of the windchimes I had hanging around the property. As an elemental, I needed fresh air, the peace of the forest, and the nearby river. I could tolerate cities, but too long out of nature drained me.

I ran from the car and hopped up both the wooden steps of the wraparound porch, then stepped over the low, tied-off chord of magic creating a block of Air. I always left one in front of the door to trip up unexpected visitors. The nice thing about elemental magic was that only other elementals could see it at work. Anyone else would stumble and make enough noise to alert me. Paranoid, but effective, given that I was the only elemental around.

Callista's words needled me as I sipped a glass of prosecco on the couch, enjoying the peaceful glow of the fairy lights I'd strung up for the solstice and left up for the new year. The manipulative old hag never lied, but the truths she told never seemed to be the ones you heard. Her statement could be about my magic, or the start-up, or—given how carefully she'd phrased her words—nothing at all. That was the trouble with Callista. Untold power and layers of secrets wrapped around dangerous fragments of truth.

The start-up, though, that bore further looking into. Callista rarely took such an interest in mundane matters, which meant Verve Health Solutions was either a threat, or not as mundane as it appeared. Maybe both.

I reached for my laptop, then stopped with my hand hovering over it. "Take a day off," I muttered to myself. Tomorrow was a holiday, and after a busy December, I deserved to sip my bubbly without creating new problems for myself. There were plenty enough of those in the world as it was.

Chapter 2

WRAL's breaking news page reported a woman found drowned in Jordan Lake, which would have been tragic enough on its own without it having happened several times already since winter started. Not the same lake, but always someone found drowned or frozen to death. Nobody could remember so many water accidents happening in the winter, and local authorities were warning heavily about water safety and the risks of hypothermia.

Something about the drownings seemed off, but I couldn't figure out what. The police weren't considering the cases connected, so it was probably my overactive detective skills looking for links where there weren't any.

A rap on the door of my office pulled me out of the rest of the morning's news.

"It's open," I sang out. When the door opened, I had my professional smile on, ready to welcome the only client I was expecting for the day.

The man who stepped in was not that client. Tall and blond, well-built, a fighter's body. Not the thin, brunette head of the board from the start-up. A weighty, black gym bag hung from one shoulder, and I eyed it warily. He could fit any number of weapons in there. The air currents shifted as the open door let warmer air in, bringing the choking, burnt-marshmallow taste of Aether into the room.

He was a high-blood elf capable of some serious damage. Fuck.

My gut clenched and a wave of dizzy fear made me glad I was still sitting. Either I had been discovered, or I would be soon. Luck runs out and skill can't save you every time, which was why all my clients were human. It reduced the risk.

That, plus most Othersiders didn't seek outside help with problems. Justice tended toward the swift and very often fatal, carried out in parallel to the human system.

Knowing that and finding it worth my life to fly under the radar, I played human. Lived human hours, kept my powers under wraps, hid my true physical strength, and didn't go to any of the events in the Otherside community that you wouldn't find a human at. Spending time with some djinn and Callista was the most damning thing I did, and they were all known to have human contacts, particularly useful ones like PIs or blood bank volunteers. As far as I was aware, there was no reason to look twice at me.

So, what the hell was an elf doing in my office, reeking of Aether and a bad attitude?

I'd been sitting too long. Forcing myself to take a breath and hoping he wouldn't see me shaking, I stood, my eyes still on that bag. As I did, I checked my shields and pulled in my own magic as tightly as I could. At the same time, I forced my body to relax and thanked the Goddess that elven hearing wasn't quite as good as that of a vampire or were. Elves had the sharpest vision, but the tripping thump of my racing heart might go unnoticed.

The thoughts skittering through my head like marching ants froze when the burnt-marshmallow scent intensified as a blanket of silence fell. It was quieter than usual outside, the cold and the post-holiday slump keeping people indoors, but what little street noise there was vanished. The sound of the door shutting seemed thunderous in the artificial calm.

He'd done something to block sound. I shifted my feet, preparing to move but not embracing Air yet. If it came to a fight, the spell he'd cast would block out the noise of whatever I had to do to defend myself. Adrenaline spiked higher and cold sweat made my shirt stick to my back.

With a serious effort of will, I pulled my mind away from the terrible ways elves could kill me and back to the immediate issue. Maybe I could get out of this the easy way—by pretending I was only human and hadn't noticed his magic trick. "Welcome to Hawkeye Investigations. I'm actually expecting a client, but would be happy to help afterward."

He studied me, a small frown flitting over his brow before the scent of Aether lessened without losing the sound dampening. He'd tied off the spell. That suggested he didn't intend to stay long and would let it unravel after he was gone. Was that good or bad?

"I need you to help me find someone," he said, ignoring me. "I hear you're the best."

I'd have to play along. "Someone must have given me a good review." I pushed through the fear and smiled, keeping it small to demonstrate humility and respect for his problem even as my mind raced, seeking what little my djinn guardians had told me about elves.

Of all the supernatural community, elves were the ones who never sought outside help. They had their own courts, their own police force, their own government. Was this related to what Callista had said, about the elves being riled up for unknown reasons? "I can see why you'd be concerned. Why don't you take a seat and tell me about your missing person, Mr.…?"

"Sequoyah. Leith Sequoyah." He sat and my heart rate eased down a notch. Not here for a bounty. Yet. Maybe? Unless he was trying to do things the easy way as well.

He shifted his chair so that it had a better view of the door, the window, and me. It struck me as habitual rather than planned, an act of preparation rather than malice. Given what I'd heard of elven politics, I supposed he'd have reason for caution. "It's my grandmother," he said when he was settled. "We're deeply concerned. She's our family matriarch."

I'll bet she is. If she was the matriarch of a high-blood family, that meant she was probably a queen. This could be bad.

"Is there any history of Alzheimer's or dementia?" I asked, playing the ignorant human. Elves didn't have trouble with any of the age-related mental deterioration humans were prone to, and only someone not supernatural would ask.

Leith frowned and shook his head. "No. She's still quite sharp despite her age. What concerns us is that she disappeared rather suddenly and blood was found in her home."

My stomach plummeted. This was definitely bad. Not something I wanted to be involved in. "I'm sorry, but violent crime is something better handled by the police. I usually get called in for wives that have run off with their lovers, or fathers who have skipped child support."

"Please, Ms. Finch. If the police are involved it will become some sort of spectacle. My grandmother is very well respected in the community. Her reputation might not recover if there's a scandal. My family would like to handle this quietly."

I leaned back and crossed my arms, studying him. Something more was going on than he was saying. No police likely meant no elven law either. That they were outsourcing to someone they thought was outside the supernatural community meant they suspected someone inside it.

Red flags went up and started waving. What was going on for a high-blood elf not to trust the elven police? I could see them wanting to avoid other supernaturals—the vamps and the djinn in particular would love to get the upper hand on the elves—but the Darkwatch was supposed to be both excellent and beyond reproach.

I was curious in spite of myself. I'd been a Watcher and a PI for too long not to be intrigued by a tale as bizarre as this one, terrified or not.

"This could go badly for me if a crime was committed," I said, hoping he'd give me a clue. "I could lose my license if the police accuse me of evidence tampering, or obstruction of justice."

"If you find evidence of a crime, I promise I'll go to the police."

"You've already found possible evidence, if there's blood and a disappearance."

Annoyance tightened his features and a flicker of Aether nudged at my aura, just shy of my tightly held shields.

You bastard. What was it? Something persuasive?

"I'll beg if needed," Leith said, smoothing his face into something more earnest even as his shoulders tensed. "I really do need your help."

Social engineering was a bland way to describe manipulating people to achieve a goal that wasn't in their interest. It was one of my favorite parts of being a private investigator, and experience with it told me he was lying. Social engineering rule number seven: make sure your nonverbals matched your words. His didn't, and if I didn't react the right way, I was fucked.

My stomach tightened as I tipped my head to the side and made my eyelids droop slightly, the way I assumed they would if his spell was actually affecting me rather than sliding off my mental shields. He hadn't cottoned on to my being an elemental, or I'd be dead. Playing human was the only way I'd see the rest of the day.

Callista's words about my passing for human came back to me and his continued ignorance gave me the tiniest flicker of hope. What if I could use this as blackmail to buy my safety?

His shoulders eased as I said, "Well…it certainly would be a shame if she was unnecessarily drawn into a scandal."

"Yes," he purred, eyes narrowed to slits of ice blue. "It would. Won't you help me?"

When I hesitated, Sequoyah's flicker of Aether pressed harder. "Of course," I said, quick and breathy. I had to do this, whether I wanted to or not. If he realized his nudges of Aether were only skating off my shields, that would tell him I was an Othersider. If he broke through my shields and got a whiff of my magic I was equally as damned as if I didn't play along. Then no amount of blackmail in the world would matter. "Damned if you do and damned if you don't" had never been so literal.

He smiled to show perfect teeth. "I knew you were the right person to come to. How quickly can you start?"

Clicking randomly on my computer mouse to give the impression of checking my calendar, I tried to convince myself that I could still get out of this and avoid the risk of elven discovery. All I had to do was tell him I was booked out, even if I didn't have anything else on the schedule.

You need the money and you definitely want to know what the hell is going on, the slowly reappearing rational side of me said. *Plus, it's not worth the risk of him finding out you've slipped the Aether net. Grow a pair. Take the job.* Winters were usually slow, which was the other part of why I was annoyed that Callista hadn't paid for the surveillance equipment I'd needed for her job. Gear was pricey, and I couldn't expense it to Verve the way I had the sandwiches I'd used to make my entry.

I needed to give Leith an answer. It was Saturday, and I usually gave myself Sunday off in the slow season. With only one debrief meeting planned for today, I could start researching the case immediately…wait, was I really going to do this?

My heart started tripping all over again, but this time excitement blended with the fear. I was tired of hiding, and had had enough of Callista. This could be my out, if I dared. I'd need to learn more about what I was getting into first. That meant stalling him just enough to do research, yet not so much that he'd go elsewhere. "I need to wrap up another case. Monday afternoon, or after receipt of the initial retainer, whichever is latest."

"No sooner?"

Entitled prick. But desperate to avoid other options. This could be good, good enough to give me something to use. "I'm sorry. While I'm highly sympathetic and sensitive to the urgency of a missing person, I do have other clients. As I said, I was expecting one when you arrived. If you're deeply concerned that there's been foul play, then I have to insist on the police."

"No…no. Monday will have to do."

Too desperate to avoid Otherside. Enough that whatever this was might really give me a way out of Callista's service, if I played my cards right. And didn't get myself killed. With a tight smile, I stood and slid my card across the desk before opening my calendar for real and noting him in. "In that case, thank you for your visit. Please send me an email and I'll invoice you—" A stack of banknotes hitting my desk made me blink.

"That's five thousand dollars," he said.

"Okay, then." I put Sequoyah in a whole new tier of dangerous. Who walks around with that much cash? "That covers the initial retainer, plus some expenses. Monday it is. If you send over a photo and—"

He withdrew a manila folder from the gym bag he'd come in with, and dropped it to the desk before he stood, zipped the bag up, and walked out, pushing past a disgruntled Amy Ulster in the corridor. I hurried to swipe the money off the desk and into a drawer while she was distracted with scowling at the elf's back. It could go in the safe after I'd soothed ruffled feathers.

"Ms. Ulster!" I called, going to the door to welcome her in. "I'm so sorry for the delay."

Her glare swung to me and my smile hardened until it was fixed to my face. The feather-smoothing was going to take a while. Doubly so once I told her how many holes there were in her healthtech start-up's security. HIPAA compliance was a bitch.

* * *

The door finally shut behind a grudgingly satisfied board member. I slumped and rested my head on my arms. I needed to start researching background information on the Sequoyah case, but a headache throbbed in a band across my brow. People might ask for your help, but that didn't always mean they were happy to get it or that they were grateful for it. Some days they were decidedly *un*grateful.

"Well. It's not every day a high-blood elf asks for help. Especially from you."

I jumped at the masculine echo of my thoughts and glared at the djinni who had just materialized in my office. "Dammit, Duke! Ever heard of a doorbell charm?" Leith had me shook and the appearance of a djinni—even a friendly one—did not help. "Why bother giving me a callstone if you're not going to use it?"

Nebuchadnezzar, who everyone called Duke when they didn't want to summon him, grinned. He was wearing his favorite shape today, that of a gangly, youngish black man with laughing eyes the color of dravite, clothed in a sharp suit. "Guilty mind?"

"I have no reason to feel guilty," I snapped, still unsettled enough to play with my pendant before catching myself. It had been a while since a djinni had been able to drop in without me sensing them first. "He came to me. I know the rules, and the dangers."

"I am so very glad to hear that." He sat in the chair Leith had vacated and wrinkled his nose at the lingering scent of the elf's magic, but withheld comment. "Are you going to help him?"

"Yes."

Duke's arched eyebrow spoke volumes. "A dangerous choice."

"But mine to make." I sighed and slumped again. The djinn were nominally on my side, since they claimed my mother had been one, and Duke was more amenable to siding with me than most. A friend, even.

That didn't mean he'd look the other way if I got too involved with the elves. The two factions had been mortal enemies for millennia, since the drowning of Atlantis, maybe. Only the Détente and the need to remain hidden from the humans kept each side from attacking the other.

"It can't hurt to build goodwill just in case," I said, disgusted with myself as soon as the words came out of my mouth. An hour after my big rush of courage, and I was already falling back into old patterns, justifying my actions.

"Just in case." Duke's lips twisted in scorn. "If you think a little goodwill will save you from elven hunters—"

"I'm a fool. I know. Bounty. Death sentence. Elementals are too dangerous for elves to leave alive. We might do something to upset their precious balance. And so on."

Duke spread his hands and offered a slight smile. "On your head be it."

"It might very well be," a contralto voice intoned to my left.

I jumped again as Grimm materialized. As usual, she looked like Lana Del Rey's twin, only with hair the arterial red of fresh blood and sapphire-blue eyes. Her plum-colored skater dress swished as she moved to lean against my desk.

"Nosy djinn," I muttered. Louder, I said, "You two cannot just pop in here like this." An annoyed wave of my hand took in the windows, tinted for privacy but not so much that someone couldn't notice the abrupt appearance of two people. It had always been their habit to appear when they pleased, but it had been happening more frequently of late. Kind of like Callista's asks. It bugged the hell outta me.

Grimm scoffed and tossed long red hair while Duke just kept his teasing smile. This wasn't the first time I'd tried telling them off only to be dismissed, and it rankled.

"Also, we had an agreement," I reminded them, knowing it was pointless but ticked enough to say it anyway. "You're not supposed to be watching. Boundaries, remember?"

"Maybe, maybe not." Duke stretched long legs out in front of him. "Regardless, you can imagine my concern when I turned a thought your way and found a barrier of elven magic."

"What did he want?" Grimm asked.

I crossed my arms. "Nope, nuh-uh. We're not doing this."

"Not doing what?" She wrapped a crimson lock around her finger, looking coy until her eyes flashed to their natural ruby and back. The eyes were always a tell. She was nervous. Or pissed. Something, but not in complete control of her emotions. Fantastic. That made two of us.

I straightened from a reflexive hunch. Djinn temperamentality could be painful. "I'm not about to be in the middle of whatever plot you two have cooked up."

Grimm pulled a face. "Why would we—"

"Enough, Grimm." Duke uncoiled from the chair and resettled the suit jacket over his shoulders with a tug on the lapels. "If you're quite alright—"

"I am," I said firmly.

"Then if you're certain you wish to take this path, perhaps we could offer some help?" The way Duke eyed me as he said that made me wary. When Grimm didn't object, I grew even more suspicious.

"Info would be welcome," I said carefully, wondering what he wanted even as a shuddery thrill ran over me at the thought of finally learning more about the people who wanted me dead. I probably should have known more about elves than I did, but I'd been sheltered in Callista's care, raised almost completely apart from the rest of Otherside and given only the barest information needed to avoid outing myself the first time I encountered another Othersider on my own. After I'd turned eighteen and moved out of Callista's house, I hadn't dared to risk drawing elven attention by investigating them.

Neither Duke nor Grimm had ever been forthcoming before; that they were now said something more was afoot. Maybe Callista was right. And maybe this was another of her ploys. Either way, I needed information. But there was a catch. Djinn never simply offered anything; there were no gifts. None without barbs, anyway. "Perhaps I could share a tale in return," I said, certain that if they were here and offering, they wanted something more than simply to check on me.

Grimm looked up from her fingernails, her pout vanishing. "Something about your work?"

"And about Callista."

That got their attention.

Keep reading *Elemental*

Find the ebook at:

- Amazon
- Kobo
- Barnes & Noble
- Google Play
- Other booksellers (including international)

The paperback is available from:
- Your local indie bookstore via IndieBound
- Bookshop.org
- Amazon

Both ebook and paperback are also available to libraries if you'd like to make a request!

Acknowledgments

Here we are at the end of another cycle of stories. As with Shadows of Otherside, I only planned so many books for Lya and Cade's story…but this isn't the last time you'll see them. A new cycle of Arden's story is coming, and there's room for the world to expand.

So for those who have been here from the very beginning, thank you for joining me through this adventure. Most especially my parents and sister, whose continuing support is always a blessing. But also to my editor, Jeni Chappelle, who always gives the best edit notes and has done so much to help guide me on this journey.

This series wouldn't be as strong as it is without the sharp eyes and strong questions of my beta reader, Callan, so a thank you to her as well!

To my Patreon supporters, I'm forever grateful that you love Otherside as much as I do! Thank you for your patronage and engagement.

Also a thank you to the ongoing support from book bloggers, Bookstagrammers, and other reading groups across the internet. I'm so deeply appreciative of those who take a risk on highlighting a book that isn't being shown on every other account, especially when that book is self- or indie-published.

And lastly, a huge thank you to the people who have not only loved the books, but also left a review. It means a lot when someone takes time out of their day to shout out something they love. It also means other readers might take a shot, enabling me to write more books. You're appreciated.

Also by Whitney Hill

The Shadows of Otherside series

Elemental
Eldritch Sparks
Ethereal Secrets
Ebon Rebellion
Eternal Huntress

The Otherside Heat series

Secrets and Truths
Curses and Faith
Menace and Memory

The Flesh and Blood series (as Remy Harmon)

Bluebloods

About the Author

 Whitney Hill is an author and speaker. The bestselling first book in her Shadows of Otherside series, *Elemental*, was the grand prize winner of the 8th Annual Writer's Digest Self-Published E-Book Awards and a Finalist in the Next Generation Indie Book Awards. Her second book, *Eldritch Sparks*, was named one of the Top 100 Indie Books of 2021 by *Kirkus Reviews*.

When she's not writing, Whitney enjoys hiking in North Carolina's beautiful state parks and playing video games.

Learn more or get in touch: whitneyhillwrites.com
More books by Whitney: whitneyhillwrites.com/original-fiction
Sign up to receive email updates: whwrites.com/newsletter

Join her on social media:
- Twitter: twitter.com/write_wherever
- Instagram: instagram.com/write_wherever
- Facebook: facebook.com/WhitneyHillWrites

Get bonus content on Patreon: patreon.com/writewherever

www.ingramcontent.com/pod-product-compliance
Lightning Source LLC
Chambersburg PA
CBHW021132190726
48288CB00008B/2611